CHYNA BLACK

Compilation and Introduction copyright © 2004 by
Triple Crown Publications
2959 Stelzer Rd., Suite C
Columbus, Ohio 43219
www.TripleCrownPublications.com

Library of Congress Control Number: 2004115363
ISBN# 0-9762349-1-2
Cover Design/Graphics: www.apollopixel.com
Editor: Kathleen Jackson and Amy Karnes
Consulting: Vickie M. Stringer

First Trade Paperback Edition Printing November 2004

Printed in the United States of America

<u>Dedications</u>

I dedicate this book to the people who believed in me most while they were here on this earth – my grandmother, Claudia 'Pat' Poe, and my grandfather, James Garfield Ervin. Also I dedicate this book to all the young women who are still struggling to find themselves throughout all the day to day drama that life brings.

Acknowledgements

Lord, when you gave me the words to write Me & My Boyfriend I had no idea that my life would change so drastically. I sit in amazement everyday at how much you have blessed me with. There is no way that I can ever doubt you and your ability to change lives. That's why I decided to make my second novel a testimony of my life. Your love is what has brought me through and I will continue to praise and believe in you. Thank you for making this past year the best year of my life.

To my handsome, chocolate baby Kyrese, there are no words in the English vocabulary that describe how much I LOVE YOU. You are my reason for living and for everything that I do. My constant source of inspiration, I love you.

Momma, you have helped me so much this past year. From watching Kyrese to helping me out financially you have been there for me. I don't know what I would ever do with out you. I love you momma.

Daddy, I still don't think that you get what's going on but you'll catch on eventually. I love you!!!

To my brother Keon, I hate that I haven't seen you in over a year. When you gone bring you big head ass home? Carlie, I know we don't talk much but you're still my sister and I love you.

Okay here we go first off to the Poe family which consists of Donald, Ronald, Lisa, Maggie, Nicole, Chantell, Tori, Matthew, Nicolas, Christian, Timothy, Tyler, Kai and Kayla thank you all for being my biggest supporters throughout this entire thing. Ya'll have truly represented!!!

To the Ervin family I want to give a shout out to Granny, Aunt Jean, Uncle Bruce, Uncle Sam, Aunt Denise, Charlene, Dorcia, Chris, Man, Lil Bruce, Becky, Aaron, Q, Michael, Deja, Lil Deja, Jamahl, Tre, Gabrielle and Quemira.

To my extended family which includes Hattie Westbrook, Angela, Asia, Aaron, Michael and the entire Blackshear family, I love you and thanks for all the support.

To my dearest and closet friends:

Alocia Roberston, you know that we have been friends since we sported Jodeci boots gurl. I love you!

What up cousin I'm putting us on the map dog. Thank you Tavia for being one of the most honest and trustworthy people that I know.

Miesha Ervin, you are my sister in Christ and I love you. Whenever I have needed you and Kevin ya'll have been there. I depend on you and our talks because you keep my head on straight when I'm about to head down the wrong path.

Jackie you are one ride or die chick gurl.

Monsieur Pascal aka Monique, thank you for helping me through one of the toughest times in my life. I will never forget how you cared for me when most didn't. My prayers and love go out to you and your mom.

Kevin, whether or not things work out between you and I, know that I love you for everything that you have brought to my life.

Debbie, thank you for coming into my life and for all the times that you helped me when it came to Kyrese.

Kelin, you will always be one of my closet friends. You just gotta quit letting certain people run your life.

Miss Danielle Santiago, keep writing gangsta stories and rocken the latest fashion. Do yo thang momma!!

Lisa Gibson-Wilson, you are the best manager and mentor that I will ever have. I really admire and look up to you. Thank you for being the DIVA that you are!!!

Last but not least to my DOG, PARTNA, HOMEY, and FRIEND TuShonda Whitaker, I never would have thought that you and I would become friends. But God puts people in our lives for a reason, a season or a lifetime. And I truly believe that you will be a lifetime friend to me. I love you gurl and we will continue to dust the dirt off of our shoulders together.

Hey Sandy, Miss Danielle, Ms. Marie, Kelly, Arnina, Mrs. Robertson, Lonnie, Robin, Keith, Ron, Miss Harris, Mr. Harris, Miss Cole, Mr. McClain, McKinley and Miss Dalton, thank you for being such good friends to me and my family.

Big ups to Miss Linda, Janea Snipes, Tiara, Sherry, Tory, Tara, Stephanie, the two Nicoles, Bob, Ray, Daryl, Chris, Barbara Jean, Tray, Shanerian, Cynthia, Dallas, Ms. Roberts and Lando.

Thank you Big D for believing in me before you even knew what my project was about.

Thank you Renaissance Management Company, Marcus & Stacy at Ujamma, Bill Beene at St. Louis American, Lime Light Newspaper, Florissant Valley Community College, Queen Isis at Q 95.5, all the Walden Book Stores, Barnes & Noble, Amazon.com, Tammy, Kevin, Karl & Steve at TCP, Joylynn Jossel & the other TCP authors, Anthony Clair, and most importantly, my city St. Louis for supporting and representing for me. I love my city and I will always rep for you!!!

To Triple Crown Publications for pushing my book and making sure my career started off with a bang. The office staff that handles my affairs on a regular, the seen and unseen – if I never meet you, nor acknowledge your work and effort, please know that I appreciate what you do.

Thank you from the bottom of my heart, Vickie Stringer, for publishing and putting my work on the shelf. You are one hell of a woman to put up with all of us crazy ass authors.

R.I.P Daryl, Aunt Sheryl, Abbie, Daddy Cole and Uncle Chester.

Nelly come holla at a playa!!!!

CHAPTER 1

JUST TO GET BY

All my drama began when I was fifteen, that's the year that I came out of my shell and broke loose. All of my womanly curves came alive and all of the old heads were peepin' me out. It kind of disgusted me at first, but eventually I got use to it. I had a banging body to be only fifteen years old. My face was innocent, but that was about it. Shit, by the time I was ten, I was in a C-cup bra. I'm seventeen now and my cup size had grown to a Double D, and with my small waist and apple bottom, all the fellas were screaming, "Drop it like it's hot!"

By the age of fifteen, I had taken notice of what my assets were. I had it going on if I do say so myself, shit I still have it going on. My stock was high and niggas in every hood wanted to invest. My girls, Asia and Brooklyn, and I had all the niggas sprung, every playa in the hood wanted a piece of at least one of us. None of us were fucking yet, so that made them want us even more.

I was all about looking good and partying. Asia, Brooke and I were always getting into something. Whether it was a house party, skating, riding around getting blazed or hanging out at home, we always had fun. We had all been tight since Kriss Kross made you "Jump" and SWV had niggas "Weak" in the knees. We were inseparable, whenever you saw one of us, you

1

knew the other two were not far behind. We were known as the ABC click, Asia, Brooklyn and Chyna, and we got hollered at on a daily basis by ballers and bums.

At the time, I had just learned what a women's body did to a man. Hell, a lick of the lips, switch of the hips and a little thigh, could get you a lot. Getting a young boy to pay for my hair and nails was a lot back then to me. Shit, I had this one dude tricking his hard earned part-time McDonald's money to me every Friday. No money, no play was my motto. You got to pay to play, so fuck what ya heard. He knew not to even talk to me if my money wasn't in hand. Don't hate, I was bout it, bout it, that's just how I rolled.

In this world, money talks so you had to pay to be with me. I wasn't some old broke down chick. Hell no, I was an exquisite piece of china and if you didn't know how delicate I was then you could step. I was like a B.E.T award, you had to trick mad money to have me on your arm, ya dig.

Fuck a nigga and a relationship cause love don't mean a damn thing to me. You see I'm a product of high school sweethearts gone wrong. My parents broke up before I was born. My momma Diane and daddy Cedric, had my brother when they were just teenagers. My brother, Cantrell and I rarely see each other these days, he's probably somewhere in Atlanta waving the Gay Pride flag, so that leaves me to live alone with my mother, Diane.

My dad and I have never been close. He tries to be a good father but he always falls short. The fact that he's never gotten over my mother makes him bitter towards me because he sees her when he looks at me. That, mixed with the amount of liquor he consumes each day, doesn't help.

Growing up on the Northside of St. Louis, there was always something poppin' off. There wasn't anything better than summertime in St. Louis. I remember everybody waiting patiently on their front porch for the bum pop man who had this one particular truck that everybody brought from, it was green and had all of the hood treats. That man had everything from twenty-five cent bags of chips, sundaes, candy bars and pickles to cigarettes, and he could make some bomb ass cherry snow cones. My grandma, whom we all called "Pat", would have me snatch her up two cold Pepsi's. She loved her some Pepsi, no other beverage compared in her eyes. Diane is like that now, after years of drinking Coca-Cola.

Pat was a cool ass grandmamma and I tend to think I get my demeanor from her. Even though hard times constantly knocked on her door, she never lost her composure. Pat never judged you no matter what your hustle was. What you did was your business, but if you asked for her opinion, you were sure to get it.

It's sad because, like me, she had issues with her own mother. My great grandma, Gloria, treated her like shit. Gloria made it well known that her oldest son, BJ, was her favorite. Gloria never once told Pat that she loved her. I learned this through one of their many arguments. Old and senile, she denied it but I knew it was true. The old woman was a very bitter and manipulative person. Even though Pat took her in after she succumbed to blindness, she still treated her badly.

Besides having Diane, Pat had four other kids. Diane was the oldest of the five children. There was Derrick, twins Cory and Tory and Lauren. Diane was the only one who had a different daddy and she never knew his name or what he looked like. The rest of Pat's kids had a darker skin complexion, and their father was a man who didn't do shit for his kids either. He had another family, so to him Pat's kids didn't exist. Pat took care of her kids by any means necessary. The lights, gas or electric may have been turned off every now and then, but they survived.

Diane was the bookworm and loner of the five and I see why she's such a control freak now. Derrick was the wild child, a thrill seeker. For Cory and Tory to have been twins, they had absolutely nothing in common. Tory was this black Vinnie Barbarino/TD Jake type brother. He used to rock suits with a briefcase to school. Cory, on the other hand, was into cracking jokes and fixing things. Lauren was just off the chain, something had to have been tied around her neck while in the womb because I swear there ain't no air up in her brain.

When I was a youngster, Lauren was in her teens and I used to straight up idolize her. No other female on the block could fuck with her style. Lauren sported Guess, Polo, Chico and Gloria Vanderbilt clothing. I used to love hanging out with her and her friends. Of course, she didn't want me around, but I didn't care cause I was kicking it with the big girls.

When I used to walk to the Arab store, this man that lived across the street used to fuck with me. He was tall with long hair and cold eyes, and those eyes still haunt me today. At first, he used to just stare at me, but one day he decided to take it a step further. Seeing me, he stepped off the porch and approached the fence.

"Hey there pretty girl," he said, licking his lips.

My momma had taught me not to talk to strangers so I kept moving.

"I know you hear me," he said, speaking a little louder.

I continued to walk and ignore him, telling myself I was almost there. My adolescent heart thumped as hard as a bass drum. I didn't understand why the scary old man kept bothering me.

"One day I'ma come from behind this fence and pull you into my house, and when I do, I'ma teach you to respect your elders. You want me to get you don't you?" He teased, sickly.

"Leave me alone!" I yelled, now running and crying.

"What you running for, I ain't did nothing to you yet. You gonna be mine one day little girl," he said, seriously.

Running as fast as I could, I tried to erase his eyes and words from my mind. Stopping in front of the Arab store, I held my chest to catch my breath. Looking back down the street, I saw him taking his seat once again on the porch. Staring at each other, I prayed that one day he would die a slow and painful death. I didn't know then that he was what we now call a child predator. Once I returned home, I told my Uncles about the frightening old man and his threats. All I know is, after that day, I didn't have any more problems out of his crazy ass.

Pat was my life as a child, she was my first love really. There ain't no love like the love of your grandma. I was her favorite, she loved her some Chyna. Everybody said I looked like her. I lived with her up until I was nine and that green house had serious problems. If the heat was on, the gas wasn't, and if lights shined, water didn't run out of the faucet. There were times when Pat had to borrow water from neighbors. We would use it to bathe, cook and to flush the toilet after use. Roaches were my friends, they were always walking around the house saying hello. We had big roaches, little roaches, mama roaches, daddy roaches and white roaches. And if you have roaches, you know that those white muthafuckers are hard to kill.

My eyes have witnessed struggle. Pat tried to play it off like she was never worried about how she would pay her bills, but I knew secretly she was worried. She would constantly sit in her chair humming and praying, wondering how she would somehow manage. But Pat being the hustler that she was would ask the mailman for some extra ends if she had to. Diane didn't like the fact that Pat depended on others to support her financially, but hey, how could you knock her, she had to stay on her grind like everybody else.

Sitting on the front porch in her peach duster, she would wait for somebody she knew to roll through then she would holla out, "Give me two dollars!" Pat didn't have any shame in her game.

One time, I was sitting outside on the porch with her when Chris, the neighborhood baller, came through.

"What you need with two dollars Pat?" Chris asked.

"Don't worry about what I need them for, do you have two dollars or not?"

"You know I got you old lady," Chris said smiling, handing her a crisp twenty dollar bill.

"Thank you Chris baby," Pat said, hugging him.

"You're welcome Pat. See you later Chyna," Chris said, winking.

Chris was that nigga, tall, dark and lovely, but he liked my Aunt Lauren, he rarely ever looked my way. I couldn't wait until I got older because shit, when it was my time, Chris would be mine. He looked real good getting into his Suzuki Sidekick with his fresh box cut. The Used Jean outfit he rocked was on point and his thick gold herringbone chain was weighing down his neck, but shit, it was a good look for that nigga.

"Chyna!" Pat yelled, awakening me from my daydreaming.

"Huh?" I answered, aggravated.

"Go in the house and tell Derrick to walk and get me some Church's Chicken."

Closing the screen door behind me, I yelled into the house, "Derrick, Pat said to come and go get her some Church's Chicken!"

"Let me get a couple of dollars Pat since I'm going to the store for you," Derrick said, coming out the house.

"I'm not stupid Derrick, you're gonna use my money to snort that shit."

"No I ain't, I swear. I just, I just need some money in my pocket."

"I ain't playing with you Derrick, you better be back here in fifteen minutes with my food and my money," Pat said, seriously.

For once Derrick came back like he promised, and I knew then that he wasn't like normal junkies. Don't get it twisted, he was a straight up junkie, no ifs ands or buts about it, but that night the monkey must not have been calling him because we all sat on the porch and shared a meal like a real family. Laughing and joking, we all cracked on Lauren and her fucked up curl.

"Whoever did that shit to ya head need to be locked up for life," Cory joked.

"Whatever, my hair looks good. I just need to put some curl activator in it," she said, fingering her hair.

"You need more than some curl activator, you need some gel, setting lotion and moose to get that shit to curl up," Cory said, cracking up laughing.

"You hear him cursing Pat?" Lauren asked.

"I heard him. You better watch your mouth Cory. But Lauren honey, you do need to fix that mess," Pat laughed.

"Not you too," Lauren whined.

"Lauren, the mushroom you had last week looked better than that," I said.

"Shut up Chyna, what do you know, you're just a kid," Lauren spat.

"Don't get mad at her cause ya hair jacked up," Derrick laughed.

When talking about Lauren's hair wasn't fun anymore, Cory left and went over his girlfriend's house. Lauren got mad and went in the house, but Derrick, Pat and I sat outside and let the cool breeze take us. For once, I felt safe, so safe that I fell asleep in Derrick's arms that night on the porch. It didn't take long for Derrick to get hooked back on dope, so Pat kicked him out and told him not to come back until he was clean.

Just before I moved in with Diane, he made a major return

back into our lives. His being back on dope had changed his whole demeanor. He had become quite, withdrawn and creepy. I made sure to stay clear of him cause he scared the shit out of me. Whenever I looked into eyes, I saw a pair of cold black eyes. For whatever reason, he just didn't give a fuck about anything or anybody. That "O Wee" (dope) makes people go crazy I swear. He would just come over clowning for no reason.

One time he clowned so bad that Pat made me run across the street to get help. I can picture that day in my head clearly. I was sitting on the floor and one of Pat's many friends had stopped by. I knew that Derrick would be coming over because he had called earlier that day. How I wished that Pat and her friend's conversation wouldn't end. My stomach hurt so bad with fear, something was just telling me that some shit was about to go down.

When Pat's friend got up to leave, I almost screamed for him to stay because then it would be just her and I there and I knew that Derrick would try something. Tears formed in my eyes as the car pulled away from the curb and rolled down the street. Back in Pat's room, which was near the kitchen, I laid on the floor staring out the back door fearing the worst.

About fifteen minutes later, Derrick came walking through the back door. Staring at him, I saw that he had a trash bag full of clothes with him. God, I prayed that he wouldn't be staying overnight. Five minutes after he got there, he and Pat began to argue because Pat wouldn't give him any money. She knew that he would only use it to get high. He was geeking so he started screaming and hollering at her. Derrick told her that she had never done anything for him and that she had better give him the money. Pat tried to calm him down but that only made matters worse. I sat on the floor in Pat's room crying. Shit, that mutha-fucker was crazy and I didn't put anything past him.

Seeing that I was crying, Pat made me run across the street to call the police. Barefooted I made the run to Ms. Mattie's house. Without even knocking, I burst through the door and raced up the steps.

"Ms. Mattie, Ms. Mattie!" I cried out.

"Chyna, is that you?"

"Yeah it's me. Derrick's over across the street acting crazy, Pat said to call the police!" I cried out to her.

"Okay Chyna sweetie. Let me get one of my brothers to go over there with her."

Hollering down the steps, she ordered her brother to go see about Pat. Staring out the window, I waited for the police. After that, the next couple of times I saw him, he had become even more dependent on drugs. He was so spiteful and hooked on drugs that he even put his then girlfriend up to calling Pat and telling her that Diane had been killed. For about two hours, we all thought that Diane had been killed cause nobody could get in contact with her because she was sleep and not answering the phone. It's sad because he didn't even live to see forty.

A couple of months later, he would try to stab and kill his girlfriend. He went down to the nursing home where she worked and stabbed her thirty-two times because she no longer wanted to be with him. He had flat out told her that if he couldn't have her nobody else would. It's funny because the day prior, he had told Lauren that we would see him on the news or in the newspaper. She thought that he was just bullshittin' so she disregarded everything that he said. Thinking that he had succeeded in killing her, he went down to the gymnasium, got a rope and hung himself.

Pat never really recovered from his death. Three years later, my beloved grandmother would succumb to ovarian cancer. The death of Pat was the last and final straw. To make matters worse, she died right in front of me. I've never hurt so badly before in my life. I had hoped that I would never feel that type of pain again, but little did I know that my path of pain was just beginning.

Now my ass has been hit so hard by this thing called love that I can't even see straight. It has me questioning myself like, what did I do wrong, wasn't I good enough, didn't my feelings count for anything, wasn't the sex good, stupid bullshit like that. Listen to me when I say, "don't ever fall in love" cause the shit will drive you crazy. You'll be looking just like me, stuck on stupid with no way to let go. If you listen to what I have to say then you can save yourself a lifetime of heartache.

Sometimes I think that I fell in love with the idea of love and not really Tyreik, and that's why I was sitting in my Jeep Liberty truck at 2 o'clock in the morning on a 'fuck him and everything he owns' mission. A full moon was out and the sky above me was dropping heavy raindrops upon the roof of my truck. Mary J. Blige's *"Never Wanna Live Without You"* was on repeat and I had just rolled up another Philly blunt.

You see, Tyreik was the first man that I ever really truly loved and when things got rough, the nigga up and left me. Trust me when I say that I have tried to get over him, but I still remember our first kiss and the stroke of his hand across my face. My eyes are heavy and my heart is low, but still that doesn't stop me. As I inhale and let the smoke go through my nose, I tell myself that he deserves everything that's coming to him.

Another hour passed by and I had dozed off to sleep only to be awakened by the loud thud of a car door slamming. I forgot that I still had the lit blunt in my hand, so when I jumped it fell into my lap. Bouncing around in my seat, I tried to avoid getting burned but ended up getting burned anyway. The white tuxedo pants that I had on now had a burn hole the size of a dime in them. Dusting the ashes off my thigh, I hit the blunt once more and then put it out. After turning Monica off, I switched to Tweet's *"Always Will"*. Resting my head on the headrest, I let Tweet's words sink into my soul while I continued waiting, and twenty minutes later Tyreik and his bitch finally arrived.

I reclined my seat all the way back to make sure they couldn't see me. Tyreik stepped out of his Navigator and walked around to the passenger side as if nothing had happened. I guess the thought of him getting some pussy made him forget, but I on the other hand hadn't forgotten a damn thing. Less than three hours ago, he and I had gotten into a heated argument in front of a room full of people and I was not about to let him embarrass me and get away with it, his ass had to pay.

I watched closely as he helped his bitch get out of the truck. Even though it was dark and there wasn't much light on the street, I could still see them leaning against the truck hugging and kissing each other. Their so-called display of affection made my stomach hurt. Taking him by the hand, she led him up the steps to her loft. I waited a couple more minutes before I hopped out of my truck. Grabbing my mini bat, crowbar and keys, I headed up the street to his truck.

I tried to walk softly so that my four-inch heels wouldn't make a clanking sound against the pavement. The fact that I had on all white with gold accessories didn't even faze me. I could have easily been spotted but I didn't give a fuck, Tyreik's shit was about to be destroyed no matter what.

First, I took my keys and scratched up the entire exterior of his truck. I carved out the word *"Bitch"* on the hood. Tyreik must have forgotten that I still had the spare set of keys to the Navigator, and it was just my luck that his dumb ass forgot to turn on the alarm system. Grabbing my pocketknife out of my pants, I cut up his leather seats, took the face off his radio and put a crack in each of his TVs. I then flattened all of his tires and then I put a dent in all four of his Giovanna rims with the crow bar.

After doing all of that in less than thirty minutes and in four-inch heels, my ass was tired. Sweat began to form on my top lip, forehead, breast and underarms, but I still wasn't done. For the grand finale, I took my mini bat and busted out his front window. The sound of the glass being shattered caused a neighborhood dog to start barking, so as fast as I could I ran back to my truck before anybody saw me. Safely back inside, I put my key in the ignition and sped the fuck off. That night I taught that muthafucker a lesson, which was I was not to be fucked with.

Triple Crown Publications presents

CHAPTER 2

I WANNA SEX YOU UP

When I got home that night, I laid in bed and continued thinking about the last three years of my life, and Asia and Brooke faces immediately popped into my head.

Have you ever known an Asian, African-American? Well up until I met Asia, I hadn't either. You would have thought she was just another pretty caramel chick with straight hair and slanted eyes, but the girl was straight up hood. Rarely did she speak of her Asian heritage. Her parents met over in Asia, they got together while her dad was stationed over there in the army. After a couple of steamy nights together, they produced Asia. Unfortunately for Asia, she never got a chance to know her mother. Ming Lee died giving birth to her and her father couldn't bare the thought of living in what now seemed like a cold country. Scooping her up, he made the trek back to the states but before leaving, he decided on giving his baby girl the country's name, her name would forever be the only reminder of his time there.

As far as Brooke goes, she's the laid back one of the group. She's always thinking, planning her next move. Anytime you look at her, you can tell that she has something on her mind. The tallest of the bunch, she could have easily made it as a model. She looked like a young Naomi Campbell, the only thing is she rocked her curly hair short.

Brooke lived a few blocks from Asia and me in a different hood. We loved kicking it over her crib cause something was always popping off on her block. Either commotion was going on in the house or outside. Brooke was the second oldest of her five other siblings. Her parents had been happily married for years, but the stress of kids and bills sometimes took its toll. Whenever they started up on one of their fights that consisted of yelling and cursing, Brooke would zone out. On a daily basis, her parents fought about everything from the dishes to the light bill. Brooke couldn't wait to break the fuck out.

By the time we hit high school, my whole way of thinking was all fucked up. Most high school guys appealed to me, but only a few of them could chill with me. Like one guy in particular named Jaylen, he and I were the same age and had all of the same classes and stuff. Everyday he bugged me about when I was going to give him my digits. Digits, do you see how corny this nigga was? Jaylen was too straight-laced for me.

He was class president and played ball. All the girls wanted him because of his status on the basketball court, but he only had eyes for me. I, on the other hand, never looked at him twice. He was cute and all, but in a brotherly way. First off, I didn't like tall, skinny, baby faced guys and Jaylen was all of those things. He had style and all but there was just no edge to him. I never understood why he even tried his hand with me. Repeatedly I told him that I didn't want him but, Jaylen being Jaylen, he would never stop trying.

One day while I sat in the lunchroom, I caught the eye of this young boy named LP, I had had my eye on him for a while. The boy always strolled down the hallways with a gangsta lean, looking like he was one of those Nelly type brothers. His build was just right, and the fact that he was tattooed up helped his look out a lot. Plus, he had a car so that was even better. The boy was going to be mine, I just had to get on him at the right time and today was the day.

Getting up from the lunch table, I excused myself.

"Where are you going?" Asia asked.

"LP is over there sitting on the radiator, I'm about to go and get on him."

"Oh word, do your thing," she said, giving me a high five.

With ease I strutted over to be where he was. He never even saw me coming and that's exactly how I liked it, I liked to pounce on my prey.

"What's up LP, you might not know my name," I said, interrupting his conversation.

Looking me over, he gave my presence an approval.

"Oh, I know your name and face," he answered, seductively.

"Oh really do you? Well um, I was wondering if you weren't seeing anybody would you like my number?"

"No doubt," he answered, coyly.

Taking him by the hand, I wrote my number on it.

Looking him dead in his eyes, I softly blew into the palm of his hand and said, "You make sure you use this number."

"Trust me I will," he smiled back.

Walking off, I knew that he was watching so I put a little extra ump to my strut. He had a good view of my ass and I knew that I would be getting a call that night. After that, whenever I was at school I was always checking for him. Anytime his name came up in conversation, I kept my ears close. LP was the first guy that I was really feeling, so ignoring my morals I invested some of my feelings into him. LP was too fine to only be seeing me and I wasn't dumb by a long shot, so it was only a matter of time before I heard some shit.

This one particular day, instead of riding home with Asia and her man Shawn like I usually did, I chose to ride the school bus home. I guess LP thought I was riding home with Asia because right in my view, he stood with some upper class chick. She was all in his face and too close for my comfort, and to make matters worse, he wasn't backing away from her. No this nigga wasn't trying to play me, I thought. I mean LP wasn't mine in words but shit I wanted him to be.

Once I got home, I paged him immediately and he called me back in less than five minutes.

"What's up?" he spoke into the phone.

I could tell he was getting high with his peoples, so me calling with my bullshit was sure to bring his high down quickly.

"Nothing, what's up with you?"

"Shit, I just got home."

"Oh word? Well um, let me ask you a question LP."

"What's cracking?" he asked, inhaling at the same time.

"Who was that you were talking to after school?"

I knew who the chick was but I played dumb for effect. Caught up, he knew he could only tell the truth.

"Oh, that was um Peaches."

"Do you and Peaches talk?" I responded back.

"Yeah we talk."

"Well, let me ask you this. Why have you been talking to me if you talk to her?" I asked, almost demanding an answer.

"What I'm saying is me and Peaches talk, but what's up wit you and me?"

Shit, at least he was honest. Most niggas would have come

with some old bullshit ass story. I had a decision to make right then and there. Either I was going to leave LP alone or keep on messing with him. There wasn't even any need to think about it, I wanted LP. The other bitch had him for now but it wouldn't be for long. LP and I continued to talk and eventually he started coming over to my house often because my mom was never at home. Him and I would chill and watch movies or I would ride with him to his hood and chill with him and his people. Sometimes we would double date with Asia and Shawn.

At the time, Peaches was his gal but I was his woman because I had LP hook, line and sinker, or so I thought I did. LP had me totally into him, he constantly stayed on my mind and I knew that he would be my first. I knew that after we had sex that would seal the deal and he would be my man. I didn't let LP know that I was a virgin because I didn't want to seem like I was inexperienced in the sex department.

One day while he was over my house after school, I made the conscious decision to give him some. As we laid on my bed, I kissed him intensely. I could have kissed him forever but LP had his mind on other things. I thought that we would have some foreplay, but shit, LP skipped straight to penetration. He must have thought it would be easy to slide up in me, but my shit was so tight it made him ask the question I dreaded.

"Are you a virgin?" he questioned.

"Nah, I just haven't done it in awhile," I replied back.

But for real, I could barely breathe because the shit was hurting me so bad. For it to be my first time, I would have to hook up with an old big dick ass nigga, I thought. I could feel his dick all the way in my stomach. When we got done my legs were shaking and shit. I didn't know what was happening to me but I felt like a woman after the pain had subsided.

After having sex with LP, that's all him and I did. I had unknowingly become his sex partner and his chick on the side. I hadn't even turned sixteen yet but LP had me open, he became the only dude that I was seeing. I didn't even know how I had gotten myself in that position.

When I paged him, sometimes my calls went unanswered. I mean what the fuck kind of shit was that? Here I was a dime piece and he was trying to play me crazy. The only time he came through was when he wanted some, and me wanting to be around him, I fell for it every time. It wasn't supposed to be that way, LP was supposed to be my man after I gave myself to him, but he and Peaches still stayed together and I wandered sometimes did she know about me.

Plenty of nights I laid up talking to Asia and Brooke about my problem. Both of them told me to tell LP how I felt about him, but letting LP know how I felt was too much for me to handle, I had never let any boy that close to my heart. I was already stressing over him as it was, and to tell him that I wasn't cool about our situation would only add to my troubles. But listening to my heart and my two best friends, I gave in.

"Hello?" he answered, half asleep.

"Wake up, I need to talk to you."

"Can't it wait Chyna, I'm sleep," he said, annoyed.

"No it can't wait. You like me right?"

"Yeah, I like you," he yawned.

"Okay and I like you too. So since we both like each other so much why is it that we still don't go together?"

"Chyna, you knew that I was with Peaches when you and me started fucking around. I mean, I like you and all but I ain't trying to leave Peaches alone just yet."

Now what kind of shit was that? He could come over on a daily basis and fuck me but he couldn't be with me. But me being young and dumb, I continued to mess with him anyway. LP had officially become my homey/lover/friend. I didn't have anyone else to compare him to and he taught me some freaky ass shit. He had to have watched a lot of porn or something because for him to be only seventeen, he put me in some weird positions. His sex game was too fast and rough for me. The only way he could make me cum was if he ate my pussy, which was a rarity. LP was only out for self when it came to sex, he never really indulged in foreplay.

That summer I learned my first lesson about men. You can never let your guard down ever because if you let a man use you once he'll do it again. LP had gotten his thing off with me, but I would make sure that it would never happen again. The next man in my life would have something on his hands because my game had just gotten stronger. I fell once but the next time it would be the man picking up the pieces.

A couple of months had passed and I had my mind right. My eyes were on the prize and the only thing that concerned me was doing well in school. We were in our sophomore year of high school. Lucky for me, LP ended up moving and transferring to another school. Every now and then we would hook up, but by then, any feelings I had for him were gone, I could fuck him and go on about my business now. I started fucking with a couple of niggas because they were giving up some cheese. Some of them I fucked, some of them I didn't.

You know that pay back is a muthafucker and I had to get LP back for how he tried to play me, so I started a rumor around school that I was pregnant by him and that I had had an abortion. I made sure that my news got back to his girlfriend Peaches. I knew that she had heard the rumor because her and her friends began to look at me funny every time they saw me, but shit, I didn't give a fuck because she knew not to even try to run up on me. If she did, I wouldn't be the only one that got hurt.

I had become scandalous and didn't even realize it. No one feelings mattered but mine, I didn't give a fuck who you were, I was going to chew you up and spit you out. Niggas didn't know how to take me cause I was so blunt with my game that it caught them off guard. Off the bat, I let them know that I was all about doe. If they couldn't handle that then they had to step. My heart had turned cold and I wouldn't allow myself to be hurt again.

One early fall night, Shawn had let Asia borrow his car and we all got together to ride on the landing by the Arch. Sitting on the hood of his truck we chilled, bass was bumping left and right. Cars filled with niggas and bitches rolled by, everybody was trying to see or be seen. I loved being out on a nice night in St. Louis. I was amped up and down for whatever.

"Girl, do you see him?" Brooke asked.

"Who?" Asia asked.

"The boy over there with the red on," Brooke pointed out.

"Oh yeah, he looks good," I answered.

"Why don't you go and talk to him Chyna?"

"I don't talk to lil boys and you know that. He looks like he's about eighteen."

"Well, what kind of guy do you want to talk to?" Asia countered.

Thinking about it, I made sure I answered carefully.

"I want somebody that is older than me of course. I want his skin to be milk chocolate and he must be thugged out. He's got to have doe and a crib of his own, basically he has to be able to take care of me."

"Damn, you want a lot," Brooke teased.

"You're damn right I do. I want it all, I want the best."

The next day at school, we all sat around the lunch table talking. Lunchtime at Norfolk High was always a mess. Students came bustling in from all different directions. Like any school, Norfolk had cliques but unlike most high schools, everybody pretty much got along. It didn't matter if you were unpopular or nerdy, everybody was accepted for who they were. There were fights here and there over he said, she said type stuff. Asia, Brooke and I kept our distance from such activities. That is until Peaches confronted me one day. I can still remember it clearly.

Peaches and two of her girlfriends cornered me in the girl's bathroom at school. I was in the mirror applying lip gloss and, at first, I didn't even notice them entering. Upon seeing them in the mirror, the reflection on their faces told it all, something was about to go down and I was prepared for whatever. Placing my lip gloss back into my makeup bag, I turned to face the girls.

"Is there a problem?" I asked.

"Is there a problem? This bitch thinks that she is tough," Peaches said.

"Yeah she does, don't she?" said one of the girls.

"Look bitch, I don't know who you think you are but you better stay away from my man," Peaches said.

I couldn't help but laugh, LP was so yesterday. We still got down from time to time but I wasn't feeling him like that anymore.

"Girl please, don't nobody want LP but you," I retorted back, waving Peaches off. "Don't come to me with that bullshit," I continued.

"Oh, so you're trying to tell me that ya'll haven't fucked around?"

"Nah, I'm not saying that, I'm saying that I don't want him."

"Yeah right, whatever bitch. He told me all about you. He told me that you have been straight up stalking him. LP doesn't want you. I kind of feel sorry for you," Peaches laughed.

"Girl, you played yourself. You're stupid, now go find a man of your own," replied another one of Peaches' friends.

"Yeah, he told me that ya'll fucked. It was a couple of times and you weren't even good, that's why he stopped fucking with you," Peaches smirked.

I had heard enough because too much of my business was being put out. LP had turned the situation around to make me look like the dumb one. LP would not get away with this but first I had to take care of his bitch.

"You know what, you got me. I confess, I was feeling LP but your story is all messed up. Your man is playing you crazy. I bet your girls didn't know that every time you called LP he was with me. I can tell you your number if you want me to. Oh, and the part about my sex game not being good, bitch please, LP could-n't get enough of this. Go and ask his mouth how well my pussy taste."

With that last comment, Peaches suddenly came charging towards me but I was simply too quick on my feet. Charging back at her, I slammed that bitch into the hard bathroom wall. Blood immediately spurted from the back of her head. I was in kill mode and could have cared less about blood. Slamming Peaches' head into the wall, I yelled all types of obscenities at her. Out of the blue, Peaches caught me with a good lick to the side of my face. As I was holding my face in shock, she kicked me in the stomach. Doubling over in pain, I tried to gather my strength. Taking hold of my hair, Peaches proceeded to hit me in the head.

"Kick her ass! Whoop her ass Peaches! Don't let that bitch get the best of you!" her cheering section yelled.

Fighting my way back up, Peaches and I went heads up. Even going toe to toe, I still put my thing down. Peaches was a lot taller than me so she should have gotten the best of me, but the bitch didn't know what to do with her height and weight. I, on the other hand, did. I used my small stature and small frame and put it to good use. I could tell that Peaches was becoming tired and winded, so I took advantage of that. Knowing sooner or later that Peaches' crew would jump in, I stepped up my game.

Fuck fighting fair, it was time to get grimy on her ass. Peaches never saw my next move coming. Pushing the bitch back as hard as I could, I sent her ass falling to the floor. Pulling my pocketknife out of my pants I flicked it open. Placing the cold knife to her throat I warned the other girls to stay back.

Focusing my wrath back on Peaches, lowly I hissed, "If you ever come at me again with some bullshit about LP, I will kill you. Do you understand?"

"Calm down Chyna, I was just playing. I didn't mean anything that I said," Peaches pleaded.

"Quit lying, I should slice your shit right now."

"Chyna, please don't. I'm sorry, I'm sorry okay," Peaches pleaded.

I saw the fear in her eyes as tears streamed down her face.

"Don't ever fuck with me again bitch," I stated, easing off of Peaches.

"Are you a'ight girl?" asked one of her friends.

"Does it look like I'm a'ight? My head is bleeding and I think that my eye is swelling up!" Peaches yelled.

Looking back into the mirror again, I checked my face. Besides having a few scratches, it was flawless. Fixing my clothes, I dusted myself off and headed out the door. A suspension was definitely in my future so I decided to turn myself in. I only ended up getting a three-day suspension, and since Peaches gave the first hit, she got more days. She wanted to tell the principle about the knife incident, but chose otherwise because she could feel my eyes on her as she told her side of the story. Never again would she fuck with me.

From then on, her and her girls steered clear of me. Word spread around school quickly that I had pulled a knife out on Peaches. Some people even started to call me "Crazy Chyna."

Asia and Brooke could only laugh when they heard this. To them, I had only protected myself.

"Chyna, ya ass over there daydreaming again?" Asia asked, snapping me back to the present.

"Shut up," I laughed.

"Asia, do you still go with that dude named Shawn?" Adrian, an associate of ours, questioned.

"Yeah, I still go with him. That's my boo, I ain't going nowhere girl."

"We know this," Brooke teased.

"Shut up Brooke."

"I haven't seen any cute dudes in a minute," I chimed in.

"Girl, where have you been at? You need to get out more," stated Michelle, Adrian's friend.

"Yeah Chyna, I just saw this one dude the other day, and let me tell you he was fine," said Adrian.

"How did he look?" I asked.

"Trust me, he was all that and then some. He was kind of tall, cocky and brown skinned, girl he was sexy."

"Did he have two platinum teeth in his mouth?" asked Brooke.

"Yeah, how did you know?" Adrian questioned.

"He kind of looked like he would kill you at the drop of a hat didn't he?"

"Yeah," Adrian laughed.

"Girl, that was Tyreik," Brooke stated, with a roll of her eyes.

"Tyreik, I heard about him," Asia added.

"Who is Tyreik?" I questioned.

"Chyna, you mean to tell me you haven't heard about Tyreik?" Brooke asked, shocked.

"If I had, I wouldn't be asking."

"Yo, the kid is large," Said Michelle.

"He's from Brooklyn so he got a New York accent and shit. He moved down here I think almost a year ago. Girl, every bitch I know wants to talk to him," Asia announced.

"The only thing though is that he's crazy. I heard he be killing muthafuckers and shit. You don't even want to fuck with him. Shit, if you make him mad he'll probably snap your neck," Michelle said, cracking up laughing.

"He gets his money through the dope game and trust me, he got dough," Adrian finished.

As the sound of the lunch bell rang, plans arose in my mind. My mind could not focus on my school work; it was in straight plot mode. I had to meet him, but how?

CHAPTER 3

CAN'T TOUCH THIS

"Chyna, come here!" Diane yelled, throughout the house.

"Hold on Asia. Ma'am!" I yelled back.

"Get off of that damn phone and come clean up your room."

"Girl, here she goes again, I'm going to call you back."

"A'ight," Asia said.

Hanging up, I rolled my eyes up to the ceiling. Diane had been in a real pissy mood. I hated when she got like this because no matter what, she always took it out on me. It was like I was her verbal punching bag. Entering my room slowly, I eyed Diane. She stood in the doorway with her "you disgust me" face on.

"Look at this room!" She yelled, into the air. "It doesn't make any sense Chyna, I don't buy you expensive clothes for you to throw them all on the floor! You don't appreciate shit I do for you! I go to work everyday to provide for you and look how you treat shit!"

Continuing to roll my eyes to the ceiling, I proceeded to ignore Diane. When she got in one of her moods she would bitch about the moon if she could. I had to go through this shit weekly. It was always, "if you don't like the way I run things around here then go and stay with your damn daddy". Since she couldn't whoop me anymore, she tried to hurt me with words.

"You think you're all that, you ain't shit Chyna! What you think, you're better than me? Do you think that you're not supposed to do anything around here? I work everyday to take care of you! Do you see all of these designer clothes, I bought them and I will take them away! I'm getting sick of your shit Chyna! One day you're going to come home to find the locks changed on you little narrow behind! I can't wait until I have my house all to myself!" She yelled.

I continued to clean my room up. Tuning Diane out seemed to make her even madder, so I did it on purpose.

She sensed this and ended her verbal bashing with, "You lazy ass heffa, I want you out!"

I had heard this time and time again before. In an hour's time, it would be as if nothing had happened. Diane talked a good talk but, in all actuality, she would never put me out. She fronted like it didn't matter to her, but the money that my daddy sent every month helped her out. It had taken for me to set up a deal with her to finally receive my portion. Yes, you read right, I had to ask Diane for my own money. Up until two years prior, she did what she pleased with the checks. Whenever I did ask for the money she would throw up in my face that she paid the bills with it.

"You have a roof over your head don't you? The lights are on and you have food in the refrigerator so don't ask me about that damn money," she would say.

But in all truth, she used it on herself. When I was old enough and hip to the game, I threatened her by telling her that if she didn't start giving me at least half of my money that I would go to my father. After a little thinking, she knew that I had pulled her card. From then on, we split the check down the middle. With this, I learned that when it comes to money even your own momma would sell you out.

The girls and I still kicked it but not as much. Everyday they made sure to call and check in, but I could tell that things were about to change. We all were being pulled in different directions in life. Shawn was Asia's whole life, and through him she had become good friends with his cousin and they started hanging tough. Brooke was too busy trying to find a way out of her parents' house. Eventually she ended up moving out and staying with her older brother. When she did move out, she had to find a job after school, so I rarely ever saw her anymore. I had to do something to bring the clique back together again. Lately, the only time we kicked it with each other was at school.

Calling them up after school one day, I propositioned them.

"Look you two, we have to get together and do something, I miss ya'll," I said, after getting them on a three-way call.

"I miss you too," Brooke said, sincerely.

"Me too, big head," teased Asia.

"How about ya'll come over here to my crib?" Brooke suggested.

"Cool, we need to see how you're living over there anyway," I stated.

"Bet. Me and T will come and get ya'll Friday," Brooke said.

I felt good knowing that things were about to get back to normal. Asia and Brooke were my family and it was lonely not having them in my life, so the upcoming weekend would be great.

The next day Brooke called and asked me to ride with her to the Southside of St. Louis.

"Girl, what are we doing down here?" I asked, not pleased.

"Look, I told you I had to come down here to pick up something. Now be cool Chyna," said Brooke.

I didn't know what Brooke was up to 'cause lately she had been real secretive. She had quit her job at the mall, but somehow she was still getting money. As a matter of fact, she had more money now then she did when she was working. Brooke always had style, but now she was flossing more than ever. The diamond stud earrings in her ears were blinding me. Brooke was my girl but I knew that I had to step my game up, because I didn't care who you were, friend or no friend, I wouldn't be outshined.

"Here we go. This is the street T told me to go to."

"Who do you know over here?" I asked.

"A couple of T's partnas live down here."

"Girl, look at those dudes over there. Damn, where have I been at?"

"You do not want any of them, trust me."

"Why don't I, shit look at him right there."

"Trust me, don't fuck with none of these niggas. I got something in store for you," Brooke replied, with a smile.

"Yeah, right Brooke."

Brooke stepped out the truck and studied her surroundings carefully. Looking left and right, she searched for any suspicious activity.

"Are you coming?" she asked.

"Oh, you want me to go with you?" I asked, jokingly.

"Girl, get ya ass out the car and come on."

It wasn't that chilly out so I opted to leave my coat in the truck. I rocked my curly hair in a ponytail and pulled it through the back of a pink Lady Enyce hat. As a matter of fact, I sported Enyce from head to toe, and to set the rest of the outfit off I had on my feet a pair of pink & white Adidas. The big gold earrings with *"Chyna"* written into the middle clanked against my face. I couldn't have looked anymore like a fly girl.

"Damn Brooke, who is this?" asked one of the six dudes who stood posted up in front of a liquor store.

"Mind your business Boog."

"Damn Brooke, why you got to be so mean?"

"Do you have my package or what?" she asked, all businesslike.

"Yeah, yeah I got it."

"Well, give it to me so I can bounce out," she demanded.

"A'ight Brooke damn, here take it."

"That's better and it better all be here."

"It is," Boog said, grinning.

"Yeah a'ight Boog, don't fuck with me."

"Bye sweetheart!" Boog yelled after me.

"What was that all about?" I asked Brooke.

"Girl, it ain't nothing."

"It sure didn't seem like nothing Brooke."

"Everything is everything C, don't worry."

Getting back into the truck, Brooke pumped some old Tupac. T, whose real name was TaRon, had some major beats coming out of his truck. As Brooke placed the key into the ignition, I spotted a 2000 burgundy Hummer coming down the opposite side of the street. The car was hot and the driver was beating too. The windows were tinted so I couldn't see the driver's face. Brooke had a wicked smile spread across her face.

"What are you smiling for?" I asked Brooke.

Blowing the horn, Brooke signaled the driver. Rolling the window down, a fine creature appeared. His features were chiseled and his glare was sinister, but looking into his eyes, I could tell that something warm lay behind his cold black eyes.

"What's up Tyreik?" Brooke said.

"Just checking up on shit, what's up with you?"

"Taking care of a little business for my brother."

"A'ight, go ahead and get on up then."

"A'ight, holla at you later."

Before I even had time to say anything, Brooke had already sped off.

"That was Tyreik wasn't it?" I asked, as Brooke laughed, "That shit is not funny Brooke, that was him wasn't it? He had the accent and everything. I can't believe that was him, damn he's fine. I can't believe you Brooke."

"When you saw him, you looked like a deer caught in headlights," she said, laughing still.

"Why didn't you introduce me? Better yet, why didn't you tell me that you knew him?"

"Because."

"Because what, Brooke?"

"Look Chyna, he and my brother get down with each other. T and Tyreik are like best friends and shit, and you know that I don't tell my brother's business. Besides, I wanted to see what everybody else had to say about him. Girl, Michelle and Adrian's asses don't know what the hell they were talking about. Tyreik can be crazy at times, and for the most part he's cool, but he'll beat a nigga down in a minute. Tyreik is all about making money for real."

The information sunk into my head heavily. Seeing Tyreik made me want him even more, we would compliment each other perfectly.

Friday couldn't have come fast enough, I was already packed and ready to go. After school I went to go get my hair and nails done. Coco, my stylist, gave me the Aaliyah 'do, you know the one were it's parted to the side and the hair hangs over your right eye. At first glance, I kind of looked like the slain R&B singer. I loved the body and bounce in my hair. Every time I turned my head, my hair bounced off my shoulders. The brand new fitted Rocawear puffy coat was a must. Underneath I had on a red fitted Rocawear shirt, low rise Seven Jeans and a pair of Adidas boxing shoes on my feet. The Louis Vuitton backpack purse set the outfit off.

After I got home, Brooke called to let me know that they were around the corner and to come outside, but I had already heard them a block away. T's bass in his Denali truck was off the meters, he had every window in Diane's house rattling and shaking. Coming down the street, they bumped *"Hot Boyz"* by Missy, it was one of my favorite songs. Brooke's brother was fine. He had tried hooking up with me a couple of times, but because T was a ho, I knew better.

"Damn Chyna, you're looking good," he stated, over the music.

"Thanks T," I uttered, rolling my eyes.

Through the rearview mirror, I could see him laughing. I couldn't help but to laugh also. T knew that we would never mess around, so hitting on me was just for fun. Back at T's crib on the Southside of St. Louis, we all got comfortable. Before long, T had blazed up a phat one. He had a case of Heinekens in the fridge so we popped them open. I had had a blunt to myself plus four Heinekens, so you know I was fucked up.

Watching Def Comedy Jam, I laughed my ass off. My stomach hurt from laughing so hard that I almost pissed on myself.

Halfway through the show, T got a call on his cell. He had to make a run. Me, having the munchies, I asked to go along. T, of course, didn't object to this offer. T only had to go a couple of blocks to meet his destination.

"I'll be right back," he said, getting out the truck.

While I waited in the car, I applied some lip gloss. Thumbing through T's CD's, I decided to put in a cat by the name of Musiq. I mainly enjoyed listening to Hip Hop, R&B was a little bit too soft for me, but instantly I feel in love. I bobbed my head to track twelve as I saw T coming out of the apartment complex, but he wasn't alone.

T and the unknown guy strolled over to the truck. I could tell that they were in a deep conversation 'cause I was all in their grill. I broke my neck trying to see the guy T was talking to, but I couldn't because they were too far away. Whoever the guy was he had T's undivided attention. Whatever they were discussing had to have been important. Without warning, T reached for the handle and startled, I jumped. As they climbed into the truck, I tried to act normal.

"Chyna, this is Tyreik, Tyreik, this is my little sister's friend, Chyna." T said.

Tyreik sat in the backseat dark as night. Even with a down coat with fur around the hood, I could tell he had a cocky build. His all black hat was cocked to the left and I could see he had a low cut. I saw that he had two platinum gangstas in his mouth. He rocked one on each side of his two front teeth. With his cell phone in hand, he said what's up and continued talking. I never even got a chance to say hi back. Through the corner of my eye, I could tell that T was holding back a laugh.

Tyreik's presence alone made me nervous, just knowing that he was sitting directly behind me had me shook. And Musiq's melodic voice made feelings rise in me that I had never felt before. Tyreik wasn't paying me any mind though, he and T carried on a conversation as if I wasn't even in the car.

After a ten minute ride, T stopped again. I wondered what T and Tyreik were up to when they both jumped out the truck and headed across the street. I didn't know what in the hell they were doing, but I did know that I didn't have any business being around.

On the other side of the street, T and Tyreik stood talking to some dudes. I spotted Boog, the guy from the other day. A couple of words were spoken between Boog and Tyreik, then Tyreik hauled off and stole Boog in the face and the next thing I knew T and Tyreik were stomping Boog. None of the other dudes jumped in or anything. From where I sat, I could tell that Boog was bleeding badly.

Walking back to the truck, Tyreik had anger written all over his face.

"Get me off this fucking block T before I kill this nigga," he stated, angrily.

I knew perfectly well what had just happened. The package that Brooke had picked up from Boog had to have been money. Boog worked for Tyreik and T and Brooke was doing pick ups for T. Evidently Boog hadn't taken heed to Brooke's warning and he must have been short with Tyreik's money. Everything was now crystal clear, Brooke was working for T and Tyreik and I feared for her safety. Even though I wasn't scared, I just couldn't wait to get back to the crib.

Nobody said a word while T drove and I knew not to ask any questions. Ten minutes later we were back in front of the apartment complex.

"I'll holla at you later T," Tyreik said, as he got out.

As I watched him walk back to his crib I felt a little hurt, he didn't even say goodbye to me. But damn he was fine, I thought to myself.

Getting back to T's place, I never mentioned the incident to Brooke or Asia. If T wanted them to know he would have told them. Besides, T was a grown ass man so I tried to put the situation out of my mind. Brooke and Asia never knew, but that whole weekend Tyreik stayed on my mind.

The following Monday in my fifth period class, I sat staring out the window. I never heard a word that Mr. Calloway, my science teacher, said. Science was the last thing on my mind because I was too busy daydreaming about Tyreik. The picture of his beautiful face would not escape my mind. He reminded me of a 50-Cent type brother but better looking. Yeah, Tyreik was sexy like that.

Doing some figuring in my head, I pretty much assumed that he had to be around twenty-three or twenty-four. With this, I pretty much figured that I didn't stand a chance of getting with him. Tyreik was a big boy alright, a little too big for me, something I hated to admit. The boy looked like he could put a hurting on my little pussy. No other dude had ever silenced me and I knew that I had to have looked like a damn fool. Tyreik had ignored me the whole time we had been in T's truck. Twisting up my lip, I figured that he had to have a woman at home. The man was just too damn fine not to, that had to have been the reason why he hadn't hit on me.

I promised myself that if I ever did get another chance, that I would make the most of it cause he was a once in a lifetime kind of nigga. True, I was a lot younger than he was, but I could teach Tyreik a thing or two.

"Chyna, the bell just rang," Jaylen said, bringing me back to reality.

"Oh, okay," I replied, trying to pull it together.

"Good job on your science project Chyna, I expect to see more good things from you," Mr. Calloway said.

"Thank you. That was nothing compared to what I can do," I boosted.

"I can't wait," he said.

"What's wrong with you? You didn't pay attention in class at all today," Jaylen asked.

"Boy ain't nothing wrong with me, I'm cool. Come on let's go," I said, waving him off.

Jaylen and I walked the crowded halls together. The whole walk to my last period, Tyreik stayed on my mind. Every word Jaylen spoke went in one ear and out the other.

"Chyna, are you listening?" he would stop and say.

"Yeah, keep going," I would answer.

The school day couldn't end fast enough for me. Jaylen would get my attention and I would listen for a minute or two, but it never failed, I would eventually drift back to Tyreik. I would picture the two of us chilling and kissing softly. Just the thought got my panties wet, and the fact that I hadn't had any in months intensified my attraction to Tyreik.

At exactly two fifteen, the last and final bell rang awakening me from my thoughts. I jumped up out of my seat like it was on fire. School had held too many distractions for me. I needed to be at home alone so I could fantasize about Tyreik. Pulling my blue jean coat on, I secured each button. The cashmere turtle-neck, brown leather skirt and brown and tan leather stiletto boots were off the chain. My hair had fallen a bit but it still had bounce to it. I strutted my stuff around school like I was J-Lo herself. With my run/walk on, I met up with Asia and Brooke at the front door entrance. Stepping out into the cold November air felt good on my skin.

Like clockwork, Shawn pulled up and scooped Asia up. That left Brooke, Jaylen and me, and five minutes later, T came and swooped Brooke up. They offered me a ride, but Diane had promised to pick me up, so I graciously declined the offer. No way would Diane dare leave me in the freezing cold. Leaning against the fence, I inhaled the cold air into my lungs.

"What time did your mom say that she was coming?" Jaylen asked.

Looking at the Guess watch on my wrist, I saw that Diane was already twenty minutes late.

"She should have been here by now," I said, rolling my eyes.

"Do you want me to stay with you until she comes?" staring at me, Jaylen smiled.

"Jaylen, you can go. I know that you have to catch the bus home. Don't miss your bus on my account, but thanks anyway."

Reassuringly, he spoke, "I want to stay with you Chyna."

While saying this, he stared deeply into my eyes. I, being the punk that I was, adverted my eyes elsewhere. Jaylen knew that he and I were just friends and I hated when he said little sly shit like that. Besides, I had bigger things on my mind.

First off, like how Diane played me for a fool over and over again. I wondered to myself how come she could never do what she promised? I never asked her for anything, so why is it when I do she can't even do that right. See, shit like this makes me hate her more and more. That's why I'm all for self now, you can't depend on anyone in this life, not even your damn parents.

"Chyna, are you a'ight? You seem like you got something on your mind," Jaylen asked.

"Yeah, I'm cool," I lied.

It had to be like thirty degrees and freezing. My legs were thick and all but the wind had them shaking like twigs.

Looking at the busy intersection for Diane's Maxima, I spotted a fly ass white Benz truck. You know that it caught my attention real quick, and whoever the driver was, he was bumping R. Kelly's *"Fiesta"* hard. As it was about to pass, our eyes connected and when they did, I knew whom they belonged to, those eyes belonged to Tyreik. If I hadn't known any better, I probably would have started jumping up and down.

"Do you know him or something?" Tyreik asked, uncertain.

I tried to answer but I couldn't, it was like I was in the presence of a superstar. My slanted eyes stayed glued to the truck. I wasn't prepared for this moment, Tyreik had caught me off guard. As we eyed each other, I hoped that he would stop and he did.

Pulling over, he said, "Come here, let me holla at you."

Strutting over to the truck I tried not to seem pressed.

"Ain't you that girl that was in T's car the other night?"

"Oh, so that's how we gonna play it. You gonna act like you don't even remember me right?"

"It ain't even like that," he laughed.

"Yeah whatever," I said, rolling my eyes.

"You waiting on somebody?"

"Yeah, I'm waiting for my mother to come pick me up. Why, you want to give me a ride?"

"As a matter of fact I do, hop in."

"Nah I'm cool, I don't know you like that."

"Oh, so that's how you gonna play it, huh?" he countered back, using my own words against me.

"Yup, that how I'm gonna play it," I smiled, showing off my dimples.

Licking his lips, Tyreik gave me the once over and I swear my whole body blushed.

"A'ight then I'ma holla at you dimples," he said, speeding off.

CHAPTER 4

JUICY

When I saw that Diane wasn't going to pick me up, I called Brooke and she had T come pick me up.

"Thanks for coming back T," I said.

"Shut up and get in," he said.

"I just saw your boy Tyreik," I stated.

"Oh word?"

"Yeah, he got a white Benz truck don't he?" I probed.

"Yeah, that muthafucker's bad ain't it?"

"Yeah it's tight. So what's up with your boy?" I asked.

Looking at me sideways, T started cracking up.

"What's so funny?" I asked, confused.

"Get the fuck outta here with that shit Chyna."

"I'm saying, what's up?"

"Girl, you better sit your young ass down and continue fucking with these little dudes, you ain't ready for a nigga like Tyreik," T replied, diligently.

"Oh, so that's your word?" I questioned.

"That's my word," he answered.

"T, now you know how I roll, I'm not like any of these silly ass hoes out here. I know the game and how it's played. I know that I'm young and all but you know how I get down. Tyreik could benefit with a chick like me on his side, but if he talking about some hit it and quit it type shit, then forget about it."

T thought about it a little. I wasn't like most broads, I knew how to keep my mouth shut and how to mind my muthafuckin' business. Tyreik didn't fuck with a lot of bitches; he was mainly about getting his cake. T told me that he would holla at Tyreik about me.

Walking in the house, I heard music blasting from Diane's room. That shit pissed me off even more. Standing in her doorway, I watched her as she sang and danced, she acted as if she didn't have a care in the world.

"Did you remember that you were supposed to pick me up from school?" I said, scaring her.

"Girl, don't be scaring me like that," turning down the radio, she asked, "what did you say?"

"I said did you forget that you were supposed to pick me up from school?" I asked, this time with more of an attitude.

"Oh, I knew there was something that I was forgetting to do," she replied, nonchalantly.

"I waited for almost an hour in the cold by myself," I lied.

"I'm sorry, I won't forget tomorrow. Now which one of these dresses do you like, I got a date tonight?"

Rolling my eyes at her, I just shook my head.

"Don't you roll your eyes at me again little girl. You got home didn't you, shit!" She yelled.

I mean it was like I didn't matter. She kept on going about her business like I wasn't even in the room. On her bed laid about five different dresses, evidently she was on her way out. Wherever she was going was more important than me. While staring at her, tears welled in my eyes.

As I stood there, never once did she ask how I had made it home. How many times have I wished for her to acknowledge me? I mean what do I have to do for her to show me some kind of attention? The only time that she recognizes me is when I do wrong. I hear her on the phone telling her friends that I'm lazy, selfish, fast and ignorant. She never tells them that she pops pills just to sleep at night. She never tells them she's money hungry and a compulsive neat freak. Shit, if my own momma didn't even give a fuck about me why should I. I told myself that there was no need for tears. There would be no more crying, tomorrow would be a new day, a new day with Tyreik in it.

Later on that night Asia, Brooke and I sat on the phone gossiping and going over our day.

"So Chyna, why didn't you tell me that you liked Tyreik?" Brooke asked.

"Damn, can T keep anything to himself?"

"T shouldn't have had to tell me, I thought we were girls," Brooke said.

"Girl shut up, it ain't even like that and you know it. It wasn't a big deal, damn."

"Well Chyna, he does look good," Asia said.

"Don't he though?" I laughed. "Brooke, you know that you got to give me the scoop on him, I don't know that much about him for real," I said.

"He rarely ever comes over here, but he was over here earlier with T and I overheard him talking about you."

"For real, what did he say?"

"I came in right in the middle of their conversation, but I heard them talking, first I heard them talking Boog and them niggas while they was here getting high. Tyreik had asked T was their money and shit straight today and T was like 'yeah.' He got to talken about how ain't none of them niggas gone step out of line since they stomped Boog out the other night. Then Tyreik brought up the situation wit you and how you shouldn't have been in the car wit them that night."

"He said what?" I asked wit an attitude.

"Yep, he said you should'nt have been in the car while they was handling they business and that T should have left you at home. At first T was on your side but then after Tyriek got an attitude so he agreed wit him."

"His ole punk ass," Asia laughed.

"Don't be talking about my brother," Brooke laughed too.

"Anyway Brooke finish telling the story," I said.

"Where was I at...oh yeah that's when Tyriek was like 'What's up wit ole girl?' T was like 'Who, Chyna?' and Tyriek was like 'yeah.' Now you know how ignorant my brother is, he started laughing and Tyriek got mad. After T stopped laughing he told Tyriek how cool of a girl you were. He told him that you were book smart and street smart and that you don't run yo mouth like a lot of the chicken heads they mess wit. He also said that who ever scoop you up got it made."

"Word?" Asia replied.

"Word but I ain't finish yet. He told T that he saw you today up at the school and that he tried to offer you a ride but that you was acten all stuck up."

"I was not," I protested.

"T told him that he came up there to pick you up and that you didn't mention shit about you and Tyriek talking. Tyreik started laughing and was like you one of them muthafucker that like to play games. So T told him that the next time he see you he gone kick yo ass but Ty told him don't do that and that he got you."

"And that was the last thing I heard them say," Brooke said, after relaying what she heard.

"I knew that nigga was feelin' me. He must have come over there after I saw him."

"Where you see him at?" Brooke questioned.

"I saw him riding past the school."

"Did he see you?" Asia asked, all excited.

"Yeah, he saw me," I answered. "Now finish telling me Brooke," I said, getting impatient.

"Okay, calm down ho," Brooke said.

"What's his real name?" I asked.

"His real name is Tyreik James."

"Tyreik is such a cute name, it fits him perfectly," I replied.

"Oh you just like the nigga Chyna, fuck his name," Asia joked.

"Whatever Asia, now continue on Brooke."

"He's twenty-two and he doesn't have any kids."

"Damn, I thought he was like twenty-four," I said.

"Ah no, wrong again. He and T are real close and when Tyreik moved down here they hooked up. They started out in the breaking and entering game together, but now they've graduated to bigger things, you know," Brooke countered.

"Got you dog," I replied.

"Now the real question is does he have a women at home with him?" Asia asked, in her ghetto girl tone.

"I don't know about that Chyna, you're going to have to find that out for yourself."

"Oh, I plan on finding that out, trust me."

A couple of days later it was a Saturday night and Brooke, Asia and I were riding around getting blazed. We rode all around St. Louis that night talking, drinking and thinking.

"Where's Shawn at Asia, ya'll usually are out doing something on a Saturday?" I asked.

"We're not on speaking terms right now."

"Well why not?" I asked, surprised because those two never argued or fought.

"Girl, he's mad because I told him he's gonna have to start wearing a rubber."

"What, ya'll ain't been using rubbers this whole time?" Brooke asked.

"We started off using them but lately that nigga been trying to slide up in me raw all the time. I ain't even trying to get pregnant so I told him, no rubbers equals no ass."

"Good for you Asia, I would have done the same thing," Brooke replied.

"Tell that nigga he better strap up and beat that shit up right," I joked.

Asia and Brooke cracked up laughing.

"What's up with you and Tyreik, Chyna?" Brooke asked.

"Shit, I haven't heard anything from him since that day, I guess he wasn't that interested."

"I thought he was really feeling you," Asia replied.

"Get ya 'hopelessly in love' ass on somewhere," I teased.

"Shut up Chyna wit ya old thug ass," she teased back.

"I'm kind of glad he didn't holla back, I might have gotten in over my head fucking with him."

Stopping at a nearby Citgo, Brooke hopped out and got some gas. That's when my phone rang.

"Hello?"

"Chyna," said the voice.

Smiling, I knew that it was Tyreik, he must have gotten my number from T.

"Who is this?" I asked, with an attitude.

"You know damn well who this is girl."

"Look, who is this playing on my phone," I grinned.

"Quit playing with me girl, it's me Tyreik, are you happy now?"

"That's much better; don't be calling my phone like you know me."

"You and your smart ass mouth gonna make me put a hurting on that pussy when I hit it."

"What? Boy, who you talking to?"

"You know I'm gonna hit that shit," he laughed.

"Whatever, Tyreik."

"Is that Tyreik? Tell him I said what's up," Asia said, excited-ly.

"Did you hear her?"

"Yeah I heard her, tell her I said what's cracking."

"He said hi Asia, now are ya'll done passing messages?"

"Where you at?" he questioned me.

"Just riding with my girls, why?"

"I want you to come see me that's why," he countered back.

"Where you at?"

"I'm at the I-Hop over by the Palace, swing through."

"I don't know Ty," I answered, nervously.

"Come on ma, give a nigga some play."

"How you know if Asia and Brooke even want to come?"

"Yeah, we want to come," Brooke said, getting back into the car.

"Bet, you ain't got no other choice now dimples. I'll see you when you get here," he said, hanging up.

I so didn't want to go see him cause just being around him made me weak in the knees. Tyreik was trying to get at my heart and I wanted him to but I was scared. He was exactly what I had wanted and more, a little too much more if you ask me. If given the opportunity, he could take my heart and run away with it. I had never given myself to a dude like that before and I wasn't planning on it anytime soon. I just wanted someone to kick it with, a nigga that could kick me down some doe and fuck me real good.

Pulling up, I spotted T and Tyreik's trucks. Admittedly, my heart was beating a mile a minute. Checking myself out in the rearview, I applied some gloss to my lips.

"Bring your old scary ass on," Asia teased.

"I'm coming, ya'll go on ahead."

"Her punk ass gonna stay in the car, watch," Brooke laughed.

"I'm coming, leave me alone!" I yelled.

Watching them go in, I tried to calm my nerves. "Okay Chyna, you can do this," I said to myself.

"What's up big bro?" Brooke said to T, walking over to the table in the I-Hop.

"Who told you to bring your big ass up in here?" T asked.

"Nigga, Tyreik asked us to come up here," said Asia.

"Shut up and sit down," T said, grabbing Asia's hand and pulling her down next to him.

"You know you need to leave that punk ass nigga you wit and get wit a nigga like me," He spoke, seriously.

"Whatever, T. When you stop being a ho holla at me."

"A'ight, when I get my shit together I'ma come swoop you up. I'm being real Asia, I want you and when I come through that nigga you wit gonna be ghost, ya hear."

"Where my girl at?" Tyreik asked.

"Here she comes," Brooke said, looking out the window.

I strutted in there like I owned the place. I rocked a fitted Rocawear baseball jacket, a white wife beater and a pair of tight Baby Phat jeans. My curly hair was freshly washed and set, I looked just like Kelis. Chewing some gum, I acted like I didn't want to be there, like I had something better to do.

"There my baby is," Tyreik smiled. "Damn, you look good. You trying to make a nigga bust two in you tonight, ma," he replied, grabbing my waist.

"You are so nasty, you need to watch what comes out of that mouth of yours," I replied, pulling away.

All the playas were up in I-Hop that night. Tyreik's crew consisted of T, Lonnie, Sam and Keith.

"That you cuz?" asked Lonnie.

"I'm trying to make her mine, a nigga been trying hard yo."

"Oh, so I still got a shot then. Come holla at a real man lil mamma," Lonnie said.

"Boy please," I smirked.

"Nigga, she straight played you," Sam laughed.

"Forget them, come sit wit me over here. So what's been up wit you lil momma?" Tyreik said.

"First of all, my name is Chyna not lil momma. I've been taking care of my business and as far as school goes, I'm in my last year you know. And you?"

"You got a smart ass mouth girl."

"You like it," I teased.

"Yeah I do, I think it's kinda sexy but check it, why you ain't want me to take you home the other day?"

"I'm not tryin' to fuck with you like that."

"If you ain't tryin' to fuck wit me like that then why are you here now?"

"Sorry to bust your bubble, but Brooke and Asia wanted to come."

"That's what your lips say but I know better, you want to be here with me."

"You think you the shit don't you?"

"Yeah I do and you do too."

"Whatever," I laughed.

"What's the problem ma, you scared of me or something?"

"Nah, I ain't scared of you."

"Then what's your problem? A nigga feeling you, matter of fact I'm feeling the shit outta you. I know you feeling me too, so let's stop all the bullshit and be together. You know you want me Chyna," He whispered into my ear.

His breath tickled my ear and he smelled so good. I tried not to look him in the face because if I did it would be over. The boy looked better and better each time I saw him. Being that close to him with his arms wrapped around me had my body feeling things it shouldn't.

"I can tell by the way you acting you want a nigga. You ain't got to be scared, I ain't gonna hurt you."

"Stop saying that, I'm not scared of you."

"Then why can't you look at me?"

Looking him square in the eyes, I tried to prove my point but that only made matters worse.

"Can I kiss you?" he asked.

"No."

"Why not?"

"Because I said so that's why. Haven't you ever been told no before?"

"Nope."

"Well I'm glad to be the first then."

"Come on Chyna quit frontin', you know damn well you gonna let me hit that."

"What?" I said, with an attitude.

"I'm just playing," he laughed.

"No you're not," I grinned.

"But nah for real, I'm gonna make you mine. I'm feeling you, I like you're style, you don't take no shit from me."

"That's what's up. So other females let you walk all over them?" I smiled.

"Yeah they do and that shit gets old after awhile. I'm looking for somebody that I can chill wit."

"And you think I'm the one?"

"Stop making this shit so hard Chyna. I want you, you want me, ain't shit else to be said."

"Who said that I wanted you?" I laughed.

"Take a chance on a nigga, quit being scared. I can understand your dilemma though; I'd be scared too fucking with a nigga like me."

"Chyna, you ready to go?" Brooke asked, coming to my rescue.

"Yeah, let's be up out this piece," I said, jumping up.

"Chill out with me for a little while longer," Tyreik said.

"No can do partna, I gotta go it's getting late."

"A'ight scary, give me a hug before you go."

Placing my arms around him, I felt his dick harden. He did that shit on purpose. He just had to give me a whiff of the dick, now he had me wanting to ride it.

"You feel that, that's all yours whenever you're ready for it," seductively, he whispered into my ear.

"That's nice to know Tyreik, now will you let me go," I said, trying to sound unfazed.

"Come on Chyna, let's go!" yelled Brooke.

"Give me your phone," Tyreik said.

Handing him my phone he put his number into it.

"Call me a'ight."

"Okay," I lied.

Walking off, I knew that I had no intention of calling him. Tyreik wasn't getting any of this, no matter how hard he tried.

Almost a week later, Asia and I ran into Tyreik again while going over to Brooke's after school to go shopping. It seemed like the more I tried to avoid Tyreik the more I ran into him. I hadn't called him like I said I would and I was starting to wonder if the brother was stalking me.

Walking into the Townhouse apartment, I saw T and Tyreik sitting, talking shit and getting blazed.

"Damn," I whispered.

Asia glared at me with a huge grin on her face. There wasn't a damn thing funny to me, I had been trying to avoid running into him.

"What up T?" Asia asked.

"You see what I'm doing, come sit over here by me," he smiled.

"Where is Brooke?" she asked.

"She ain't made it home from school yet. She should be here in a minute."

"What's up Tyreik?" Asia asked.

"Shit, what's been up with you?"

"School, that's what's been up."

"Now that you're all caught up, let me hit the blunt," I said, aggravated.

Taking the blunt from T, I inhaled slowly. I needed that shit to calm my muthafuckin' nerves. Tyreik's eyes had been glued to my breast since I had walked through the door and the shit made me uncomfortable as hell. I was trying my best to ignore Tyreik but he just looked too damn good, besides I didn't want to deal with the fact that I had played him. It was too much for me to deal with, I couldn't even stand still, I had to get up outta there.

"Give me your keys," I said to Asia.

"Why?"

"I left my phone outside in the car," I lied.

Playing along with me, Asia handed me her car keys. Outside, I stood on the driver's side rummaging through my purse, searching for a piece of gum. I had the door opened and was bent over leaning on the seat when Tyreik approached me.

"That's how I like it," Tyreik spoke from behind.

"Oh, is that right?" I asked, still playing it cool.

"Damn right," he replied, grabbing me by the waist.

"No you don't have your hands on me."

"Correction, I have my arms wrapped around you."

"Well you need to back up off me," I demanded.

"Let's be real Chyna, you don't want me to let you go do you? You like the way this feels just as much as I do," he replied, rubbing my thighs.

"You need to quit rubbing all up on me and let me go," I said, trying to control my breathing.

"Come on Chyna, you know you want me just as much as I want you."

"You're one arrogant ass nigga," I said, trying not to notice the fact that he was playing with my zipper.

"I'm just stating the facts, you the one lying to yourself. This feels right Chyna, you and me. Damn, I want to fuck the shit out of you," he said, inhaling my Sweet Pea body splash.

"Well, you can forget that shit."

"Whatever," he said, licking and kissing my neck.

Who in the fuck do he think he is, I thought to myself. There was no denying who he was, he was the nigga getting my panties wet with just a kiss on the neck. I had to get away from this nigga, but I was stuck between a rock and a hard place literally. His dick was rock solid and he made sure that I knew it. Biting my ear, he licked and sucked and that shit was feeling too good to me. I had completely forgotten that we were standing in a parking lot.

"That feels good, don't it?"

"Mm, hmm," I moaned.

"Let me touch you Chyna."

He didn't even give me a chance to answer before he had stuck his hand inside my panties. Gliding his hand around my pussy, he found that I was already wet.

"I knew you wanted a nigga," he bragged. "Let's go back to my crib," he said.

I couldn't say a word because Tyreik had my lips trembling. Biting down on my lips, I tried not to scream.

"Stop Tyreik, we can't do this."

Rotating his fingers faster over my clit, I felt like my body was about to explode. Grabbing his hand I tried to steady his pace.

"Why not, you're almost there, quit fighting me ma," pinching my nipples with his other hand, he continued. "Let's go back to my crib."

I couldn't fight it anymore and the moans that I had tried to suppress were coming out full force.

"Damn Tyreik," I moaned.

"It feels good, don't it?"

"Yes," I moaned, cumming.

"I knew ya ass was frontin'," he laughed.

"Whatever, Tyreik," I stormed off, totally embarrassed.

Grabbing me by the hand he pulled me back.

"Now what's your problem?" he asked, aggravated.

"You know that wasn't even right."

"I can't help it you're a freak," he said, laughing.

"Is that what you think of me?" I asked, hurt.

Pushing me back up against the car, Tyreik held me tight.

"You know I'm feeling you so don't even trip. I want you and I'm gonna make you mine, so you just need to stop fighting me girl."

"Why do you want to be with me Tyreik? I'm so much younger than you."

"Age ain't nothing but a number," he grinned. "Besides, you don't act young, you got it going on with your fine ass. I'm trying to see you tonight."

"I can't cause I got a test in the morning and besides my momma would kick my ass."

"A'ight that's cool. So are we gonna do this shit or what?" he asked.

Playing dumb, I asked, "Do what?"

"You still playing games Chyna, you know exactly what I'm talking about. You and me, are we gonna be together? I want you to be my woman. You know you already mine anyway," he said, staring me dead in the eyes.

This nigga had a pretty good chance of breaking my heart if I let my guard down. I wanted to be with Tyreik and I liked him a lot, but something inside of me was saying run and run fast.

"I don't know Tyreik, give me some time okay."

"That's cool, no pressure. But check this, you gonna be mine whether you want to be or not."

The next day I was getting ready for school when Diane and I had a heated argument. You know that she and I didn't have the typical mother/daughter relationship, she couldn't stand me and I could barely tolerate her funky ass attitude. Now more than ever, she and I were getting into it on an everyday basis. I guess that you could say that it was a typical morning in my house. I was preparing for another hectic day at school while Diane walked around the house bitching as usual.

"Chyna, get your shit together so we can go!" she yelled.

"Here I come momma, dang!" I yelled back.

"Don't be momma danging me girl, I'll come in there and slap the shit out of you!"

"She gets on my muthafuckin' nerves," I hissed, as I placed my books in my book bag, not knowing that she was within hearing distance.

"What did you say?"

A sharp pain ran through my chest, I couldn't believe that she heard me.

"I said, what did you say?" she demanded, walking up on me.

"Momma, go on wit all that yelling, I don't even feel like it this morning."

"I don't give a damn what you feel like this morning. This is my goddamn house and if I feel like starting some shit I'm gonna start it. If you don't like it..."

"You can get out," I said, finishing her words for her.

The next thing I knew, I was holding my face and crying because Diane had hauled off and smacked the shit out of me.

"What you hit me for?" I said, yelling.

"You might be big shit up there at that high school, but I'm the Queen B up in here, ya hear me? I told you that I was two seconds off ya ass and that you were gonna get your little feelings hurt. I'm your mother, not one of your little girlfriends."

"Oh, so now you wanna play momma?" I asked, laughing.

"You little ungrateful bitch, I'm gonna fuck you up, just keep on getting smart wit me."

"Do you actually think that I'm scared of you?" I said, staring her down.

At the point, she realized that I wasn't playing and backed up off me. I wanted her to hit me again because God knows I was gonna wear her old ass out, momma or no momma.

"Find your own goddamn way to school since you so grown. And your ungrateful ass better not ask me for a damn thing, nah. Now we'll see who'll get the last laugh. You gonna realize that you ain't shit, I control all of this up in here. Without me, you ain't got nothing. Where ya damn daddy at, he ain't gonna do shit for ya ass, I'm all you got so remember that. Now marinate on that while I'm gone," Diane said, leaving out the door.

Sitting down on my bed, I cried because I knew that she was right, Diane was all that I had. Drying my eyes, I remembered that I had only until the end of the school year to put up with her bullshit. Slamming the front door behind her, I heard Diane start up the Maxima and peel off. Now how was I supposed to get to school? Asia and Brooke probably were already gone and Jaylen was car less just like me. The only person that I could call on was Tyreik. Grabbing the phone, I decided to give him a chance.

"What's up Dimples, why you ain't at school yet?"

"I just got into it with my moms and she hit me," I cried.

"Yo, I'm on my way. Be outside cause I'm like five minutes away, a'ight?"

"Okay," I sniffed, wiping my face.

Tyreik must have been speeding because he got to my crib in less than five minutes. Hoping into his truck, I smiled weakly.

"You a'ight?" Tyreik asked.

"Yeah, I'm cool," I lied.

"You ain't got to front for me Chyna. I know that whatever went down between you and ya old bird got you twisted."

"Nah, I'm cool."

"Where she hit you at?" he asked, ready for war.

"Right here," I said, pointing to my right cheek. Touching my skin there I squirmed some because it still stung.

"Listen Chyna, you can tell me anything. Whatever you tell me will stay between you and me and I will never hold anything that you say against you. You believe me right?"

"Yeah, I believe you," I almost whispered.

CHAPTER 5

THE BEGINNING

It was November 20, 2000, and my first period class that day was Social Studies 101. The class had been discussing The Russian Tea Party and my mind had finally found its way back to the classroom. Ty and I talked from time to time, but I still wasn't sure so I kept my distance. He continued to press the issue of us being together, but I needed time to think so I told him that I couldn't continue to talk to him until I was completely sure. I literally had to force myself not to think about Ty.

I had to ace the test we were about to be given because on the last one, I had only scored a "B" and Diane nearly shit her pants when she saw it. A "B" was far from bad, but Diane expected perfection. As soon as the test started, my name was announced over the intercom for me to come to the principal's office with my things. A million thoughts ran through my mind with things that I could have possibly done and I couldn't come up with anything. Pushing the office doors open, I found the school secretary on her computer.

"Excuse me," I spoke lightly.

"Oh sweetie, your dad just called and said that you all have had a family emergency and he wants you to come home. He's outside waiting for you."

Tears welled up in my eyes because something bad had to have happened 'cause my daddy had never even been to Norfolk before. Throwing my coat on, I raced outside. As soon as I reached the gate, I saw that it wasn't my daddy it was Tyreik. My breathing had slowed and butterflies rose up in my stomach.

"What's up Chyna?" he smiled.

I couldn't say anything. The fact that the school guards were staring at me, and Tyreik's presence being so strong, I was speechless. As I got inside the truck I inhaled his scent.

"So what's up?" he asked again.

"Nothing," I said, confused by the whole situation.

I didn't expect for him to come back at me so soon, but instead of me showing my insecurities, I played it real smooth.

"What's going on? Why are you picking me up from school? Where are you taking me? You ain't kidnapping me are you?" I asked, all in one breathe.

"Nah, it ain't even like that. I just wanted to chill wit you, you know."

"We could have done that when I got out of school." I stated.

"I didn't feel like waiting until then, besides I got business to take care of later."

"Oh," I replied. "So where are you taking me?" I asked, again.

"We're going to my crib, is that okay with you?" he asked.

"Yeah, that's cool."

I hope he don't think he's gonna hit this without giving up some cheese first, because if he does, he's got another thing coming, I thought.

Pulling in front of the apartment complex, I saw that it was the same one from the other night. Tyreik lived on the second floor. From the outside it didn't look like much, it looked like your typical apartment building, but the inside of Tyreik's apartment was off the chain.

In his living room he had all black leather furniture. He had added African art for a touch of color. He had a flat screen TV on the wall. The dining room was black and gold, the table and chairs were black with gold trim, even the china was black and gold. Studying my surroundings, I saw that everything was neat and clean. Tyreik had style and I liked that.

"Ay, you want something to drink?" he yelled, from the back of the apartment.

"Nah, I'm cool," I said, sitting on the couch and removing my coat.

"You can turn on the flat screen if you want!" Tyreik yelled, from the back again.

"I'm cool!" I yelled back.

Making myself comfortable, I took off my white and pink Air Force Ones and got situated. Twirling my hair, I waited for Tyreik to return. Oh and when he did return, I almost shitted on myself. I thought that I had made myself comfortable, but this nigga had really stripped down. His coat and t-shirts were now gone, the only thing he had on was a wife beater, jeans, socks and house shoes. His chain still lay across his chest and his muscles were on point for real. The boy was cocky as hell. Sitting down next to me, I scooted over to give him some room.

"You got a nice place."

"Thanks," he said.

Leaning forward, he grabbed the remote and scrolled through the channels. I watched his every move. My eyes scanned over his back with pleasure. Catching me off guard, he started up a conversation.

"How long have you known T?"

"Oh, um, since I was about nine or ten," I said.

"Word?"

"Yeah, Brooke and I have been friends since then. How long have you known T?" I questioned.

"For about a couple of years," he answered.

"Where are you from because I know that you are not from here?" I giggled.

"Have you ever heard of Flatbush, Brooklyn?"

"I think so."

"Well, that's where I'm from."

"Word, I've always wanted to visit New York. How is it up there?"

"It's cool if you like to live in a fast paced environment."

"Do you miss it?"

"Sometimes I do, but not for real."

"Do you have any family up there?"

"Nah, not for real," he replied, glumly.

"Oh, sorry to hear that," I said, sadly.

"It's cool yo."

As he leaned back on the couch, I watched him watch the TV and I could tell that he had hurt in his eyes. Suddenly and without any knowledge of my actions, I eased over and laid my head on his chest. I didn't care if I was being bold or not, I had to touch his skin. I melted into his chest as I rested my body on his. I guess he didn't mind because he wrapped his arm around my waist bringing me closer to him. I had never felt so at peace in my life and I could tell that he felt the same way too because he didn't seem so tense anymore.

Sitting in that position, we kicked back and watched TV in silence. While watching Regis and Kelly, we both fell asleep. When I awoke, I tried to adjust my vision. Where in the hell am I, I thought? Staring around the room I realized that I was still at Tyreik's place. When I tried to move, I felt a hand pull me back. A smile spread across my face when I realized that I was not alone. Ty had brought me to his bedroom while I was asleep. That was sweet right?

Looking at him, I knew that I was in deep with him. Tyreik had me going and I never wanted to leave him. Rubbing his face, I tried to wake him and it didn't take much because the slightest touch of my hand awakened him. Grabbing my hand tightly he scared me because he had the death grip on me. The look in my eyes must have alerted him that I was afraid because he let me go and apologized.

Sitting up, I eased myself away from him. Shit this nigga was crazy.

"What was that all about?" I asked, kind of afraid.

"My bad, I'm just not used to sleeping with anybody."

"I see," I said, with a roll of the eyes.

"Come here," he said, demandingly.

Taking me by the arms, he placed me on top of him. Holding my face, he brushed my hair away from my eyes. Staring deeply into my eyes, I saw that he was contemplating something serious, it was like he was trying to figure me out.

"I'm gonna get locked up fuckin' with you," he stated.

We both broke out laughing.

"Look Tyreik, I like you and if I chose to mess with you that's my business," I said, assuring him of my position.

"I hear you talking."

It was funny how comfortable we were together. Tyreik had his arms wrapped around my waist and I had my head lying against his chest. Laying in silence we both drifted into our own thoughts. Tyreik and I didn't have to talk to understand each other, we knew exactly what was about to happen. Tyreik was the type of brother that girls only dreamed about, he was the kind of guy that you only saw in videos or magazines. Tyreik was the total package for real.

Once I got to know him better, I learned that Tyreik was misunderstood not crazy. He was a private person and he only truly opened up when he got to know you better. Tyreik was smart, he knew that you had to instill fear in niggas. His motto was "you either kill or be killed" because if you let someone get over on you once they'll try to do it again. It wasn't that hard to figure out, I understood perfectly.

When we had our morning talks, I learned about Tyreik's family. His mom, Lizette, was a prostitute and his dad, Big Redd, was her pimp. They both still lived out in New York and neither of his parents ever had time for him. Big Redd spent his time pimpin', flossing and building his stable of hoes. Lizette was his bottom bitch, she had been down with him from the start.

Big Redd was thirty years old when he scooped the young naïve fifteen-year old girl up. She could have easily been a Jet Beauty of the Month. Lizette had run away from home because she couldn't continue living underneath the strict rules of her Christian parents. When Big Redd approached her with the idea of hoeing, she looked at it as easy money. Big Redd became the young girl's savior and any and everything that he told her she believed. As the sun is yellow, if he said it was blue, she believed it.

In August of 1977, Lizette learned that she was pregnant with Tyreik. Because of her fear of Big Redd, she tried to keep her pregnancy a secret, but once she hit her second trimester her secret was out. The skimpy outfits that she was required to wear did no justice to her growing stomach. One night out on the strip, Big Redd confronted her. Cornered, she had no choice but to tell him the truth. Big Redd became furious when he learned of Lizette's unexpected arrival.

"How can I put you out on the strip now ho! I can't do anything with you, you are of no use to me! Don't nobody want no pregnant pussy, bitch!" Furious, he slapped her down to the ground.

"Daddy, I'm sorry! I knew that you wouldn't be pleased! I'm sorry Daddy Redd, please forgive a bitch!" Lizette pleaded.

"Forgive you? Bitch, is you smoking that dope? Are you crazy ho! Where are you and your bastard baby planning on living? Cause if you didn't know, Big Redd don't want crumb snatchers!"

"Daddy Redd, this baby right here is yours."

Slapping her face again, he grabbed her and said, "Bitch, I know that you don't expect me to believe that baby is mine when you fuck about ten different Johns a night!"

"But Daddy Redd, I only go raw wit you. You got to believe me Redd."

Big Redd wasn't trying to hear that shit, he didn't put shit past a ho. Even though he cared for Lizette more than he did the other hoes, he still didn't trust anyone. The only thing that mattered to him was his money.

Throughout the rest of her pregnancy, Lizette didn't receive the finer things that she had been accustomed to anymore. No longer on the block, she was flat out broke. Big Redd only gave her enough doe for fare to the doctor's office, toiletries and food. Each and everyday that she spent alone in that house, she grew to regret keeping the unborn child. The thought of adoption had even crossed her mind, but who would want a whore's baby.

May 22, 1978, was the day that Tyreik was brought into this world. Lizette had to go through the painful eighteen-hour labor alone, she didn't have any friends and none of the other hoes liked her. Her family had disowned her and now Big Redd had too, and that hurt because she truly had believed Big Redd when he said that he loved her. The only reason he still allowed her to live with him was because he knew that she had no other place to go, and plus, when she got her shape back she would be of good use to him again.

The long labor was a horrific one. The whole time that she was there she cried, physical and emotional tears poured out of her. She didn't have anyone there to tell her that she would be okay and no one was there to hold her hand. The look on the nurses faces showed disgust and disdain, she knew that they pitied her. The birth of her son would forever change her. Lizette had become bitter and unsympathetic during the nine months, no one cared for her so why should she care. No longer was she the same young woman searching for love and acceptance, her love would be the streets.

"Fuck my family, Big Redd and this baby!" she screamed, as Tyreik was being born.

The doctors asked her if she wanted to hold the newborn, she coldly answered, "No."

Despite his mother, every nurse in Labor & Delivery fell in love with Tyreik, he was a beautiful baby. From his chocolate skin to his wavy black hair, he was perfect. When Lizette arrived home from her stint in the hospital, she returned to an empty house. For the first time she didn't feel the need to cry. As Tyreik began to cry, she rummaged through a plastic bag for formula. She was down to her last can of milk and the last of her money had been spent on the cab ride home.

Thankfully, Big Redd finally decided to show his face. When

he heard the wail of a crying child he went ballistic, yelling throughout the house, "Didn't I tell you not to bring your bastard baby back here with you bitch! Didn't I tell you Lizette! You must think I'm playing or something? Do you hear …?"

But he couldn't finish his sentence. The first sight of the little boy bundled up in Lizette's arms softened his tough demeanor. Taking him from his mother, Big Redd asked the child's name.

"I named him Tyreik James," Lizette responded, resentfully.

Admiring Tyreik, he fell in love. Big Redd still wasn't ready for kids, but Tyreik was already there, so he had to make the best out of a bad situation.

Most of Tyreik's adolescent years were spent alone. Soon after he was born, Lizette turned to drugs. The streets became her family and crack was her best friend. Big Redd made sure that Tyreik was well taken care of, but often he was not around. Different people babysat him each day, but by the time he was thirteen years old, Big Redd got locked up for soliciting young girls to prostitution. He ended up serving ten years upstate. Tyreik never, if rarely, saw Lizette because she was a straight up crack head. That's when Tyreik got hip to the B&E game.

When I learned all of this, I looked upon Tyreik in a whole new light. He had survived so much and here I was complaining about Diane and my problems. Diane didn't have shit on Lizette. He said that I reminded him of her, the only difference between her and me were my dimples and my wild curly hair. Tyreik told me that that was the reason he barely said anything to me on our first meeting because seeing me had conjured up too many memories. The memories of Big Redd and Lizette had long been buried until that night.

Little did I know then, but Tyreik would become my main focus in life. Initially, I still tried to keep school a priority but whenever my cell phone rang and I saw Tyreik's number, I put school aside. I would only attend school about two or three days a week because my days were spent with Tyreik. Sooner than I thought, my "A" average had already fallen to a "D" average. The teachers saw this and admittedly became concerned.

Coming in from another day of skipping school and spending it with Tyreik, Diane confronted me.

"What is this I hear about you missing days at school? Your English teacher, Mr. Bryant, called me to see if you were alright. He told me that your grade has fallen from an "A" to a "D" Chyna! You have some major explaining to do!"

Of course I made up a lie, I was not about to tell Diane about my escapades with Tyreik. Hell, she would have had my ass in a second.

"Momma, Mr. Bryant is trippin', my grades are straight, you'll see. Report cards will be out in about a month or so and you'll see my grades are on point."

Saying this, I bought myself a little time. I figured that I still had time to bring my grades back up. With confidence, I shrugged Diane's news off and went about the rest of my day.

CHAPTER 6

SINCERELY YOURS

You don't even know how much I loved being around Tyreik, I really and truly looked up to him. Anytime he told me something I would listen intently, everything he said was important to me. Being around him hipped me to a lot of shit that I didn't even know about. Prior to meeting Tyreik, I knew a little bit about the dope game. He taught me about ounces and kilos. I learned how to cut that shit up, cook it and package it. Tyreik only let me do it once though and I thought that it was fun, it was like an experiment in science class.

My personality even changed being around him. I already was a mean little something, but being around Tyreik and his cocky ass attitude boosted it to a whole other level. Tyreik, like me, just didn't give a fuck.

One day while we were out having lunch at Hoolahan's, this bitch kept on mean mugging me so I had to put the bitch in her place.

"You got something on your lip baby, let me get that off you," Tyreik said, wiping my lips.

"Thank you, baby," I smiled, while eyeing the bitch up and down.

Her and her friends would look at me and then start whispering and shit. By the time dessert came I had had enough.

"Excuse me sweetie, I need to go take care of something," I said, pushing my seat back.

"Fuck them hoes!" Tyreik yelled, as I made my way across the restaurant.

Fuck that, I thought. The bitch was about to get chin checked if she didn't stop staring.

"Do ya'll got a problem wit me or something? Cause I swear ya'll been down my throat since I got here."

"You must be the new flavor of the month," The caramel colored chick replied, with her lip turned up.

"Excuse me?"

"You heard right, I said you must be the new flavor of the month. I was with Tyreik before he started fucking wit you. I can't believe he's fucking with high schooler's now," she and her friends laughed.

"Bitch, don't be mad cause I got him and you don't."

"Are you done?" Tyreik asked, hugging me from behind.

"You got the nerve to hug this bitch in front of me?" The caramel colored chick asked.

"Damn right I'm gonna hug her in ya face. You my girl ain't you?" Tyreik asked, looking at me.

"Damn right," I smiled.

"Well then the shit is settled. Let's go home baby, my dick is hard and I need to taste the kitty," He said, licking my neck.

"Ya'll heard, my man's dick is hard and he needs to taste the kitty, so see you when I see you," I laughed, walking away with Tyreik.

Tyreik and I had officially been boyfriend and girlfriend for over a month. He and I spent a lot of time together snuggled up during that cold winter in 2000. But it amazed me how he had so much restraint because never once did he try to have sex with me. I started to question my sex appeal when it came to him. I wore all of my tightest shirts and jeans and Tyreik could barely keep his hands off me. We kissed, licked, rubbed and sucked each other daily, but whenever we got to that point, he would back down. Hell, his foreplay was enough to make me cum at least twice, but you know a freak like me wanted more.

I had gripped his "daddy long stroke" a couple of times to see what he was working with and I was pleased to know that my man was packing some heat. I wanted Tyreik inside of me so bad that sometimes I even begged for it. Thinking back, I think that Tyreik was trying to torture me on purpose. He would have this wicked smirk on his face every time he saw how bad I wanted him and he wouldn't budge. After a while I just stop asking.

Fucking around with Tyreik, I ended up missing finals all together. I was totally fucked so I had decided to tell Diane the truth. I was going to tell her right before the Christmas break, but before I had the chance to, I got caught.

Tyreik and I had planned on shopping that day but I had left my Visa at home. Yes, I had a Visa at seventeen. Diane had gotten it for me for my sixteenth birthday. It was around noontime, so I asked Tyreik to swing by my house. I had forgotten that Diane had changed her shift at the bank and it was just my luck that she had come home for lunch that day. With no sight of her car, I thought that the coast was clear. Little did I know that her car was parked in the garage. I hadn't plan on being that long but Tyreik had to take a leak.

As I put my key in the lock, I laughed at Tyreik doing his pee pee dance. When I opened the door, I saw Diane there standing.

"What in the hell are you doing home from school Chyna, and who is this?" She asked.

Frozen, I stood in the foyer shocked but Tyreik could have cared less.

"Look, I got to go piss, I'll be right back a'ight," he said, while kissing me on the cheek.

"Oh hell no, Chyna have you lost your damn mind! And where do you think you're going? Chyna, you better get your little friend!"

"I'll be back man," Tyreik spoke, reassuringly.

"Chyna, I'm going to kick your ass! You better tell your little friend to leave my house! Oh I get it, this is the nigga you've been fucking! You must think I'm dumb don't you! I know that your fast ass would hang yourself sooner or later! I've been up to your school and I've seen your attendance record! You've missed twenty days of school and your grades, we're not even going to talk about your grades!"

"Momma, it ain't even like that."

"Am I missing something? Tell me what I'm missing Chyna! I know the story all too well! You met this low life and you've let your pussy lead you instead of your brain!"

By this time Tyreik had returned.

"Come on Chyna let's go, I ain't got time for this shit yo."

"My daughter ain't going anywhere with you, I want you out of my house!"

"Look, I'm trying to respect you on the strength of Chyna but you need to chill!"

"Who do you think you're talking to lil boy?"

"Man fuck this, Chyna let's go!" Tyreik yelled.

"Baby, calm down," I said, gently.

I knew that Tyreik would kick Diane's ass if I didn't calm him down. He already didn't like her after I told him how she treated me.

"That's it, I'm calling the police," Diane warned.

"All that ain't even called for momma!"

"Chyna, this is the last that I'm going to tell you to tell your lil' boyfriend to leave my house."

Staring up at Tyreik, I saw that he was passed pissed off. I didn't know what to do. On the one hand, Diane was the woman who gave birth to me, but on the other hand, I had Tyreik. If I told Tyreik to leave, he would leave me for sure.

"Chyna, I'm getting ready to go, are you coming or what?" He asked me, sternly.

"Momma, just let me go and talk to him. We'll talk when I get home I promise."

"Chyna, if you walk out of that door with him, you will not, and I repeat, will not step foot in my house again!"

Diane was serious so I made the best decision for me at the time.

"Chyna, fuck all this bullshit, you know that I got you," Tyreik replied.

Taking one last look at Diane, tears filled my eyes. Nothing hurts more than the pain that comes from loved ones. Diane would rather see me out on the streets than to love and support me. I always knew that she didn't want me around because I had become a constant reminder of what was, all of the failed relationships and hardships in her life were my fault. The only thing that I wanted was to make her proud of me. This would only be another disappointment on my list of many.

"Let me get my stuff then."

"You ain't taking a damn thing out of here. Since you want to be so grown, have him buy you some new clothes."

"Shut the fuck up you, she don't need shit up in here! Let's go Chyna!"

Turning to leave, Diane asked for my keys. As I placed the keys on the table, tears fell from my eyes.

"When he breaks your heart and puts you out, and believe me he will, don't come back here."

"Trust me I won't," I replied, as I slammed the door shut.

That day we didn't make it to the mall as planned. The entire ride back to Tyreik's place was spent with me crying hysterically. I couldn't believe that Diane had actually put me out. My face was red and my eyes were swollen with tears. Tyreik tried to console me but I was inconsolable. Here I was, seventeen and homeless, I had no money, nothing. Yeah Tyreik said that he would take care of me, but I'm no dummy, if he decided that he didn't want to be with me anymore I was surely out on the streets.

Lying on the bed in my new crib, I continued to cry. Tyreik had gone out to get us something to eat. His, *I'll be right back*, had already turned into an hour and a half. Thinking that I should let my girls in on what had happened, I called them.

"Chyna you're lying, Diane did not put you out," said Asia, in disbelief.

"I'm telling you the truth she put me out, I ain't got shit but the clothes on my back," I said.

"Damn Chyna, that's fucked up. We wear the same size so you can borrow some of my clothes," Asia assured.

"Thanks Asia, I'll probably have to take you up on that offer."

"So you're really going to live with Tyreik. You know that

you're welcome to stay with me and T, I'm pretty sure that he wouldn't mind," said Brooke.

"Yeah, Chyna, I don't think you staying with Tyreik is a good idea," replied Asia.

"Why wouldn't it be a good idea?" I asked.

"I mean you don't really know him that well," Asia responded.

"He may want you there for now, but how long do you think that will last?" Asked Brooke.

She had a good point there. What had I gotten myself into? If Tyreik decided one day that he wanted me to leave, where would I go? My head began to hurt again with thoughts of doubt running through it. I couldn't let my girls know, because me telling them that I too had doubts would only make the situation worse. Holding my head, I heard the front door open.

"I'm going to call ya'll back."

"Chyna wait, we got to talk about this," Brooke demanded.

"Okay, I'll call you back later," I answered, as I hung up on them.

"Tyreik, is that you?"

"Yeah it's me, come here."

Jumping out of the enormous bed, I headed to the living room. To my surprise, Tyreik had the living room filled with bags of clothes from all of my favorite stores. More tears came to my eyes as I looked at all of the bags. He had thought of everything, each bag was filled to the brim. He got me Rocawear, Baby Phat, Enyce and more. He had even gone to Victoria Secret's and bought me new bra and panty sets, he had even added a couple of sexy negligees to the bunch.

Hugging his neck, I kissed him for what seemed like forever.

I didn't know why I had let Asia and Brooke put any doubt in my mind when it came to Tyreik. I had to have been important to him, if I wasn't he wouldn't have been going through all of this for me. He didn't have to tell me, I already knew that he loved me.

CHAPTER 7

CAUGHT UP IN THE RAPTURE OF LOVE

Christmas had come and gone and the New Year was fast approaching. To me, life seemed to be looking up. Despite the fact that I had been kicked out of my house, dropped out of high school and was living with my drug dealing boyfriend, I was happy. I didn't have Diane on my back every damn minute of the day. I controlled my own destiny, with Tyreik there, of course, guiding me along the way. I didn't see what the point of school was, I was smart and I didn't need no high school diploma to tell me that. Eventually I would get my GED and once I acquired it, I would attend classes at one of the community colleges.

For now, the only thing that I had on my agenda was kicking it. The only thing Tyreik expected from me was to keep a clean house and to have something on the table for him when he came home. I knew how to burn in the kitchen so he stayed fed. Tyreik was my knight in shining amour and he spoiled me rotten, everyday was like Christmas in our house.

For Christmas he got me a brand new Jeep Liberty. You can't even understand how excited I was. It was about time that I had my own whip to ride around in and I couldn't wait to sport my shit around the city. Brooke and Asia didn't believe me when I told them the news, I literally had to go to each of their houses to show them. It seemed like after I got my whip, the girls and I started to grow even farther apart. I just didn't understand why they couldn't be happy for me. They constantly told me that I wasn't the same person anymore and that I had started to change once I got with Tyreik. They even said that I put Tyreik before everybody, including them, which I didn't understand.

When Asia and Brooke were out doing their thing, I sucked it up and stayed cool. I didn't understand why they couldn't be happy for me. Tyreik was my man and they were my friends, how was I supposed to choose between them. It seemed to me like they looked past the fact that he was taking care of me, the only thing that they saw was the fact that I was putting my own happiness first for once. Secretly, I began to resent them for this, they had to have been jealous. Yeah jealous, that had to have been it. My own satisfaction is what mattered and I had to go for self. They only thing that would matter from here on out was me, myself and I.

With all of the clothes and money that I had, Tyreik and I still hadn't fucked yet. Shit, I was starting to wonder if the nigga was gay. Whenever I was in the same room with him, I would be turned on. It was like I was a dog in heat so, me being me, I brought the subject of us having sex up.

Lying in bed nestled under his arms, I said, "Baby, how much longer are you gonna make me wait?"

"What you talking about Dimples," he said, half asleep.

"Why haven't we fucked yet?"

"I haven't fucked you because I don't want to just fuck you, I want to make love to you Chyna. I want you to be my wife one day and someday be the mother of my kids. Don't you think it's hard for me to lie next to you every night and not touch you like I want to? A nigga like me would've been tore ya shit up, but I see more in you than just your physical appearance. I want you to need me Chyna, not just want me."

After that statement, there wasn't shit else that I could say, Tyreik taught me everything I needed to know. He schooled me on how to act, dress and how to get what you wanted out of life. I thought that the way I dressed was on point, but to Tyreik it was a little too girlish to him. My shirt, tight jeans and tennis shoe game wasn't sexy enough for him. It kind of hurt my feelings when he told me this. There I was thinking that my shit was tight and to him I looked like a little girl. Tyreik was an important man and his woman had to look good, so I did what I had to do to make that possible. I wanted to make Tyreik happy so I changed everything about myself to please him.

While he was out one day, I went to the mall and picked up a few new items. My Baby Phat, Rocawear and Enyce clothes were a thing of the past. My wardrobe would now consist of Chanel, Dior, D&G, and Diane Von Furstenberg. I replaced my Adidas and Nikes with stiletto heel pumps. I even went as far as to cut and straighten my hair. I had Coco cut my hair to reach just above my breast.

As my hair fell to the floor, I cried tears of sadness, Coco even cried too. Diane would have flipped her wig if she saw Coco cutting so many inches off my hair. It was all worth it though 'cause Tyreik was all that mattered anyway. He would definitely be surprised when he saw me. I even had Coco teach me how to apply makeup.

Leaving the shop, I felt and looked like a new woman. Hurrying down the highway, I rushed home so that I could beat Tyreik home. Quickly, I showered and dressed. Looking at my new reflection in the mirror, I knew that without a shadow of a doubt I looked HOT. The seventeen-year old Chyna had gone bye-bye, I could now easily pass for twenty. I had on a slinky black Versace dress cut with its back out all the way down to my butt. My new style was banging.

Hearing the sound of keys being placed inside the lock, I sat on the bed and prepped. The scene was all set, I had candles placed everywhere, the bubble bath was drawn and I had T buy us a bottle of wine to go along with the meal that I had prepared.

"Chyna, are you here?" he called out.

"Yeah, I'm back here in the bedroom. Come here, I have something I want to show you."

"It smells good in here, what have you cooked girl?"

"Come here first, then I will tell you."

Tyreik couldn't have been more surprised. As soon as he hit the doorway, his jaw dropped. There I was sitting on the bed scantily dressed with my bare silky legs crossed seductively. To shock Tyreik was a lot, so I knew that my shit was tight.

"Damn baby, what did you do to yourself?"

"Do you like it?"

"Damn right I like it, shit, come here," he said, grabbing his dick.

Slowly I eased my way off the bed and made my way over to him. Taking me by the hand, he pulled me close and held my tiny waist in his hands. Wrapping my arms around his neck, I kissed his lips and we kissed for what seemed like hours. Letting me go, he asked me to turn around for him, he needed to see all of me. With a little twirl, I stood with my voluptuous backside facing him, all the while standing in my video girl stance. Tracing his fingers down the crease of my back, he stopped once he reached my butt. Bending over slightly, I gave him a better view.

"Do you like it?" I asked, nervously.

"I can't believe you got my name tattooed on you."

"Tyreik, I know that we've never even brought this up before, but I love you and I would do anything for you. I thought that this would be a nice way to show you how much I appreciate everything you've done for me."

"I love you too girl, I just ain't that big on words and shit, but I do love you."

Smiling gleefully, I kissed his face. Taking me into his arms, Tyreik picked me up and placed me gently on the bed. Kissing my lips softly, I prepared myself for what was finally about to happen.

"Are you sure that you want to do this?" he asked.

Hell yeah I thought, but instead I opted for a more suttle yes.

"A'ight now, I'm giving you a fair warning Chyna."

"Whatever nigga, you act like your shit is all that."

"Okay baby, I tried to warn you."

I was not trying to hear that shit, getting my freak on was my main concern. Hunger and yearning was written all over Tyreik's face. Taking my hands into his, he placed them above my head. With my hands in one of his, he used his free hand to massage my breast. Kissing each other like never before, Tyreik peeled my dress off without me even knowing it. I was buck naked in a matter of seconds. Placing both of my breasts in his mouth, he licked and probed. He sucked on my mountaintops like they were going out of style.

Flicking his tongue across my nipples made my whole body shudder. Savoring the sensation of his tongue, I bit into my lip. Tyreik trailed loving kisses down my stomach and made his way to my inner being. His fingers continued to pleasure my nipples as his tongue seduced my pussy. Tweaking and pinching my nipples, he toyed with my body with no remorse. Tyreik had never gone down on me before like this so I enjoyed every minute of it. His tongue did things that I know are illegal in all fifty states. Finding the thing that makes a woman go crazy, he sucked on my clit. The other niggas I fucked with knew nothing about this hidden treasure.

I was worn out and we hadn't even gotten to penetration yet. Not wanting to admit it, but Tyreik was a lethal weapon in bed. He was far more advanced than I was in the sex department, and I had gotten off at least three times in about an hour's time.

Tyreik hadn't even gotten off once, so I knew that I had a lot more in store. He didn't even give me a chance to catch my breath before he went directly to another form of foreplay.

Taking my hands again, he found my center with his fingers. Massaging my clit slowly, I moaned from pleasure. My own fingers had done this plenty of times, but Tyreik's felt even better. I hated that Tyreik wouldn't let me touch him, but knowing that he was in control turned me on even more. I shrilled with sheer delight as he went in and out of me, I couldn't take it anymore, he was torturing me. My whole body was on fire and I was beyond warmed up.

"Come on baby, put it in," I begged.

"I don't think you're ready for that yet."

"Come on Ty, please."

"Umm, let me think about it," he grinned.

Suddenly I had Superman strength. I flipped his two hundred pound ass over like he was a mere pancake. Lying back, he placed his hands behind his head like I was a joke. Rocking back and forth, I worked him slowly. Tyreik laid there like he was watching a rerun of the Jefferson's, I guess he thought that was all I had to give. Building momentum, I worked my hips like I was in a Sean Paul video. My ass went left, right, to the side, and up and down, Tyreik couldn't deny my power anymore. He started to moan and slap my ass from the feeling that my hip treatment was giving him, that shit was feeling good to his ass. Face to face, he lifted my ass up higher and higher so he could run himself in deeper and deeper. Scratching his back, I yelled out his name.

"That shit feels good, don't it?" Tyreik questioned, hungrily.

"Yes baby," I responded back.

"Is this my pussy?"

What the fuck kind of question was that, is this his pussy? Hell yeah this was his pussy. He was the one putting a hurting on it, but I played along with him because the shit turned my young ass on.

"No." I countered.

"This ain't my pussy," he growled.

Flipping me over, he went doggy style on my ass. Gripping my waist tightly he rammed his dick all the way up to my stomach. Shit, doggy style and Tyreik's big dick was too much for me to handle all at once.

Tyreik slapped my ass and repeatedly asked, "Is this my pussy?"

And I repeatedly answered, "No."

Our little game had me going, it was like we wanted to find out who would break first. Going even faster, my ass bounced up against his thighs making a clapping sound.

"Is this my pussy Chyna?" he grunted.

Nearing another orgasm, my body began to tremble.

"Baby, I'm about to cum," I told him.

"It feels good to you baby, this my pussy ain't it?"

"Yes baby, yes!" I yelled out in ecstasy. "Oh Ty, it feels so good!"

"Chyna, I'm cumming too baby!"

"Cum with me!" I demanded.

Holding the sheets with a vice grip hold, I came all over Tyreik. Juices came running out of me like running water. The fact that Tyreik came inside of me didn't even cross my mind, the only thing that I knew was that I had had the best sex ever. Sex with Tyreik was like a contact sport of some sort, we both tried to outdo each other during our escapades.

Pulling the satin sheets over me, I laid there in heaven. While Tyreik went to the bathroom, I gazed at the ceiling feeling inspired. Returning to bed, Tyreik got in and laid close to me. Holding me closely, he kissed my gently on the forehead.

"That was some crazy shit yo. I ain't never got down like that with a chick. Are you sure you're only seventeen?" he teased.

"I told you I wasn't no joke boy."

"Get the fuck out of here," Tyreik laughed. "I'll give it to you, you held it down. You threw that shit back at the God, but you talk so much shit Chyna, you could barely keep up."

"Whatever," I laughed.

"Oh Ty, it feels so good, don't stop get it, get it," he teased again.

"But what about ya ass nigga? Who pussy is this? Is this my pussy? Ya pussy feel so good Chyna," I joked back.

"On the real, that was on point. I knew that shit would be good. I'm already crazy about your lil ass. Shit, fucking you is only gonna fuck my head up even more," he stated.

"No it's not, you know that I love you."

"I love you too but before you came along, I had my mind right. My mind was strictly on business but since I've been with you, I haven't been on the grind like I should."

As he continued to talk, I began to get angry. We had just shared what to me was a special moment and here he was complaining.

"Tyreik, I didn't ask you to spend so much time with me. You chose to keep your ass at home, you chose to be around me twenty-four seven. If you need to take care of business then do it, but don't try to blame that shit on me," getting out of the bed, I almost began to cry.

Grabbing my arm, Tyreik pulled me back.

"What Tyreik?" I asked, with tear filled eyes.

"Come here."

"What?" I asked again, not wanting him to see me cry.

"You know it ain't even like that Dimples."

I tried to conceal my smile, but when he calls me Dimples, I grin every time.

"I'm not trying to blame anything on you, I'm just saying I have never been in a serious relationship before. I'm just trying to keep my business straight and I also want to make you happy, a'ight."

"I understand that Tyreik and I just want to make you happy too."

"Oh word?" he asked.

"Word," I answered.

"Well then come to Atlanta with me."

"For real?"

"Yeah, I got to handle some business down there. Me, you, T and Brooke are going to go down there Martin Luther King weekend."

I couldn't wait to get out of St. Louis and go to Atlanta. We were to leave that Friday, so that meant I only had a couple of days worth of shopping to do. I had to buy luggage and a couple of new outfits to compliment Atlanta's weather, but first I had a phone call to make. Checking my so-called best friend Brooke was the first thing on my list. I couldn't believe that she had held such vital information from me. It seemed to me that me going to Atlanta too was a last minute decision on Tyreik's part. Brooke had actually planned on going out of town for the weekend with my man and she wasn't even going to tell me, and that hurt a lot. Now what type of shit is that? This really led me to believe that Brooke's feelings towards Tyreik were far more than what she led on to be. She was my girl and all but she had been acting kind of shady for a while. I would most definitely have to keep a close eye on her.

Picking up the phone, I dialed her number ready to confront her.

"Hello?"

"What's up girl?"

"Shit, what's up with you?" she asked.

"Nothing much, guess what?"

"What?"

"Tyreik, T and I are going to Atlanta this weekend," I stated, fucking with her to see how she would react.

"So he finally told you, huh?"

"Yeah, it's funny that I didn't hear about it from you."

"Chyna, I told you that I don't discuss my brother's business with anybody."

"Not even with your best friend Brooke, to me that's pretty fucked up."

"Not even with you Chyna, my best friend," Brooke responded, coldly.

"Well I think that's pretty shitty. You had to know that Tyreik was going to tell me sooner or later. I would have eventually found out that you were going too. To me it seems like you're trying to keep secrets from me. Tyreik is my man now. I understand that he is your so-called boss and all but you have to remember that you do have a loyalty to me too. There is fine line between getting money and friendship Brooke."

"Chyna, you know that I love you like a sister, there are just some things that I cannot and will not talk to you about, and Tyreik is one of them. I'm not trying to keep any secrets from you if that's what you think, I just don't want to get involved in ya'll relationship."

"And why is that?" I asked, heated.

"It's not that I don't think that Tyreik is good for you, it's just that I know Tyreik a lot better than you do."

"I don't care how well you think you know him, he is my man and I know him a hell of a lot better than anybody else. We do live together or haven't you noticed Brooke."

I was going off on Brooke and I knew that I had to calm myself down before I said something that I would regret. We both were taking things too far and I had to be the bigger person and patch things up.

Calming myself down, I continued, "Look Brooke, I don't want to fight with you, but if you know something about Tyreik that affects me tell me, that's all I'm saying girl."

"I understand. I do be tripping sometimes don't I?" asked Brooke.

"Yes you do," I laughed.

"It's just that things have been getting so heavy lately out here, you know. I have to stay focused Chyna, that's my whole thing."

I had questions that were burning to be asked but I opted to stay quiet. Just how deep had Brooke gotten herself with Tyreik and T? They both seemed worried when it came to the business.

A tiny bit of fear began to grow in my heart. If something happened to Tyreik I would truly die. One day I would ask her the questions that were in my head. We would talk eventually, but not tonight, and especially not over the phone.

That night, Brooke and I held a fairly normal conversation, but things had already changed. Our friendship was being tested and I honestly didn't know if it would survive.

CHAPTER 8

GAME RECOGNIZE GAME

Friday came faster than I had ever expected. There I sat on the 9:00 a.m. flight headed to Atlanta. Holding onto Tyreik's hand for dear life, I glared out the tiny window. Tyreik laughed at me the entire plane ride there. I didn't care, this was my life that I was dealing with and I didn't find a damn thing funny, I was scared out of my mind. T and Brooke sat a row behind us fast asleep. Tyreik wanted to get a quick nap in but I wouldn't let him because if something were to happen, there was no way they would be asleep when it happened.

Overjoyed didn't even describe my feelings as I stepped off the plane, I was so happy that the thirty minute plane ride had ended. Inhaling the fresh air, I fell in love with Atlanta on sight; the city was lively and cultural. Tyreik had rented us a 2001 black Mercedes Benz C Class for our weekend stay, while T rented a 2001 Cadillac Escalade. Brooke had made reservations for us to stay at the W Hotel. She said that it was one of the finest hotels in the US and she was right.

Our suite was so plush it could fit into our apartment back home. Brooke and T had their own suite a floor above us. Gazing over the Atlanta skyline, I looked upon the city, the sun was shining brightly and down below people were bustling about going on with their day. The weather there was much different from back home; it was cold but not as cold.

As I stared in amazement out of the wall-sized window, Tyreik came up behind me and wrapped his arms around me.

Kissing his cheek, I said, "I love you."

It wasn't long before his hands began to roam. Since the first time we made love, Tyreik had wanted me every minute of the day. I wanted him too because his left stroke was the death stroke. Caressing my breast, my nipples began to rise. It was so erotic, the thought that somebody could see us. Tyreik didn't waste any time, he went directly for my jeans, and unzipping them, he placed his hands insides my panties and opened my lips. Stroking me with his fingers, he kissed my neck. The combination felt so good but I wanted to please him.

"Let me take care of you for once," I said.

Turning myself around, I kneeled on the floor. Taking his instrument in my hands, I placed him in my mouth and played with his tea bags. My technique worked, I had Tyreik going crazy. The combination of my mouth wrapped around his dick and my hands stroking his balls were lethal. Like I said, LP was my sex instructor; he taught me the art of sucking dick. It didn't take much before he was ready to blow.

Relieving himself on the floor, we continued on. Standing back up, I eased my jeans off. Tyreik turned me around and entered me from the back. Taking it from the back was by far my favorite position. Placing my hands on the window I held myself up. Tyreik had me humming in a matter of seconds, that boy's sex game was Grade A forsho.

Staring out the window at the people down below took me to new heights of ecstasy. Just the thought of somebody watching us made me want to cum and with that, I did and so did Tyreik. Our quickie and jet lag sent me straight to sleep. We had a big night ahead of us so I took a quick shower and a nap.

Earlier, after much pleading and prodding, I learned that Tyreik and T were down here to hook up with a new distributor. They had never met the dude, but heard that he had the best cocaine around. T's man named Big Ron had hooked the meeting up and they would meet the mystery man that night at 10:00.

Awakening from my slumber, it felt as if I had been asleep for years. Jet lag mixed with an orgasm had me tired than a muthafucker. I awoke to find it dark and me alone in the huge hotel suite. Finding the clock, I saw that it was 8:30 p.m. Never before had I slept so long during a nap, but fucking with Tyreik could do that to me.

My coochie had been sore and swollen all week long. I didn't know what the hell was wrong with me. At first I thought that Tyreik might have given me the dead man's disease. Scared out of my mind, I called Asia and she explained to me that I was in fact okay and didn't have any venereal disease. The only problem that I had was that my man was putting a hurting on my little pussy.

"Brooke, you know where Tyreik's at?" I asked, after calling Brooke's room.

"I think he said he was going down to the bar."

"A'ight, thanks."

After hanging up, I slipped on my clothes and took the elevator down to the main floor. It wasn't hard to find him because he was one of only four people in the bar, and the only black one at that. He was so into the game, and to me, what seemed to be his thoughts as well. I hadn't noticed it before, but a lot was weighing on him.

Tyreik was a serious man anyway, but this deal meant a lot to his growing empire. T and him were pushing a lot of weight around St. Louis, but they needed more so that they could expand. Their distributor couldn't produce such a mass quantity, so Tyreik and T had to take their business elsewhere. Tyreik only had so much coke left and he needed this deal to be a success. If this meeting didn't go well, they would have to start from scratch and Tyreik didn't want to have to do that and neither did I. I had become accustomed to living well and couldn't deal with watching our expenses. Rubbing his shoulders, I caught his attention.

"What's up baby?" he said, turning his attention to me.

"Nothing, I was just a little scared up there all by myself. You could have woken me up sweetie."

"Nah, you needed to rest. I could tell that you were tired," he said, with emphasizes on tired.

"Whatever, boy," I laughed, hitting him playfully on the arm.

For a couple of minutes, he sat and I stood in silence. He watched the game while I watched him. Tyreik was always in control and rarely ever showed his feelings, but I could tell that he was disturbed. His eyes may have been on the game, but his mind was somewhere far away. I wanted to know what was troubling him but I was too afraid to ask.

"Are you okay baby?" I asked, while tracing my fingers across his cheek.

"I'm good why, what's up?" he said, now looking me in the eyes.

"I'm just worried about you that's all, you seem preoccupied."

"I'm straight, stop worrying. Once this deal goes down we're gonna be set C. The God is taking care of business, you ain't gonna ever have to work if you don't want to after this shit."

Gazing into his eyes, I saw hope and determination. My man just wanted to make me happy that's all. I knew that there was far more going on, but I also knew that whatever it was I wasn't prepared for it yet. Ignorance is bliss and I wanted to be as ignorant as I could be so, me being me, I continued to live in my so-called fantasy world of life.

"I'm getting ready to go back up, are you coming?"

"Nah, I'm going to stay down here for a little while longer. You go on back up and start getting ready because I know how long it takes you to get dressed," he teased.

"Oh you got jokes. Okay I'm leaving but hurry up, I don't like being up there all by myself."

"A'ight, give me a kiss," Tyreik demanded.

Giving him a quick peck on the lips, I kissed his forehead as well. Not wanting to, I pried myself away from his embrace and left the bar. Hitting the lobby, I gazed over my shoulder taking one last look at him. Tyreik must have thought that I was already gone because he had placed his head in hands, the sight of this sent tears to my eyes. I hated that he was hurting and desperately wanted to fix what was broken. The fact that Tyreik was shutting me out cut deeply at my heart. He had always been there for me and I needed to return the favor. A fire was brewing all around me and I didn't even realize it.

The Velvet Room was packed to the brim, the crowd was filled with people mingling and getting their party on. A couple of local celebrities were even in attendance. I spotted JD and Janet Jackson sharing a table with Usher and Chili in the VIP section. The atmosphere was hype and people were everywhere. The DJ had me hype as well, I wanted to hit the dance floor and do my thing but Tyreik would have had my head. I knew that I wouldn't be able to do anything until the deal had gone through.

You would have thought that we were celebrities by the way people stared at us as we walked by. Our shit was tight so they had no choice but to stare. Tyreik sported a black Sean John suit jacket, a plaid long sleeve Sean John shirt and a pair of blue jeans. The waves on his head were busting, but Tyreik had to keep it gangsta, he just had to represent and put on an all black STL hat. The crisp white Air Force Ones on his feet made his cycle complete. I had unbuttoned a couple of the buttons so that his iced out chain could show.

Oh and me, you don't even want to know about me. My hair

reminded me a lot of that girl that sings *"I Hate You So Much Right Now"*. The black D&G corset dress clung ever so snuggly over my curves. My bronze colored makeup, chandelier earrings and Stuart Weitzman heels completed my glamour girl look. T looked good as always. Keeping it gangsta, he sported a red leather All Star jacket, white T and MFG jeans. Brooke looked like she had stepped straight off the runway. Her crème mini dress barely covered her ass. T didn't approve of the provocative outfit but Brooke and I knew that the dress was a must. We were slaves for fashion and that dress would have every bitch in the club wishing she was in it.

Seated in the VIP section, we all ordered a drink. The fake ID Tyreik had set me up with worked out well. It had gotten me into the twenty-one and older club, and now it was getting me drinks too. The other half of our party was late, so we all sat in silence awaiting the mystery man's arrival.

The DJ continued to spin hits while I sat irritably. It wasn't because I was tired of waiting on our guest, I was agitated because Tyreik's ass was so wound up. We had barely spoken a word to each other since his return from the bar. We practically got dressed in silence. The huge hotel suite seemed like a can of sardines, we could hardly go without bumping into each other. It was understandable that he was nervous, but damn Tyreik was taking this whole meeting thing a little bit too far.

This nigga wasn't talking to T, Brooke or me. It wasn't like Brooke and him talked much anyway, but damn, I sat right next to him and he barely acknowledged my presence. To make matters worse, he hadn't even said anything about my dress. Now you know that hurt my feelings. With my arms crossed, I sat there rolling my eyes and sucking my teeth. Usually this would get his attention, but tonight I didn't exist.

"Excuse me, but the rest of your party is here," the waitress said to Tyreik.

This mystery man had me past intrigued, I had to see this nigga so I could see what the big fuss was all about. Studying the crowd, I saw two guys who looked to be in their twenties approaching us. If these two guys were our guests, I was sure to be in trouble. They both were cute but the brown skinned one was fine, his demeanor reminded me a lot of Tyreik. The dude looked a lot like the rapper Camron and he had a cockiness about him that interested me. Snapping myself back to reality, I watched as Tyreik and T stood to greet the guys. Suddenly Tyreik's nervousness disappeared and a big smile appeared on his face.

"Tyreik, is that you nigga?" the brown skin guy asked.

"Dame cuz, I know that ain't you, oh and is that my nigga JB?"

"Yeah nigga, it's the God, the one and only JB."

Giving each other a pound and a hug, they continued to talk amongst themselves.

"I haven't seen you since that night son," the Dame guy said.

"I know and I heard about the bid you and my man here did. Yo, thanks for not ratting on a nigga. I got mad respect for ya'll niggas for real," Tyreik said, speaking from the heart.

"Oh no doubt son, you know that I'm far from a snitch nigga," spoke JB.

"I still appreciate that shit. Yo, good looking out dog."

Now Tyreik had always had a New York accent, but never before had it been this thick. The boy had gone straight Brooklyn on me, it was like a whole new Tyreik was standing before me. T was even looking at his ass like he was talking a foreign language.

"I can't believe this whole time I was holding this meeting with my fam. I've straight up been stressing and shit son, I even had my girl worried and shit."

It was about time, I had begun to think that he had forgotten about me.

"Yo, my bad. Dame and JB, this my girl Chyna."

Looking into Dame's eyes, I hated that I felt a twinge of an attraction. Holding my hand out to shake his, he opted to kiss it and I'll be damned if his lips didn't feel good against my skin.

"Hey watch that shit nigga," Tyreik joked.

I tried laughing the whole thing off, but it was hard to forget the way his lips felt on my skin. I don't think anyone but me noticed, but Dame's eyes had been on me the whole time he and Tyreik were talking.

"Oh and this is my partna in crime T."

"What's up cuz?" T said, giving JB and Dame a pound.

"Yeah, my homey told me about you. It's good to meet you," JB replied.

"And this is his little sister Brooke," Tyreik said.

"I don't mean to be disrespectful, but T dog you have a beautiful sister," Dame said.

"It's cool cuz, I hear that shit all the time," T said, laughing.

Brooke's whole body lit up with a smile and I saw immediately that she liked Dame. She had had a smile a mile wide pasted on her face since Dame had arrived. After situating ourselves around the table, the boys continued to talk.

"So what's been up with you B?" JB asked.

"You know I've just been doing my thing in St. Louis with my man here. We've been getting down for a while now. I moved down there a few years back, and as soon as I got down there I hooked up with T. Shit, we've been doing the damn thing ever since. I would ask how you doing but shit, I already know," Tyreik said.

"I don't mean to brag but shit, I'm doing my thing. After we got out we made our move too. JB and me came down here and got on the grind yo. It's a lot of money to be made down here Tyreik. While I was down, I hooked up with this cat and got a connect to his Columbian friends. Word to my mother, them Columbian niggas have hooked a nigga up."

"I hear you talking B," replied Tyreik.

"So what's up, are we going to talk business or what?" T questioned.

"I see your man here is all about business, I like that shit," Dame spoke.

"Damn right, I'm trying to get this shit over with so I can get on one of these bitches. A nigga trying to cut something tonight," T said, high as a kite.

"I hear you B, I hear you talking," Dame said, while eyeing Brooke.

"Look, I'm willing to talk business with you because you are family, but alone," Dame said.

"Chyna baby, will you excuse us while we talk for a minute, and take Brooke with you please."

"Okay baby, we need to go the powder room anyway. When we get done we'll be over by the bar," I said, grabbing my clutch purse.

Kissing my Boo on the cheek, I excused myself from the table. As we stood to leave the table, Dame also stood. We were upstairs and had a flight of steps to go down, so Dame extended his hand to help us down. Tyreik was far more interested in his conversation to help. I know that I wasn't supposed to feel this way but I had anticipated the touch of Dame's hand again, I liked the way his skin felt on mine. I hoped that no one had noticed the way that I gazed over at him from across the table.

The thoughts that ran through my mind made me sick to the stomach. I loved Tyreik so how could I be lusting after a nigga I barely knew. I tried to shake the feelings off as I looked back at Tyreik. Staring back at me, Tyreik gave me a wink of the eye. Quickly I remembered how much I loved him and there was no way that Dame could compare, Tyreik was all the man that I would ever need.

"Girl, Dame is too cute," Brooke gleefully replied, as we entered the restroom.

"He is a cutie, but my Boo got him beat," I responded, trying my best to cover my true feelings.

"Anyway, did you see the way that he looked at me? Girl, I'm on his ass."

"Do that shit cause he's got plenty of doe and he's fine. Shit, he sounds like a catch to me."

CHAPTER 9

SUCKA 4 LOVE

After our talk in the ladies room, Brooke and I made our way over to the bar area. I didn't want to get too plastered so an Amaretto Sour was the perfect drink. Brooke, on the other hand, needed a stiff one so a Vodka Martini did her just right. The girl needed something to calm her nerves because she was really feeling Dame. I had never seen her so wound up over a guy before. I was happy for her, it made me happy to see my girl feel the way I felt for Tyreik.

Looking across the room, I could tell that the meeting was going well. Tyreik's confidence and cocky attitude had come back in full force and it felt good to see a smile back on his face. Tyreik's happiness was the only thing that I cared for at the time. Sipping on my drink slowly, I felt a presence from behind.

"Ay shorty, you looking good, you wanna dance with a playa like me?" Some Gerri Curl brother with a bright yellow suit, fedora and stank breath had the nerve to ask me.

"Um, let me think about it. Ah No! I'm here with my boyfriend, sweetie," I retorted, snobbishly.

"Well then how about you sexy?" the bug-a-boo asked Brooke.

"I don't even have a man and the answer is no," laughed Brooke.

"Oh I see ya'll tryin' to play a brother. Well then fuck you and fuck you too, I can't believe you bitches gonna try to play a pimp like me. Ya'll can't roll with a nigga like me anyway, fuck ya'll bitches," He spat, as he walked off.

Brooke and I fell out laughing. The comments that he made about us didn't even register in our minds. His Gerri Curl, four gold teeth and stank breath had us dying laughing.

"Was that nigga bothering ya'll?" questioned Dame.

I wondered had he been standing there the whole time.

"Nah, we're cool, aren't we Chyna."

"Yeah it's cool. We get hit on all the time so the shit, don't even bother me no more," I said, confidently.

"Damn, you're confident just like your man," Dame joked.

"I sure am, you have to be or you'll get walked all over."

"I feel you; my boy has done well for himself," he said, while tracing my body with his eyes.

Self-consciously, I turned my attention elsewhere and tried to act as if I didn't notice his blatant disrespect for Tyreik.

"So Brooke, do you think that it would be a'ight if I called you sometime?"

"Sure I'd like that," She answered, gleefully.

Shit, the meeting was over, so where was Tyreik? I was starting to feel like a third wheel, I needed my man to hold and caress me.

"There my baby is," said Tyreik, as he wrapped his strong arms around my tiny waist.

Now that's what I'm talking about, my baby was always right there when I needed him.

"Hey baby, so everything's okay?"

"Oh yeah I'm straight, we're on our way," he said, excitedly.

"Good, I'm happy for you baby," I said.

"You ready to party or what?" Tyreik asked.

"And you know this man," I answered, in my best Chris Tucker impersonation.

"Oh and yo, you're looking good in that dress ma," he seductively spoke into my ear.

"I thought you didn't even notice."

"Every nigga in here noticed that shit. You got every chick in here beat Boo, that's why a nigga like me got with your fine ass," he replied, grabbing a handful of my ass.

"Oh, so that's the reason you're with me?" I asked, trying to act mad.

"Whatever C, you know I got mad love for your little ass."

Hugging each other, we stood in silence by the bar until the DJ did the unthinkable, the man had the nerve to play *"I Love You"* by Faith Evans. Pulling Tyreik to the dance floor, we danced to my song. Even with the loudness surrounding me, I still could hear Tyreik's heartbeat while I laid my head on his chest. I ignored the fact that the girls in the club mean mugged me the whole night, they were just jealous because they wanted to be me, and if I were them, I would have wanted to be me also. Tyreik only had eyes for me, and despite my moment of weakness, I for him. I had Tyreik wrapped around my finger or so I thought.

We didn't make it back to the hotel until about 6 o'clock that morning. When the club let out, we all decided to grab a bite at the Waffle House. The Waffle House in Atlanta was like a liquor store in St. Louis, you had one on every corner. Honestly, up until that point I had had the perfect vacation. Tyreik's boys were cool, especially Dame.

With a couple of drinks in my system, I put my sexual feelings aside and began to look at him as a friend. Once I did this, my whole attraction for him went away or so I thought. Dame was a flirt and nothing more, he had eyes for my girl and my girl only. The four of us had our double dating thing going on as we sat sharing a booth. Tyreik had never been more relaxed in his life since I had known him. He really must have trusted Dame and JB. Don't get me wrong, he trusted T as well, but for some reason he hadn't let his guard down completely like he was doing now.

T and JB skipped out on breakfast with us due to the fact that they had hooked up with some chicken heads at the club. Pussy was on T's mind, so it didn't take much for him to ditch us. By the time we finally returned to the hotel, my body had officially shut down. I hit the bed and was out like a light. Seven hours later I was awakened with a slap on the ass.

"Wake up sleepy head," Tyreik said, loudly in my ear.

"Boy have you lost your damn mind, leave me alone!" I yelled, agitated.

"You better wake ya ass up if you want to go shopping."

"Shit, you ain't said nothing but a word," I said, fully awake now.

In less than hour I was dressed and ready to go. Tyreik and I hit Lennox Square with a vengeance. We added more shit to the shit we already owned and hadn't even worn yet. Little did I know, but the shopping spree was only a lead up for what was about to come. Tyreik was about to ask me that ride or die question. Right before I got my foot in the car, he stopped me dead in my tracks. Pinning me up against the side of the Benz, he held my hands close to his heart. Right then and there in the middle of the parking lot, he asked me the question that would literally knock me out.

"What are you doing, people are looking at us?" I asked.

"Fuck them, I got something I need to talk to you about."

"What is it baby, you know that I got you."

"Yeah, you say that shit but do you really mean that shit?"

"What the fuck is going on Ty, you're starting to scare me. You know that I would do anything for you," I said, confused and hurt.

I watched as he studied his environment, I could tell that he was pondering his words. Regret was written all over his face, but why? Whatever he needed to say was very hard for him to do. I continued to pry until I found out what was going on.

"Tyreik, what is it baby, talk to me?" I questioned, still confused.

Looking down at his feet, he said, "I need you to take an early flight out tomorrow."

"Why?" I asked, with tears in my eyes.

This was it he was leaving me. I couldn't breathe because the air in my lungs had escaped me. If Tyreik was planning on leaving me I would die.

"Don't cry baby, I just need you to carry a little something back home with you for me."

"What? Why me?" I asked shocked, while pushing him away.

"Listen, I already have a record and so does T. Security is going to be on my ass extra hard, I can't carry that shit on me," he said, taking my hands back.

"Okay, what about Brooke? She's the one that works for you, not me."

"Look ma, I didn't want to tell you this but Brooke already has a warrant out for her arrest back home."

"What?"

"Yeah, she got a couple tickets that she ain't paid yet and one those times she was caught wit weed in the car. You're clean baby; I just need you to carry this weight for me this one time. After this deal we'll be good and you won't have to want for shit."

I didn't know what to do; my man was asking the unthinkable. The person I loved was putting my life in jeopardy all because he wanted a slice of the American pie. If I said no then there would be no us. I loved Tyreik more than I loved myself. Hurting him was something that I couldn't bare doing. I knew that this is what comes along with being with a hustler, I had just chosen to ignore this part of his life. Up until this point, his being a hustler hadn't affected me. I had wanted a thug and a thug is what I had gotten.

"Please baby, do this for us," he pleaded.

My whole body had gone numb. I stood there shaking with fear. This was my life that I was dealing with here. If I got caught I would be in jail and then what? Looking into Tyreik's eyes, I saw that I had no other choice. He had loved me when no one else did. It had been two months and I had not heard a word from Diane or my father, my own parents didn't care about my well being. I owed Tyreik my life, I thought.

Drying my tears, I inhaled deeply and said, "I'll do it."

Squeezing me tight, Tyreik hugged me with all of his might. The touch of his face against mine only sent more tears to my eyes. I became so weak that Tyreik had to help me into the car, he had drained me with only one question. Leaning the seat all the way back, I closed my eyes and tried to make the question and the answer disappear.

CHAPTER 10

THE MIDDLE

I had tried not to cry during the plane trip, but it was too hard not to. The more that I tried not to cry, the more the tears seemed to build at the rim of my eyes. On the outside, I sat stoned face with a confident demeanor. I don't know what got me through the whole ordeal but God, because before that day I had never prayed. I needed something or somebody to help me get home safely so I asked God for help. I promise you, that thirty minute ride home seemed to have lasted at least an hour.

Tyreik told me to watch everybody and everything around me. He said that a person's body language said a lot about what they were thinking. He said that if anybody seemed to be out of place that I was to ditch the package immediately. Shit, everybody looked suspicious to me. When I wasn't praying, I was thinking about Tyreik. If you would have told me two days ago that I would be sitting on a plane with cocaine taped to my body, I would have called you a fucking liar. I still couldn't grasp the fact that my man was putting my life in jeopardy all for the mighty dollar.

The morning before I left, we didn't say a word to each other. Tears streamed down my face as he taped the kilos of coke to my chest and thighs. Tyreik could barely look me in the eyes. I had hoped that at any moment he would say that this was all a big joke, but that moment never came. The more that I thought about it, the more I came to realize that this whole thing had been planned way before my knowledge of it. T, Brooke and Tyreik had this planned from the start. Everything was becoming clear to me. Tyreik had held out on telling me about the trip to Atlanta because he knew that he would ask me to carry the weight back home for him.

Brooke didn't tell me either and she knew the whole time, that's why she made that comment to me on the phone. You know the one when she was like, *"Oh, he finally told you"*. I'ma fuck that tall, lanky, bitch up, I thought. Brooke was supposed to be my best friend and she had betrayed me for the first and last time. The fact that she would place my life in danger hardened my heart even more. Revenge is a muthafucker.

I was supposed to be this nigga's wifey and he couldn't even clue me in on the business. Brooke's ass had been lying to me for months, and for what, just so she could get some doe. I wondered did Asia even know about Brooke's warrant. I bet you that she didn't even know. None of them bitches had bothered to let me in on the biggest decision of my life.

Studying my surroundings carefully, I departed the 747 plane with my carry on luggage in tow. My heart was beating a mile a minute. Everyone around me seemed to be staring at me, or was I just being paranoid. I couldn't take anymore of this second guessing myself, so I quickly made my way through the crowded airport terminal. The little bit of a heartbeat that I had left went faint as a hand grabbed my shoulder. Caught, I didn't know if I should run or face the music. If I ran, I probably could make it because I wasn't but a few feet away from the entrance doors. Tyreik said that Boog would be outside waiting for me in a rental car. I couldn't run because the hand on my shoulder was not letting up. Dropping my bags, I put my hands to my face and cried.

"Fuck, fuck, fuck," I whispered to myself.

"Chyna," the voice said to me.

Hold up, I know that voice I thought. Taking my hands away from my face, I turned around only to find Jaylen.

"Jaylen," I said, shocked.

Jumping up into his arms, I hugged him.

"What's up? What are all the tears for, I know that we haven't seen each other in awhile, but damn," Jaylen joked.

"Shut up Jaylen," I said, as I hit him playfully on the arm.

"Where have you been girl, I've missed you."

"I've missed you too boy."

"So, what's been up with you?"

"Shit, nothing much."

"Why did you just up and drop out like that Chyna? You know that it's our last year, you could have hung in there for a little while longer. Norfolk High ain't been the same without you."

"Circumstances just got in the way man."

"I heard that you moved in with that nigga Tyreik."

"Yeah I have," I answered, dryly.

Remembering the task at hand, I rushed the conversation.

"You seem a little stressed, what's going on?" Jaylen asked, overly concerned.

Not being able to answer him honestly, I switched the subject back to him.

"While you sitting up here questioning me, what are you doing here Jaylen?"

Before he could answer, I heard the sound of a car horn

blowing. Looking out of the glass revolving door, I spotted Boog waiting impatiently.

"Look Jaylen, I gotta go. I'm going to catch up with you later, a'ight."

"But wait, I got something to tell you!" He yelled, over the crowd.

"I'll call you!" I yelled, over my shoulder.

Once outside, I hopped into the rental and Boog began to barrage me with a ton of questions. "What in the fuck were you in there doing? What took you so long? You trying to get us knocked or something?" he yelled at me.

"Yo, who in the fuck do you think you're talking to? Have you forgotten who I am nigga?" I yelled back.

"My bad. But damn Chyna, a nigga been stressing all day over this shit."

"Park the damn car over there so I can get this shit off me and shut the fuck up," I said, irritated.

With the tinted windows up and Boog standing outside of the car, I stripped down. Ripping the tape from my body, I packed the kilos of dope in the duffle bag sitting on the backseat. The Dior outfit that I had on would be ditched as soon as I got home, I didn't want any reminders of this day. Changed and ready to go, I let Boog back in the rental car. Driving me to a nearby mall parking lot, he showed me the rental car that I would be driving home.

The ride home was a smooth but long one. I looked in the rearview mirror every other minute to make sure that I wasn't being followed. Stepping out the Honda Accord, I sighed a sense of relief because I was finally home. I never wanted to leave St. Louis again. I hadn't slept a wink the night before so I was dead on my feet. The adrenaline rush and fear had subsided and all I wanted was a bed to rest my head on.

In an hour's time, Tyreik would be home so I showered and put on a pair of pajamas before he arrived. I really didn't know how I would react when I saw him. The question had emotionally drained me and I had fallen asleep as soon as I hit the sheets. It was midnight by the time Tyreik brought his ass home, he should have been home hours ago and I was pissed.

I lay in the bed half awake, half asleep when he strutted into the bedroom. No words were spoken as he stripped down to his boxers and lay down next to me. He laid there for almost an hour before he decided to touch me; I know this because I was watching the clock. I wanted him to reach out and touch me; I wanted to hear him say that he was sorry and that he wouldn't put me in that position again. I wanted him to make love to me passionately and slowly. I needed him to take the pain away.

Holding me in his arms, he kissed the back of neck. I don't know if he knew that I was awake or not, but he whispered in my ear the words I had been dying to hear.

"I love you," he said, kissing me again on the neck and returning to his side of the bed.

Once again tears formed in my eyes, but this time I was determined not to cry. The trip to Atlanta, the question and cocaine would all be chalked up to a bad dream that I had had. I was determined to believe that I had not done what I had done for Tyreik and, me being me, did just that.

Two weeks had gone by and things between Tyreik and me were pretty much the same, he still was avoiding me and I still didn't have anything to say. Tyreik had even picked up the habit of coming home late just so he could avoid me. At first, I didn't mind because he was still feeling guilty and he should have. After a while it became old and I became frustrated, I longed for the touch of his hands on my body. We hadn't had sex in almost a week and a half and I had begun to wonder if he was giving my dick away.

It just so happened that the night that I was going to forgive him, he came in at three o'clock in the morning. Now I don't know about you, but I didn't play that shit, Tyreik was totally disrespecting our home and me. The boy hadn't even bothered to pick up a phone, for all I knew he could have been locked up or dead. You know that I had to clown his ass when he got home.

As soon as I heard his keys hit the door I played sleep. He walked in the room smelling like Cool Breeze mixed with weed. I didn't even give him a chance to sit down before I pounced on his ass.

"Where the fuck have you been all night?"

"I've been out chilling, why?" he answered, unfazed.

"What the fuck you mean why? It's three o'clock in the morning Ty, that's why!" I yelled.

"I'm saying, why are you so worried about where I've been, your ass been giving me the silent treatment for weeks, why should I come home? It's like I've been living here by my damn self!" he yelled.

"Cut the bullshit Ty, this is me you're talking to, I don't want to hear that shit. You've been coming home late because you know that your ass was wrong for asking me to carry that shit for you. Your coming home late ain't got shit to do with me, it's your conscious that's eating your ass up. You only have yourself to blame, so try again nigga," I barked at him.

"Yo, who the fuck do you think you're talking to. I'ma slap the shit outta you C, you better calm your little ass down. This was a big run for me and all I did was ask you to carry a little weight for me. Damn, you act like I asked you snort that shit or something."

"You might as well have. Shit, what if I would have gotten caught Tyreik? Did you think about that? Let me guess, ah no. I can't believe I did that shit for you. It's cool though because I got something for your ass. When I start coming in the house at all times of the night don't say shit to me," I said, pushing him over the edge.

"You know all that shit you talking is gonna get your little ass beat. You actin' real stupid, you need to chill the fuck out."

"Nah fuck that shit, you caused all of this, you hurt me I didn't hurt you. You're the one that put me in an uncomfortable situation. You knew that I wouldn't say no to you so now you feel guilty. Well guess what, you should."

"Kill all that noise ma."

"Nah, you're gonna listen to me!"

"I ain't got time for this shit, I'm up," he said, grabbing his coat.

You know that I think I'm Mighty Mouse and shit, so my little ass hopped out the bed so quick I surprised even myself.

"You ain't going anywhere!" I yelled, snatching his coat from him.

"See, that's the stupid shit I'm talking about. Fuck that coat, I'm still leaving."

Watching him walk out of our bedroom made me even more heated. You would've thought I was Flo Jo the way I ran after him. Shooting past him, I blocked him from leaving out the front door.

"Yo, T what up? I'm coming through cuz, Chyna over here trippin'," Tyreik said, into his cell phone.

"I said you're not going anywhere!" I screamed, slapping his phone out of his hand.

His brand new Cingular flip phone broke as soon as it hit the marble floor.

Grabbing me by the arms, Tyreik yelled, "What the fuck is your problem? You trying to make me hurt you Chyna, is that it? Do you want me to hurt you? Ain't that a bitch, you broke my brand new muthafuckin' phone!"

"Fuck that phone, let me go!" I screamed.

I swear to God I had never seen Tyreik so mad. His eyes were bloodshot red and his nostrils were flaring, but fuck that shit, I ain't never been scared of no man.

"Let me go!" I yelled again.

Pushing me hard into the wall he let me go, the grip that he had on my arms caused them to turn red.

"Don't you ever put your hands on me again!" I spat at him.

"Shut the fuck up. Take you ass back to bed and leave me the fuck alone!"

"And if I don't, what you gonna do, whoop my ass?"

"You better shut the fuck up before I put ya ass in the trunk!"

"Fuck you, then leave, I don't even give a fuck!"

The walk back to the bedroom was the longest walk of my life. I didn't know if he was going to leave or stay, but what I did know was that Tyreik had hurt me again. We had officially had our first fight and I hadn't even seen that shit coming. Just a few weeks ago we were the happiest couple on earth. Man, I tried to keep it gangsta but my punk ass started crying like a baby as soon as I hit the bedroom. My chest was heaving up and down and I could barely breathe. Everything seemed to be falling down around me. My eyes were so clouded with tears that I did-n't even notice that Tyreik was standing right before me. Taking my hands into his, he lifted me up and held me tight.

"Come here, I'm sorry Boo. You know I ain't going nowhere, I ain't gonna leave you, I got your back. Look, I didn't want to do that shit but I had to. I got big plans for us C, but you just gotta ride wit a nigga. I know that I'm pushing things a little too far. You ain't just some chick to me, I'm trying to make you my wife and the mother of my kids ma. I ain't trying to be up in here arguing wit you. I'm sorry for laying my hands on you though. I got love for you C, you my girl, I ain't trying to let shit come between us," Tyreik said, apologizing.

Tilting my head up gently, Tyreik kissed my lips lightly, taking all my pain away with one kiss. All the hurt and pain that I had felt was quickly replaced with lust. Ripping his shirt off, I kissed his chest and it was on and popping then. With one swift move, my man had my nightgown off and my thong on the floor. Pushing me down onto the bed, he took my nipple into his mouth, the sensation felt so good. Arching my back, I moaned with delight. Tyreik had me sprawled out on the bed gripping the sheets. Making his way down, he circled his tongue around my navel. Kissing my stomach lovingly, he began to play with my clit. Circling his thumb around slowly, he slipped a finger in and the combination of the two was lethal. My God, I was seeing stars.

"Damn, I want to taste you," he said, staring me in the eyes.

Licking his fingers, he savored my juices. Taking his head down, he spread my lips apart and kissed my pussy. Stroking me with his tongue, he made me reach new heights.

"Damn baby, do ya thang!" I screamed.

"You taste good baby."

"We missed you too baby."

Yelling out his name, I came all over his face.

"Shit Ty, goddamn boy," I said, still cumming.

Wiping his face, Tyreik stripped down and got on top of me. With one leg on his shoulder, Tyreik hit me with the death stroke. Hitting all four corners I tried not to orgasm, but goddamn, Tyreik had me speaking in tongue. I tried to grab the sheets, but that shit wasn't working, I was literally climbing the walls. His ass was drilling my shit, I knew his ass missed this good pussy.

Teasingly, he rubbed his dick against my pussy. We went at it like crazy, me pleasing him and him pleasing me. Our sexual bond was something that could never be broken. Tyreik and I knew each other too well and we couldn't get enough of each other. Afterwards we lay together talking, catching up on the past few weeks that had been left unspoken.

Another month had passed and everything that had gone down between Tyreik and me had been forgiven and forgotten. I could never hold anything against him because I loved him too much. I couldn't say the same thing about Brooke, her unspoken truths left me very distrustful of her. Don't get me wrong, she was still my girl and I would always be there for her, but I had come not to expect much from her. The whole working for Tyreik and T thing was going to her head. I was getting money thrown at me on the daily but I wasn't about to let that shit gas me up, because all this shit could be gone tomorrow. Tyreik and T's asses could be locked up on any given day. My baby had the streets on lock though, Dame kept my man supplied.

The shit was selling so fast that Tyreik always needed to re-up. The more money he made, the more his attitude started to change. He never really gave a fuck in the first place but now he had started to make it crystal clear. Dead bodies were poppin' up all over St. Louis. It was always gang or drug related on the news, but I knew better. Half the niggas coming up dead were ballers. Some of the cats like Zack, Coach and Mickey were holding major weight. Once Tyreik put his shit on the streets, he started dippin' into the other dealers' pockets.

Tyreik didn't know I knew, but I had started hearing about niggas talking shit about him being taken out. I knew that he was shook by this because he had started wearing a vest whenever he went out. I knew my baby could handle himself so I didn't worry. I was more worried for his adversaries because Tyreik could be a sick muthafucker when we wanted to be.

CHAPTER 11

COME AND TALK TO ME

Spring was fast approaching and feelings of summer started to rise in all of us. Like flowers blooming, we all had begun to grow and change. I still hadn't talked to my mother, I rolled by her house a couple of times just to check on her, but my pride would never let me make that walk to the door. I rarely talked to my father, so that didn't hurt as much.

I had just come in from getting my nails down when I learned of Dame's arrival. I couldn't have been more surprised when I came in to find him and Tyreik getting lifted together.

"What the fuck took you so long?" Tyreik barked.

"Damn, am I on a time limit now," I barked back.

He had been getting on my damn nerves, twenty-one questioning me all the time. Every time I went somewhere or did something he had an attitude.

"See, that's the shit I be talking about Dame, she got a smart ass mouth."

"She cool man, leave her alone," Dame laughed.

"Anyway forget him, how you been Dame?" I asked.

"I'm good, you?"

"Besides having to deal with you know who, I'm fine. Let me hit that," I asked Dame.

Passing me the hydro, I inhaled and winked at Tyreik. He hated when I smoked 'cause he thought that it was so unlady like.

"That's some good shit," I coughed.

"I got that straight from Brooklyn," Dame stated.

"Have you been back home nigga?"

"Nah, I'm never going back to Brooklyn. I got a surprise for you though. What ya'll doing tonight?"

"Shit, nothing."

"Well then it's all set, I'm having a little get together tonight."

"Damn nigga, you just got into town and you already having parties and shit," Tyreik joked.

"Come on now, you know how I do. I had Brooke plan this for me weeks ago. Meet me tonight at the condo I'm renting," Dame said, standing up.

"Let me walk you out," I said, trying to be polite.

"A'ight B, I'ma holla at you later," Tyreik said, giving Dame a pound.

"Holla at me B, see you later Chyna," Dame replied, giving me a hug.

Inhaling deeply, I inhaled his scent and damn, he smelled good. I kind of didn't want to let go but remembering Tyreik, I checked myself.

"See you later," I responded, breathing heavily.

"I wonder what that nigga got planned," Tyreik said.

"I guess we'll just have to wait and see."

I know this might sound strange but that night I wasn't much into dressing up. I pulled my hair back into a ponytail and adorned my ears with hoop earrings. A yellow spaghetti strap tank top, a denim pleated mini and heels were my look. I didn't even want to go out but Tyreik insisted that I come. I had a headache out of this world and a sista was seriously PMSing. Kicking it at Dame's was not my idea of fun. Tyreik had promised that we wouldn't stay long, so I agreed to go.

Cars were lined up for what seemed to me like blocks. As soon as we entered, Tyreik was bombarded with hugs and pounds. Niggas from around the way had mad respect for him. Leaving him to his groupies, I made my way around the house. People were everywhere. Dame even had caterers, waiters and waitresses. Over the crowd of people I could see Brooke, the bitch was tall as hell. Standing next to her was my girl Asia.

"What's up baby girl?" shrieked Asia.

"Hey girl," I said, hugging Asia. "Brooke," I said, with a head nod.

"What's up Chyna?" She replied, with a hint of hurt in her eyes.

"It took ya'll long enough, girl this party has been jumping," Asia danced.

"I wasn't even gonna come. I'm tired, my head hurts and I think I'm about to come on."

"Shit you should have stayed your premenstrual ass at home," Asia said, jokingly.

"I really should have but Ty said we wouldn't stay that long."

"There that nigga is over there," Brooke pointed out.

Staring in the direction of which she was pointing, I spotted my baby. There he stood amongst a crowd of niggas with a phat blunt in his mouth.

"Girl, you can hang that shit up, ya'll ain't going nowhere no time soon," Asia laughed.

"A bitch hungry than a muthafucker. Tell one of those wait-ers to fix me a plate," I demanded.

"Damn bitch, calm ya hungry ass down. You better fix your own damn plate," Asia responded.

While I got my grub on in the kitchen, I spotted Tyreik talk-ing to some chick. Brooke was walking past me so I stopped her to ask about Miss Jane Doe.

"Yo, who is that over there talking to Ty?"

"Oh that's Tyreik's surprise. That's Rema, his partna from Brooklyn, she came down here with Dame and JB."

"Oh really," I replied, annoyed.

The bitch and I hadn't even said a word to each other and I already didn't like her. Besides the fact that she was drop dead gorgeous, the bitch was all up in my man's face. Whatever they were discussing had Tyreik's undivided attention, his face was lit up with a smile. I thought I was the only one that made him smile so bright. You know that my friends only made the situa-tion worse, right?

"Who is that girl over there talking to Tyreik?" Asia asked.

"Some chick he knows from New York named Rema," I said, with an attitude.

"Is it just me or is she all up on your man?" Asia instigated.

To be honest with you, the more I watched them the more jealous I became. Every other second, the bitch would touch his chest or hand on the sly. I knew that the bitch was flirting. They stood face to face just a laughing and talking. I guess Tyreik forgot that I was there. He hadn't even come to check up on me to see how I was feeling. His eyes stayed focused on her.

Unbeknownst to me, my lip began to curl and my, "no he didn't" face was on. Rising from my seat, I strutted my ass across the room.

"Ah,um," I said, pretending to clear my throat.

Turning around, Tyreik looked to be pissed that someone was interrupting his conversation. With one eyebrow up, I gave him the now what look.

"Oh, what's up baby?" He said, after realizing it was me.

"It looks to me like I need to be asking you that question," I said.

"Don't even trip Chyna, this is Rema, Rema this is Chyna."

"His girlfriend," I added.

"Nice to meet you," she responded, flakily.

"Sorry that I can't say the same. Tyreik, I need to talk to you."

"Why you trippin', we were just talking," Tyreik asked, confused.

"I don't give a fuck!" I shouted, angrily.

"Look, I'm gonna holla at you later," Rema replied.

"Yeah, we'll see about that," I spat.

"Whatever," She said, with a roll of the eyes.

"Yeah, whatever," I countered back.

Grabbing me by the hand, Tyreik dragged me to the nearby bathroom. Locking the door behind us he started to go off.

"What the fuck is your problem!" he yelled.

"No, what is your problem!" I yelled back.

"Ain't shit wrong with me, you the one sitting up here trippin' and shit over some bullshit!"

"I ain't embarrassing nobody, you embarrassed yourself. You the one standing up there grinning all up in some other bitch face!"

"We were just talking, that's some straight lil girl shit you on."

"Oh, so now I'ma lil girl," I laughed.

"You're acting real childish Chyna, grow the fuck up!" he yelled.

"You grow up!" I yelled back.

"Your cra...!"

"Don't even think about calling me crazy, I saw you wit the bitch. Don't even try to play that shit off Ty. Tell me, how do you two know each other so well?"

"We're just friends Chyna damn, quit being so insecure!"

"Now you wanna flip and call me insecure? No matter how hard you try to deny it, there's much more going on between you and Rema than meets the eye."

"Fuck this, you're not about to ruin my night. Act silly if you want to, just don't say shit else to me tonight," he said.

Standing there left alone in the bathroom, I stood astonished. He was straight trying to play me crazy. Exiting the bathroom, I was beyond pissed. Going after him, I searched the whole house but couldn't find him.

"Have you seen Tyreik?" I asked around.

No one knew where he was or where he had gone. Searching outside, I found him and T by the pool getting blazed.

"Tyreik!" I yelled.

"Chyna, leave me the fuck alone," he said, calmly.

"Excuse us T, but we need to talk," I said, ignoring him.

"I ain't got shit to say to you."

"Well I got plenty to say to you. Let's see where do I begin? First of all, why did you let that bitch rub all up on you?"

"Leave him alone Chyna," T said, trying to warn me.

"Don't tell her ass nothing T, when I slap the shit outta her she'll shut the fuck up then," Tyreik laughed.

"Nigga, you ain't gonna do shit!" I yelled, poking him in the head.

"Touch me again Chyna and I'ma beat ya ass," he said, seriously.

You know me, I just had to prove a point. I pushed him in the head again, this time only harder. Tyreik grabbed my wrist and twisted. The bloodshot eyes were back so I knew that I was in for it.

"Let me go Ty that hurts," I whined.

"I told you ya silly ass not to touch me. Why you always gotta fuck with me Chyna!" He yelled.

"That hurts Ty, stop," I cried out.

Tyreik was twisting my wrist to the point where, if he were to apply more pressure, he would break it.

"Let her go man!" T demanded.

"You better stop fucking with me Chyna," he spoke, calmly.

"Please Ty stop, it hurts," I whined.

Pushing me away he let me go. Holding my wrist, I saw that he had bruised my arm.

"I'm up, find your own damn way home!" Tyreik angrily barked.

"I know you're not going to leave me out here by myself."

"Come on T."

"You gonna leave her for real man?" T asked, concerned.

"Fuck her, since she wants to act silly she can find her own damn way home!" Tyreik yelled, walking off.

"No, fuck you Ty!" I yelled after him.

I didn't give a fuck that people were staring at me like I was crazy because I was. This nigga had just played me out like I didn't know the game. He liked the attention Rema was giving him. I wouldn't trust that bitch with my dog let alone my man. Friend or no friend, the bitch had to go.

"You a'ight?" Dame asked, coming out of the house.

"I'm cool Dame, thanks."

"Damn, did he do that to your wrist?"

Embarrassed, I didn't answer.

"Does it hurt?" he questioned.

"Yeah, a little bit."

"Come on back inside it's getting cold."

Back inside, I sat on Dame's bed. He sat in front of me wrapping my wrist up. Staring at my wrist I wanted to cry, Tyreik was straight turning me into some kind of weak ho.

"You a'ight?"

"I can't believe he did me like that."

"Are ya'll always like this?"

"No," I laughed. "It's only been like this lately. I don't know what's wrong with us, one minute were cool and then the next minute we're killing each other."

"Just hang in there with him, he's just going through something right now, that's all lil momma," he said, trying to help.

"I'm trying to but it's hard. I know that that's your girl and all but what's up with her? She was all up on my man, and when I confronted Ty about it, he had the nerve to get mad."

"Was he all up on her?"

"No."

"Well then what's the problem?"

"The problem is that he should have checked her ass."

"I feel you, if I had a women like you I wouldn't let another bitch near me," he said.

Sitting there we stared at each other. At any moment I felt he would kiss me. Moving in closer he touched my face. I didn't know why I was allowing him to get that close to me, I was most definitely tripping. Just as Dame was about to move in Brooke and Asia walked in.

"There you are girl, where have you been? We've been looking all over for you." Asia said.

Standing up, Dame turned and kissed Brooke on the cheek then he left out.

"What happened girl?" Asia asked.

"Me and Ty got into it big time. I clowned his ass and he had the nerve to try and flip the script on me. We were outside arguing and I hit him. Then he grabbed me by the wrist and nearly broke it."

"Let me see. Ouch, that looks like it hurts," Brooke said.

"Where is he now?" Asia asked.

"He and T left, he said I had to find my own way home," I cried.

"That's fucked up girl, don't cry," Asia replied, hugging me.

"I can't believe he did me like that," I said, crying harder.

"Girl, you better stop crying, there are some fine ass niggas out there, you better go get you one. There are plenty of guys trying to see you Chyna, fuck him, Ty ain't the only nigga on the planet. Go in that bathroom and get yourself together, then we're gonna party," Brooke said, trying to console me.

Fuck a party, my life was falling apart. Tyreik had me strung the fuck out, I didn't know which way I was going half the time. Our relationship had taken a turn for the worst. All the arguing, cussing and fighting stuff would have to stop.

Getting my cell out, I called him. After letting the phone ring about ten times, I hung up. After calling him again four more times, he still wouldn't pick up. The last time I left him a message, *"Baby it's me, pick up the phone man. I miss you and my wrist hurts. I'm sorry for coming at you like that, I just couldn't stand watching that chick touch you. I know you still love me so please come and pick me up. Love you, bye."*

It was 4:30 in the morning when he finally decided to come pick me up. I had fallen asleep in Dame's room. The party was still going strong when I was awakened by the sound of Tyreik's voice. Opening my eyes, I saw him standing over me still mad as hell.

"Are you coming or what?" he asked, pissed.

Jumping up, I hugged his neck. He didn't hug me back but I didn't care.

"I love you Tyreik, don't ever do me like that again," I said, kissing his face.

Kissing his lips, he wouldn't kiss me back and that turned me on even more.

"Kiss me baby," I begged.

Sucking his lips, I pushed my tongue into his mouth. With a few strokes of the tongue, Tyreik let his guard down. Sucking my tongue, he grabbed a handful of my ass.

"Baby, don't leave me again," I pleaded.

"You gotta stop fucking with my head Chyna."

"I know, I'm sorry."

Kissing me deeply, Tyreik placed me up against the wall. Pulling my skirt up he played with my clit.

"Tyreik, make me cum," I moaned.

"I don't know if the God should bless you."

"Please, that feels so good," I panted.

Circling his fingers around my clit he entered me. Finger fucking me, he continued to play with my clit. Just as I was about to cum he pulled out.

"What are you doing? Why did you stop?" I asked, confused.

"Tell me you love me."

"I love you, now make me cum."

Picking me up, Tyreik took me into the bathroom and placed

me on the sink. Pulling his dick out, he teased me with it. Gliding it up and down my pussy he made me promise not to ever act like that again.

"I promise Ty, now fuck me," I begged.

Entering me slowly, he slid all the way up to my soul. Eyeing each other we connected on that level. Arching my back I savored every stroke. Taking both my legs he held them up and pumped harder.

"You're the only one for me Chyna, believe that. I love you girl."

"I love you too Tyreik. Oh baby, I love you!" I yelled.

"This my pussy?"

"Yes boy, it's all yours," I moaned.

Licking his ear, I fucked him back.

"Damn your pussy feels good."

"Ty baby, I'm about to cum!" I yelled out, in ecstasy.

"No you're not," he grinned and slid out.

Opening my eyes, I looked at him like he was crazy. Laughing, he wiped his dick off and pulled his pants back up.

"What are you doing?"

"Until you get your mind right my dick is off limits to you."

"Boy please, you better get back over here and finish."

"No can do sweetheart," he grinned, wickedly.

"Come on Ty, don't do me like that," I begged.

"Say my name for me" he said, biting my nipples.

"Damn Tyreik, quit teasing me and put it back in," I demanded.

"A'ight baby, calm down," he laughed.

"Come on Tyreik, I need to cum."

I don't know what had come over me, it was like I was some kind of mad woman. My ass was craving for the dick. Getting down off he sink, I turned around. I trembled as Tyreik hit it from the back.

"Damn girl, I'm going crazy fucking with you," he groaned.

"I love you baby," I whined.

"I'm cumming Boo, damn your pussy is wet."

"I'm cumming too Ty."

Calling his name, I came harder than I had ever came before. My lips were quivering and my arms, thighs and legs were shaking.

Ramming his dick in me slow and hard, Tyreik asked, "That was some good dick wasn't it?"

"Yes," I moaned, still cumming.

"Do you trust me?"

"Yes."

"Then you gotta stop trippin' all the time," he said, still pumping me hard.

"Okay Tyreik, you hitting my spot baby. You gonna make me cum again."

"Cum for me again, I like to see you cum."

Hitting my G Spot, Tyreik made me cum even harder than before. Looking through the mirror we watched each other climax. Collapsing on top of me, Tyreik placed loving kisses all over my back.

"Damn Boo, that's one of the best shots I've ever had. I ain't never came like that before."

"We need to argue more often, don't we," I laughed and he did too.

Getting ourselves together, we laughed at the night's events. Tyreik apologized for hurting my wrist and I apologized for going off on him. To be honest with you, I didn't even care anymore cause I had my baby back. As long as I had my baby I was cool. I trusted Tyreik, he wasn't going anywhere, I knew that he loved me.

CHAPTER 12

IF YOUR GIRL ONLY KNEW

April 16, 2001, was a beautiful spring day, but I wasn't enjoying it. I sat by the phone awaiting Tyreik's call. He had promised that we would spend some time together that day. It was 4:00 p.m. and he was already an hour and a half late picking me up and my patience was running low. If there is one thing that I hated, it's when someone says they're going do something and then don't. This had been going on for a while, him making promises and not keeping them.

For the past month or so, he had been lying to me on a regular basis. He constantly left me at home alone wondering where he was or who he was with. Whenever he was at home, he would have an attitude and start fights with me for no reason. It seemed like no matter what I did it was never right. I made sure that he stayed fed and that the house was clean at all times. I tried to be cool about the situation because I said that I would trust him, but I really wanted to fuck him up.

Tyreik had started complaining about small petty shit. Soon after the complaining started, he began to come in the house at all times of the night. When I did confront him on this, he would either ignore me or say that I was trippin'. He always justified his staying out late with he was working. Bullshit, something was up but I couldn't pinpoint it. Sometimes when I called him on his cell he wouldn't pick up or when I two-wayed him he wouldn't reply. Everyday that passed and the bullshit ensued I became crazed with anger.

It got to the point that I started to skip meals and spaz out at any given moment. Whenever I became angry, I would tremble with fear because I knew that on any given day the truth would come out. I had to find out what the problem was. Talking to Tyreik was like talking to a brick wall, so I got no answers from him. When I asked him if he was cheating, he would become upset and turn the situation around and accuse me of cheating. He would say that I was being weak, immature and insecure. Then we would argue because I hated when he called me immature or childish. I didn't understand why he couldn't just meet me halfway and be truthful.

If Tyreik couldn't get his way or deal with the situation, he would just up and leave. Here I was trying to keep us together and he was treating our relationship like it wasn't shit. The more I tried and didn't succeed, the more I cried. I didn't know it at the time but I had become depressed, my tears had become my best friend.

I didn't want to talk to Asia or Brooke about my problems because I didn't want to hear I told you so. My relationship with Tyreik was so fucked up. First we would argue, then he would leave, I'd start crying, he'd apologize, and then the next day, the cycle would continue. We were on the verge of breaking up and I knew it, but I tried lying to myself so that none of this would be true. My instinct told me that he was cheating but I had no proof.

Calling his phone again, he finally picked up.

"Where are you?" I asked.

"I'm out getting money Chyna, why?" Tyreik said.

"Why, what the fuck you mean why? You said that we were going to do something together today Tyreik, that's why," I said, with an attitude.

"Damn, I did say that didn't I? We're just gonna have to get up tomorrow ma because I'm busy."

"We don't do shit together as it is because you're never at home. You don't answer your phone when I call you. I don't need this bullshit, you promised Tyreik."

"What the fuck Chyna. A nigga trying to stack his papers and all you can do is bitch and complain. I'll see you when I get home a'ight, I gotta go," he said, trying to hang up.

"Tyreik, if you are not here in fifteen minutes I'm leaving and I mean it," I warned.

"What the fuck you gonna do Chyna, go back home," he laughed.

"I'm not fucking playing Tyreik, fifteen minutes."

"A'ight damn," he said, hanging up.

Fifteen minutes came and went, and still there was no sign of Tyreik. He must've thought I was playing, well guess what, I wasn't. I grabbed my car keys and got the fuck up out of there. I rode around for a while then went to the movies. When the movie let out, the sun had gone down and nightfall had appeared. I called home to check the messages to see if Tyreik had been home and he hadn't. I had a message from Adrian and Michelle asking me if I wanted to go out clubbing. T had left a message telling Tyreik to call him. I called Tyreik's cell phone and checked his voice mail. He had to be dumb as hell if he thought I didn't know his pin number. I checked his messages daily, but never came up with anything except the usual, until that day.

"You have one new message." The operator said, "first message 2:13 p.m. today, *"Tyreik, this is Rema. I'm over Dame's house, come pick me up. I miss you baby."*

I wanted to cry but I couldn't. Rage was the only thing I felt, it had taken over me. I made a quick u-turn and headed home.

I ransacked and tore up all his shit. His clothes torn, jewelry broke, furniture fucked up, revenge on a cheating boyfriend priceless. I threw every plate, bowl and cup up against the wall. By the time I finished destroying the place, it looked like a tornado had blown through. Sitting in the middle of all my mess, I cried freely. He told me to my face that he wasn't and wouldn't cheat on me, and I believed him.

My momma told me that he would break my heart but I didn't listen. I was totally blind when it came to Tyreik. I truly believed him when he told me that he loved me. How could he play me out like that? I had dropped out of school, left home and carried weight for him. I sacrificed everything just to be with him and what had he really given me, nothing but a headache. I knew that I shouldn't have fucked with him.

The phone began to ring. Distraught, I answered it.

"Hello?" My voice quivered.

"Chyna, is that you?" Dame asked.

"Yeah, it's me."

"What's up, you sound like you're crying?"

"Dame," I cried.

"Where's Tyreik at, is he there?"

"You know damn well he's not here Dame, don't play dumb wit me! You can stop covering for him, I know everything!" I yelled.

"What you talking about?"

"I know he's with Rema."

"Damn, how did you find out?"

"Does it matter how I found out, all that matters now is that I know."

"I'm coming to get you. Don't go nowhere and please don't do anything crazy."

'Too late," I said, hanging up.

Dame had been speechless when he entered the apartment and found the mess I had made. Following Dame back to his crib, I cried the whole way. Sitting at his kitchen table, I blew my nose.

"Here, drink some tea," Dame suggested.

"Thank you," I said, in a daze.

Dame didn't talk, he just allowed me to cry and get all my feelings out.

"You cool now?"

"No I'm not cool, I just found out that my man is cheating on me."

"I'm sorry you had to find out that way ma."

"Yeah me too, so how long has this been going on?" I asked.

"You really want to know?"

"Yes, I really want to know Dame," I said, with an attitude.

"A'ight, it's been going since the party I had."

"I can't believe this shit, this nigga has been cheating on me for a month. I would tell people that Tyreik would never cheat on me, how dumb am I?"

"You're not dumb ma, you're just in love with that nigga."

"I can't believe I let that nigga play me! I believed every bull-shit story he told me! All that shit about he loved me and would never hurt me was a bunch of bullshit! I turned my back on my family to be with him. I can't go back home, I don't have a job,

I even dropped out of school just to be near him!" I yelled, heated.

Pacing back and forth, my temper rose to its boiling point.

"I believed him Dame, I believed him."

"Face it Chyna, a nigga's gonna be a nigga."

"Well that's not good enough for me! I gave him my all and I believed him when he said that he wanted to marry me! He told me he cared for me and that he would always take care of me! When I tried to talk to him, he didn't console me he walked away! I can't believe my momma was right!" I continued to yell. "What am I gonna do now? I can't go back home and I'm most definitely not going back to Tyreik's."

"You can stay here tonight," Dame offered.

"I don't want to bother you with my problems Dame, I mean you barely even know me."

"Ain't no thang, I want you to stay."

"Are you sure?"

"I'm sure, now go take a hot bath and then I'm gonna feed you, I know you're hungry."

Thinking about it, I hadn't eaten all day. The bubble bath was just what I needed, I came out feeling cleansed and refreshed. Dame had let me wear a T-shirt and a pair of his jogging pants. I still felt like I was floating on air, I didn't know where I was going or where to turn; my mind was all fucked up. There was a pain in my chest and a weakness in my heart that I didn't think could ever be fixed. Tyreik's indiscretions had broken me down physically and mentally. It felt like I was dying a slow and painful death.

Dame had everything set up. He had ordered in Chinese food and had a bottle of wine to go along with it. He had impressed me once again.

"You didn't have to go through all of this just for me, I could have fixed a sandwich or something."

"You're no sandwich type broad so don't front, plus I wanted to do something nice for you," he said, with a smile.

That smile would be the death of me. Taking my attention away from his face, I eyed the food like a hungry beast. My body had been drained from all the crying I had done and it needed to be replenished. We ate in silence not knowing what to say.

"Did Tyreik and Rema mess around before we got together?"

"Yeah, when we lived up North they did."

"Why did she come down here? Oh wait, I already know the answer to that, she wanted him back."

"Pretty much."

"Did they hook up over here often?"

"A couple of times they did."

"Now I have a question for you."

"What's up?"

"Why are you telling me all of this? You're supposed to be Tyreik's boy, right? But you're selling him out to his girl."

"Is that how you see it?"

"Ah, yeah," I laughed.

"I'm a grown ass man, I ain't got time to play games and shit. You wanted to know the truth so I told you. Tyreik is my boy but he's dead wrong for doing you like that. You're a beautiful girl Chyna, any nigga would die to be with you. I don't know what that nigga's problem is."

"You think I'm beautiful," I blushed.

"You know you're bad. You're one of the finest chicks I've ever seen."

"So what's up with you and my girl?" I asked, switching the subject.

"We cool, she's trying to take things slow and I can understand that."

"That's so sweet. At least you're respecting her wishes, Tyreik wouldn't take no for an answer when I met him."

"I would've done the same thing," he said, with a sexy grin.

"Whatever," I said, rolling my eyes.

"I'm full, I can't eat another bite," he said.

"Me either. I'm tired, do you mind if I go to sleep now?"

"Nah, go ahead. You need some rest after today," he replied, with open arms.

Hugging him, he rubbed his face up against mine. Kissing me softly on the cheek, he made his way to my lips and lightly we touched lips.

Stopping him, I asked, "What are you doing?"

"I'm making you feel better," he said, kissing me again.

"We can't do this, what about Tyreik and Brooke?"

"Ma, your man is out with another chick right now, and me and Brooke are just friends," he spoke softly, licking my neck.

"She's still my friend Dame and Tyreik is yours," I moaned.

"Nobody has to know except you and me."

Laying me down on his bed, Dame took control of my body. Physically I was there with him, but mentally I was somewhere else. I saw myself committing the ultimate betrayal but refused to stop myself. I wanted to hurt Tyreik and Brooke for what they had done to me. Images of Tyreik with Rema filled my head. I regretted ever meeting him and letting him into my life, I regretted everything we shared.

That night, Dame and I had sex and nothing more or less. There was no feeling to it, at least not on my part, it was just pure animalistic sex. He laid it down, but confronting Tyreik was all that I could think about.

The next morning I woke up lying next to Dame, who was still knocked out sleep. Remembering the night before, I felt guilty. If Brooke ever found out about what I had done our friendship would be over. I couldn't believe that I had done that to her. How could I face her after all that had transpired? Damn, I had fucked up big time. I had to get out of there. Snatching my clothes, I dressed quickly and left. Back in my car, I checked my phone and saw that Tyreik had called me twenty-seven times. I knew that facing him and dealing with his lying and cheating ass would be the hardest thing I would have to do.

CHAPTER 13

BREAK UP 2 MAKE UP

"Where the fuck you been at?" Tyreik barked as soon as I stepped through the door.

Walking past him, I gave him the silent treatment.

"Chyna, I know you hear me! Why you fuck up my shit?" he yelled.

Rolling my eyes, I said, "If you would have come home like I told you to your shit wouldn't gotten fucked up!"

"What kind of answer is that?"

"I told you to come home in fifteen minutes. What, you thought I was playing? Why you ain't come home last night Tyreik?" I asked, calmly.

"I told you I was out taking care of business."

"Quit lying, tell the truth Ty! Where were you?"

"I'm not gonna tell ya dumb ass no more, I was out getting money!"

"Lie number one!"

"Lie number one, what is that supposed to mean?"

"It means you're a fucking liar Tyreik! You weren't out taking care of business all night! You were out with Rema nigga, now what?"

Speechless, he just stood there looking at me.

"Now what you got to say, huh, I don't hear you hollering now!"

"I wasn't with no damn Rema! You need to quit being so jealous. Quit being so fuckin' insecure all the time," he replied, waving me off.

"Tell the truth for once in your life! Your lies have caught up with you, I know everything! I know that you were with Rema last night! I know that ya'll have messing around since Dame's party!" I yelled.

"I don't know what you're talking about."

"Oh, so I'm lying?"

"You're crazy Chyna!"

"Oh, so I'm a liar and I'm crazy," I laughed. "Just tell the truth Tyreik, I can handle it, I'm a big girl, you won't hurt me."

"Fine, I was with Rema, is that what you want to hear!" he yelled.

"No, that's not what I wanted to hear! I wanted to hear you say that you loved me and that this was all a lie!"

"I do love you but you be trippin' sometimes!" he yelled.

"No you don't Tyreik!" I yelled back.

"If I didn't love you I wouldn't be with you!"

"Why did you fuck her then?"

"I don't know why, I just did."

"Bullshit, you know why you did it! You did it because you still have feelings for the bitch! Yeah, I know that you and Rema used to fuck with each other! You didn't know I knew but I did! But you know what, I don't want to hear your sob story Ty!"

"Oh, so that's it, we're not even gonna talk about it."

"Oh, now you want to talk! When I wanted to talk you didn't, remember? You were too busy chasing pussy! I gave you a chance and you fucked up, so…"

"So, what?" He asked, getting angrier by the second.

"I can't forgive you Tyreik. So…" I said again, this time my voice cracking.

"So what, what the fuck are trying to say!" he yelled, coming near me.

"I'm saying it's over."

Face to face, we just stared at each other. Heat radiated off Tyreik's body. Looking at me, a tear fell from his eyes. I had never seen a man cry before. I couldn't believe I had this nigga straight up crying.

Raising his fist, I jumped back. Charging at me, he had backed me up against the wall. Instead of punching me, he punched the wall. I just looked at him like he was stupid.

"Okay, what was that for?" I laughed.

"That shit ain't funny, you need to quit playing games!"

"When are you going to get it, I'm not playing."

"Look, I'm sorry. That shit between Rema and me is over with, a'ight. I don't want to be with her, I want to be with you.

Just give me another chance so I can make this up to you. Give me a kiss," he said, changing his tone.

"Nigga is you crazy?"

"Come on let me make you feel better."

"Tyreik don't touch me. I don't want your trifling ass nowhere near me."

"Come here," he said, grabbing my waist and pushing me back up against the wall.

Kissing me on my lips, I began to cry. I knew that I wasn't going anywhere, I just needed to make him suffer a little bit. I may have been stuck on stupid, but I loved him and I was not about to let him go. He was making a complete fool out of me but I didn't care. Nobody had ever made me feel the way he did, I was crazy in love. The more he kissed me, the more I became turned on. Kissing him back, I nibbled on his ear but then I stopped.

"Get off of me!" I yelled, pushing him off me.

"What's wrong?" he asked, pulling me back up against him.

"I smell that bitch's perfume all over you," I said, heated.

"I'm sorry, just let me make it up to you," he whispered, sucking on my neck.

Making his way down, he unzipped my pants, pulled them off and then took off my thong. Holding onto his head, I lifted my leg up so that his tongue could find its way to my pussy. Stroking me gently with his tongue, he made me cry out in ecstasy. I tried to fight the feelings of pleasure, but the combination of his tongue and his hands on my thighs had me torn. The next thing I knew I found myself lying on the floor with my legs up in the air and Tyreik cumming inside of me.

A month and a half later, I found myself feeling sick on a

daily basis. If I wasn't throwing up, I was too tired to even walk. But when my monthly friend had forgotten to stop by, I immediately became worried. Also Tyreik had begun to complain about his penis hurting, and when I saw that his balls were swollen, I ordered him to go get his shit checked out.

After a little hesitation, Tyreik got tested and guess what, he had contracted Chlamydia from sleeping with Rema and me at the same time. Embarrassed was not the word to describe my feelings when I had to go to the clinic. The doctor at the clinic checked me for all STDs and said that I was HIV negative, but that I had indeed contracted Chlamydia. Oh, and guess what, I was pregnant too. There I was seventeen, a high school dropout who had gotten kicked out of her mother's house, who had Chlamydia, was pregnant and only 90% sure who her baby's daddy was. Now ain't that some Maury Povich shit for yo ass.

I didn't know what I was going to do. Getting pregnant was not in the cards for me. It had never even crossed my mind that having unprotected sex could lead to me becoming pregnant. I knew right off Tyreik would want the baby, that wasn't even the problem. The problem was I just didn't know if I wanted it because I wasn't prepared to become somebody's mother. Plus, there was the fact that I knew there was a slight chance that Dame could be the father tore my insides up. Yes, Dame and I had used protection but while he was cumming the condom broke.

The doctor at the clinic said I was almost two months pregnant. Tyreik and I still weren't even talking. I tried keeping my pregnancy a secret but Tyreik could smell the pregnancy all over me. I tried denying it by saying that I was sick from the antibiotics the doctor had given me to treat the Chlamydia. Tyreik knew that I was lying, so he insisted that I take a pregnancy test. When the test came back positive, I did my best impression of being surprised and shocked at the same time.

Tyreik was ecstatic when he learned that I was pregnant. Immediately, he started making plans for us to move into a house and get married. I wanted nothing more than to marry Tyreik despite his flaws, but I couldn't lie to him or myself.

Sitting him down one night before bed, I told him the truth about how I felt, well not the whole truth.

"Tyreik, we need to talk about this whole pregnancy thing," I spoke, nervously.

"What is there to talk about? Once you turn eighteen this summer, we're gonna get married and move out of this apartment. I already found us a fly ass crib out in Black Jack, Missouri. We're gonna be straight ma, I got you. You know I'ma take care of mine."

"That's not it Tyreik. I'm… I'm… I'm just not sure if I want to keep the baby," I finally said.

"What the fuck you mean you don't know if you want to keep the baby!" he yelled.

"I'm saying I don't know if I'm ready for a baby. I'm only seventeen Tyreik; there are other things that I want to do with my life," I spoke, looking down at my feet.

"You can still do whatever it is you want to do, but you're not killing my baby," he said, scolding me like I was a child.

"Tyreik, you cannot make me keep this baby. What kind of mother would I be if I woke up each and everyday regretting even having this baby? I wouldn't want to do that to you or the baby."

"What's the real problem Chyna, why don't you really want to keep it?" he asked, sounding suspicious.

"I told you I'm not ready," I lied.

I couldn't tell him that it sickened me to even think of holding the tiny baby in my arms. I couldn't tell him that I became depressed every time I even thought about keeping the baby. I couldn't tell him about Dame and our one night together. I couldn't tell him that I was selfish to the point where I wanted to keep my figure more than I wanted to keep our baby. I couldn't tell him that kicking it at the club and smoking weed was more important to me. I couldn't tell him that having a child would only slow me down. I couldn't tell him that I didn't love this child at all. I couldn't tell him any of this because his happiness meant too much to me.

"Chyna, you know how I grew up. I told you how my momma didn't give a fuck about me. She didn't want me but damn, at least she kept me. You cannot kill our baby Chyna, it wouldn't be right. Maybe you could grow to want it as the pregnancy progresses. Just think about a little boy with your hair and my smile. Come on Chyna, do this for me," he pleaded.

Looking into those sad eyes, I saw just how much he wanted this baby. I had tried to avoid this conversation since the moment I found out that I was pregnant. I knew that Tyreik would pull the orphan card and that I would cave in. I had to make Tyreik happy because his being in my life was all that I wanted.

"Okay Ty, I'll keep it," I spoke through gritted teeth.

"Good, I promise you everything is gonna be okay," he replied, hugging me.

Barely hugging him back, my heart broke because I knew that deep down this child would never see the light of day.

That night after Tyreik and I talked, I lay in bed next to him and thought back on the story of how he told me he was raised. By the time Tyreik was eight he had learned what a ho and a John was. His first sentence was *"Bitch better have my money"*. Tyreik told me that one day he and Big Redd were sitting in his pearl white Chevy Caprice when he learned the art of hoeing.

"You see pimping ain't easy son. I have to be about my bitches at all times or one of those pigeons will fly the coupe. Since I've been in the game, I've only had one hoe leave my stable and you best believe that bitch got cut the fuck up the very next day," Big Redd said, while taking a puff from his Cuban cigar.

"But Redd why you care if a ho leaves? From what I see you got too many hoes to be worried about one," Tyreik asked.

"Ty, it's the principle of the whole thing. You have to make a hoe fear you; you gotta put fear in their heart baby. If a bitch wanna step out of line or leave me, the bitch gonna leave in a body bag, ya dig?"

Nodding his head, Tyreik agreed.

"Oh, and another thing, never and I mean never, fall in love cause it'll be ya downfall. A bitch ain't good for shit, the only thing a bitch is good for is to cook, clean, pimp and fuck."

"What about momma, she was ya ho and you loved her."

"Ya momma was different at first. She was fresh, pure and ripe when I picked her up, the world hadn't gotten to her yet."

"When I was a baby did ya'll mean to have me?"

"I ain't gonna ever lie to you Ty, you wasn't supposed to be here but shit happens. All I can say is ya momma ain't been right since she had you."

"Why don't she love me Redd?"

"I don't know Ty, that's something that you're gonna have to take up wit ya momma."

A few weeks had passed before Tyreik saw Lizette again. She only came around when she needed to cop some money for a fix from Big Redd. Since she was the mother of his child Big Redd held a special place in his heart for Lizette. Tyreik was sitting at home by himself watching a rerun of Soul Train when Lizette made one of her unexpected visits.

"Where ya damn daddy at boy!" she yelled in a drunken slur.

"He's gone ho watching."

"That nigga can't never let a ho be," she laughed a toothless grin.

"Momma."

"I told you about that shit, my name is Lizette not momma."

"Sorry momma, I mean Lizette. I wanted to ask you something."

"What is it, shit?" She asked, searching the living room couch for spare change.

"Why don't you act like the mommas on T.V.? They love their kids, why don't you love me?"

Snatching him up by his collar, she yelled, "Cause this is real life nigga not some damn T.V. show! My own momma and daddy don't love me so why in the hell would I love you. Love is overrated anyway, you ain't missing shit. Now I know ya daddy left you some money so give it to me," she said, searching his pants pockets.

"I ain't got no money!" Tyreik yelled, trying to push her off of him.

"You gonna raise ya hand to me muthafucker!" Lizette screamed, enraged.

Pushing him to the floor, she tried to take his pants off so that she could whoop his ass when Big Redd walked in.

"What the fuck you doing to my son bitch?" he yelled, back-handing her.

"That lil muthafucker hit me," Lizette said.

"She was trying to take my money so she could go get a hit Redd," Tyreik said.

"Go in your room for me Ty."

Knowing what was about to happen, Tyreik did as he was told and went to his room and closed the door. Even with the television turned all the way up, he could still hear Lizette's cries for help. Immune to her cries, he laid there and went to sleep because from that day on he made a vow to never love or care for a woman.

When Big Redd was locked up for prostituting teenagers, social services placed Tyreik with Lizette's parents in Harlem. When he walked through the doors of their two family flat, pictures of Jesus, bibles and crosses were scattered throughout the house. Tyreik was thirteen and wanted to roam but his grandparents' rules were too strict. They expected for him to go to church seven days a week. Tyreik had never even seen a bible before so all that religion was too much for him.

The first day there, he said his grandmother put blessed oil on his forehead and started speaking in tongue. The next day he ran away. It didn't take long for the authorities to find him since he didn't know his way around. Four more times he did this before his grandparents gave up and stopped looking for him. Just a few months shy of his fourteenth birthday, Tyreik was homeless and living on the streets until the day he met Dame. Dame and he became fast friends and from then on he stayed with Dame and his family until he was seventeen.

Even after thinking about all of that I still knew that the baby that I was caring would never be born.

It was the middle of April and I was beyond depressed. The more my belly grew, the more I grew to hate the baby. I know that sounds cruel but that's how I felt. I was only two and half months pregnant but my stomach had already begun to harden and show. All day long I would sit in the bed, watch T.V. and cry. It would take a miracle to happen for me to even crack a smile. Tyreik tried his best to make me come around, but I knew that having the baby would be the biggest mistake of my life. Everyday I would go back and forth between keeping it and having an abortion. One minute I wanted it and then the next minute I didn't. Tyreik had gotten to the point that he didn't want to hear or talk about it anymore.

I hadn't seen the girls in over a month so they didn't know of my latest dilemma. I made Tyreik promise that he wouldn't tell a soul about the baby. I told him that I would tell people when I was good and ready, which would be never.

Tyreik had planned a special night out to try and cheer me up. Brooke, Dame, Asia, T, Tyreik and I all went to dinner at Calico's Restaurant. I had learned from Brooke that Asia and T were now seeing each other. He stayed true to his word and swooped her up when he got his shit straight. I couldn't believe it was that easy for Asia to leave Shawn. I couldn't believe it, Asia and T an item, who would have thought.

The morning sickness faze of my pregnancy had subsided and I constantly craved Lay's Flaming Hot Potato Chips. After getting my hair done for the first time in weeks, I felt okay about going out. I knew that I would have to run into Dame sooner or later, I had just hoped that it would be later, much later. I hadn't seen nor spoken to him since that night and that's how I planned on keeping it. He would only be another problem that I would have to deal with.

I tried every excuse in the book to get out of going to the dinner, but Tyreik wasn't having it, he didn't want me to spend another night cooped up in the house. I hadn't dressed up in weeks, so it felt kind of good to be in something besides a T-shirt and jogging pants for a change.

Entering Calico's, I spotted the crew immediately, they were seated in the middle of the room at a huge table. I had to act as if everything in my life was perfect. The little pink off the shoulder shirt and pink and black striped pleated skirt showed off my growing figure. My legs were already thick and strong but now I had some big ole thighs and legs. I had Coco straighten my hair and I wore it flat ironed going to the back. I looked pretty damn good despite the fact that I was in hell.

'There they are!" Asia yelled.

"You are so ghetto," Brooke laughed.

"Shut up." Asia laughed too.

Standing up, T and Dame gave Tyreik a pound and me a hug.

"Damn Chyna, you gettin' thick as shit," T teased.

"No I'm not," I nervously replied.

"Yes, you are girl, your skin is glowing and shit," Asia pointed out.

"No it's not; it's just the makeup I'm wearing."

"I don't care what you say, I think you're pregnant," Asia continued.

It was like all eyes were on me. Everybody at the table including Tyreik eyeballed my stomach. Damn, Asia and her big mouth, I thought.

"I can tell by the look on your face you're pregnant," Asia shrieked, running over to me.

"Well now that everybody in the whole damn restaurant knows my business, yes I'm pregnant," I said, rolling my eyes.

"That's why we haven't seen your big ass," Asia joked.

"Whatever," I laughed.

"Congratulations, my nigga's gonna be a daddy," T said, giving Tyreik a hug.

"Yeah, you know I got a little boy in there," Tyreik smiled.

"Nigga, you don't know if it's a boy or a girl yet. Chyna ain't that far along, are you?" Dame asked.

Avoiding his eyes, I answered, "No."

"How many months are you?" He quizzed.

"Damn, Dame, why?" I snapped, paranoid.

"Damn Chyna, the man just asked you a question, calm your ass down," T replied.

Checking myself, I apologized. "I'm sorry, it's just my hormones fucking with me."

"Yeah, she be spazzing out on me all the time so don't pay her no mind," Tyreik assured Dame.

Throughout the entire dinner, my legs and hands wouldn't stop shaking. I felt like the walls were closing in on me. I had Tyreik to the left of me, Dame on my right and the baby in the middle. I stayed quiet throughout the course of the night. For the first time in my life I wished that I could disappear.

Dinner was finally over and T, Asia, Brooke and Dame had decided to catch a movie. I, of course, asked to go home instead. As we got up to leave, Tyreik asked Dame to walk me out to the car while he paid the bill. I had hoped that I could go the entire night without having to talk to him, but I guess lady luck was not on my side.

First, Dame put Brooke in the car and then he walked me to Tyreik's Benz. My heart couldn't take the questions that I knew he was about to ask. I just wished that he would die and then all of this would be over. For a minute it seemed like he wouldn't ask me anything but, of course, I was wrong.

"You know what I'm about to ask you, don't you?" Dame said.

"No I don't," I said, nonchalantly.

"I think you do Chyna."

"If I knew I would've said that I did. Look, if you have something you need to ask me just go ahead and ask me Dame, quit beating around the bush and shit," I spoke, with an attitude.

"A'ight it's like this, is that my baby you're carrying?"

Rolling my eyes, I huffed and said, "No."

"I know you're lying. If it's my baby I'm going to find out eventually."

"There ain't shit for you to find out Dame," I said, turning to face him. "Tyreik and I are having a baby and instead of you trying to cause trouble, you should be happy for us."

"I just need to know because if there is a chance of that being my baby, I think Tyreik and I should know."

Now he had the game all fucked up with the shit he was talking. Tyreik wasn't going to find out a damn thing. Dame needed to be shut down real quick.

"Okay Dame, we need to get some things straight. First of all, stay out of my muthafuckin' business. Secondly, we used a condom so this could not be your baby. And, last but not least, what happened between us was a one-night thing, so don't start catching feelings on me now."

"Tyreik is my boy, I shouldn't care about him?" Dame asked.

"Um excuse me, but if I remember correctly you didn't care about his feelings when you were fucking me," I snapped.

Stepping to me, he softly said, "You're sexy when you're mad, you know that right." Caressing my hair he continued. "But check this out, I will find out the truth one way or another. I know you're lying Chyna, that's my baby and when I find out, my boy will know everything. You know, like how when I kissed your neck you moaned," he grinned, devilishly.

Looking at him clearly for the first time, I came to realize that Dame had more than a few screws loose in his head. This muthafucker was actually threatening me on the sly. If he told Tyreik about that night, my whole life would be fucked up. Tyreik would do more than just kick me out, he would kick my ass. I couldn't let my lie continue on, I had to do something and fast.

Hugging me, Dame whispered into my ear, "I promise I'll love you and our baby if you just let me."

"Ay dog get off my gal!" Tyreik yelled, scaring the hell out of me.

"You know I had to congratulate the mommy," Dame smiled, rubbing my back.

I didn't like his touch so much anymore. I could barely stand the sight of his crazy ass but I had to play it cool for Tyreik's sake.

"I still can't believe it man, I'ma be a daddy," Tyreik grinned.

"Me either, nigga."

"Yo, I need to ask you a question B."

"What's good dog?"

"Ty, I'm going to go sit in the car," I said, feeling very uncomfortable.

"No baby wait, you should be here 'cause this involves you too."

This was it, he must have found out about Dame and me. I didn't know if I should run, cry or try and defend myself. My legs started trembling and sweat formed on my forehead, I swear it felt like I was about to pass out.

"Dame, you've been my boy since PS22. You've been loyal to a nigga when most niggas would've snitched. Don't think that I'm going soft, but you're like a brother to me dog and I would be honored if you would be my son or daughter's Godfather."

I damn near fell out when I heard the words Godfather, now things were really getting out of hand. Fuck being the Godfather shit, he may be the father, I thought.

"So what you got to say nigga, you in or you out?"

"What you think, I'm in," Dame said, hugging Tyreik.

CHAPTER 14

DANCE WITH THE DEVIL

My life was falling apart at the seams and the more I tried to pull things together, the worse it all became. The fighting between Tyreik and me had started again. Once I told him that I had made up my mind about having the abortion, he hit the roof. Anytime I mentioned the word abortion, he would fly off the handle and cuss me out. Then there was Dame's old crazy ass hounding and harassing me everyday. He would call the house all the time for dumb shit just so he could talk to me or he would drop by without calling so I would be caught off guard. Whenever he was given the opportunity, he would black-mail me about the paternity of the baby. I was either going to lose my mind or have a nervous breakdown.

I was already three months pregnant, so I only had another month before it became too late for me to get an abortion at all. After much stress and deliberation, I finally made the painful decision to call Planned Parenthood. My scheduled appointment was for May 14, 2001.

Telling Tyreik that I had made up my mind was the hardest thing I ever had to do. Up until that point in my life, I knew how much he wanted a child and the fact that I could and wouldn't give him one was hard for him to grasp. I promised him that once I got my life back on track that I would be more than happy to give him a child. Tyreik could care less about later, he wanted the baby that I held in my stomach now.

One day while we were in the car coming from the grocery store the conversation of my abortion arose.

"Ty, I promise that once I get myself together I will give you the baby that you want, just give me some time," I begged.

"What's wrong with the baby that you're carrying now?" he stressed.

"It's just not a good time for me to have a baby right now Ty. I'll even use the money that I've saved up for the abortion."

"Have you lost ya muthafuckin' mind girl?"

"What?"

"You're fucking serious aren't you?" he yelled.

"Tyreik, just listen to me, I'm sorry," I cried.

"I promise once my shit is straight I'll give you as many kids as you want. I just…. I just can't do it right now. Just trust me a'ight," I sobbed, wiping my nose.

"I'm done, do whatever you want to do, it's your body. I can't make you keep it if you don't want it, can I?"

"I'm sorry."

"It's cool," he said, inhaling deeply.

"Will you come with me then?"

"You're asking for too much Chyna."

"I know, but I can't do this without you."

"Whatever, if that's what you want I'll go with you. I don't want to talk about this shit no more," he sternly spoke.

A week later I went to my first appointment with the counselor with Asia and Brooke. They had me in there asking me a whole bunch of nothing. I had to look the chick square in the eyes and let her know that I was 100% sure of my decision. They gave me a Pap smear and an AIDs test. The Chlamydia had cleared up so everything came back negative. I got the chance to see the baby when they did the ultrasound to see how far along I was. It wasn't really much to look at honestly. The only thing my heart would let me see was a tiny ball. The next week I would be back for the actual abortion.

Tyreik had barely touched me throughout my mini pregnancy. I guess he didn't want to become too attached to the baby, which is something I could understand. The night before the abortion while we lay playing sleep, Tyreik brushed his hand across the lower part of my stomach, which was now the size of a soccer ball. I didn't think he would keep his hand there but he did for the rest of the night.

You don't understand how hard it was for me to hurt the person I loved more than life itself. I know that I was hurting him deliberately, but it was for his own good. If there was a slight chance that my baby could have been Dame's, I knew that having an abortion was the best thing to do. It would have hurt Tyreik even more to know that I was carrying another man's baby.

When the alarm went off, I woke up to find that Tyreik had already dressed and gone. I figured he was out clearing his head so I didn't trip. My appointment was for 8:45 a.m., so I showered and dressed. One of Tyreik's T-shirts and a pair of jogging pants were all that I needed for that day. Asia and Brooke called to check up on me and to tell me that they loved me. They offered to come but I told them to stay home since Tyreik would be going with me.

It was 7:15 a.m. and Tyreik still hadn't returned home. He had specifically said that he would go with me so I didn't know what the hold up was. I tried calling his cell phone twice but he didn't have it on. Growing impatient, I decided to leave hoping that he would meet me there. The fact that he couldn't even ride with me pissed me the hell off. Tyreik could be cold sometimes but I never knew that he could be this cruel.

When I stepped outside, for some reason everything seemed sunny and bright. The birds were chirping extra loud, people were cheesing extra hard and traffic wasn't even all that bad. Then out of nowhere I caught a flat tire. I knew that it was just a matter of time before lady luck bit me in the ass.

Pulling the Jeep over, I stepped out and examined the damage. I couldn't change a tire if I tried, so I called up roadside assistance. The way things were going I was going to miss my appointment. I cursed the car, my life and the flattened tire as I kicked it. Just as I was about to hit the last number, a car pulled over to help me. Flipping my phone shut, I eyed the driver but couldn't see what the person looked like because the windows were tinted. Whoever the person was, he or she had a clean ass ride. Not looking at the car anymore, I stooped down to examine the tire some more.

"Thanks for pulling over to help me, my tire just caught a flat," I said, still looking at the tire.

"No problem, you know I always got your back," the familiar voice replied.

"Jaylen!" I screamed.

"What's up baby girl?"

"You nigga, I've missed you," I said, giving him a hug.

"I can't tell that, but I can tell you something else," he said, touching my stomach.

"Oh, that," I rolled my eyes.

"Damn, is being pregnant that bad?"

"For me it is."

'Talk to me, what's going on?"

"It's a long story Jaylen. I'll talk to you about it one day but right now I need you to fix this tire for me."

"I got you, pop the truck for me."

"What are you doing out this early in the morning?" I asked.

"I was on my way to school. You know some of us still go to school Chyna," he teased.

"Whatever, Jaylen," I laughed.

"Graduation is next month, are you coming?" he asked, while fixing the tire.

"I don't know, maybe."

"You should come, everybody misses you. I really miss you," he said, with a smile.

Smiling back, I said, "I've missed you too Jaylen."

"There, all done," he said, standing up surveying his work.

"Thank you Jaylen."

"Look, there's something I need to tell you," he stated, seriously.

Glaring at my watch, I saw that I only had thirty minutes until my appointment.

"Jaylen, I have somewhere I need to be. I promise that I will call you okay. I love you and thanks for the help!" I yelled out the window, pulling off.

I felt bad for leaving him standing there like that, but I had bigger issues at hand. I called Tyreik as I sped off down the highway but he didn't answer. I figured that he was already there or either on his way, so I didn't trip.

Entering the brightly colored facility, I was shocked to find so many girls there my age or younger. It had to have been at least fifteen girls there, not including me. All of them, including me, sat patiently awaiting our dance with the devil. It was also amazing to me that out of those fifteen girls, the majority of them were white.

Checking my watch, I saw that it was 8:27 a.m., so I tried calling Tyreik again. This time when I called his cell phone it was on and he still didn't answer. Each and every time that I called him and he didn't answer, I became angrier and angrier. This was his way of getting back at me for my decision. He was actually going to make me go through the abortion alone. I couldn't call Asia or Brooke because, by the time they would have gotten here, the procedure would have already started. I couldn't believe Tyreik could be so cold, he knew that there was a chance that I could die if things didn't go right.

Staring around the room, I noticed that I was the only one alone. My eyes stung from the tears that were trying to form in them. For the first time in my life I realized just how alone I was in this world, I didn't have anybody but my damn self. I had always felt this way, but now it was more noticeable and evident.

Picking up my cell, I tried calling him again. This time I left him a message begging him to come and be by my side. I had only five minutes to go before it was my turn. I wanted to break down and cry, but instead, I pulled myself together and prayed to God, asking him to please not let me go through this alone.

Walking into the tiny room, the first thing that I noticed was the machine that would ultimately seal my unborn child's fate. Closing the door behind me, the nurse gave me the opportunity to undress. As I changed clothes, my mind once again drifted to Tyreik, I wondered where he was and how he was feeling. Myself, I wasn't feeling a thing but anxiety, I couldn't wait to get the whole thing over and done with.

Opening the door, I spotted the nurse and told her that I was ready. Easing myself onto the medical bed, I placed my feet into the stirrups. I wished that Diane could have been here with me. The thought of me dying on that table was killing me softly. Gazing around the room, I noticed that no color or liveliness was around. I guess there was no need for that anyway. Once the doctor entered, he assured me that everything would be okay.

There were four of us in the room, the doctor, the nurse, the nurse's assistant and me. As he started, I focused my attention on the ceiling. The light above me just kept drawing my attention, and for some reason, it seemed like the light only shined on me. Am I doing the right thing, I thought? Lifting my head up, I let the nurse place the oxygen mask over my nose and mouth. I had chosen to be put under instead of being awake, I didn't want any reminders of the day. As soon as I began to inhale, I began to get nervous. Now more than ever I needed my momma to be by my side.

"Okay Miss Black, I'm going to need you to count backwards from ten to one," said the nurse.

"Ten, nine, eight," I said, trembling.

"You have to calm down Miss Black, everything will be fine," the nurse reassured, while patting my hand.

At any moment I prayed that Tyreik or Diane would burst through the door and race to my side, but the clock continued to tick and I was still lying on the table alone.

"We promise Miss Black, that you are in good hands. We will not let anything bad happen to you, I promise," the doctor spoke, reassuringly.

Nodding my head, I continued to count, "seven, six, five," and by the time I hit four, I closed my eyes and let one single tear slide down my face.

An hour later, I was awakened by the sound of muffled cries. Prying my eyes open, I tried to remember where I was. Looking to my right, a young girl who looked to be a couple years younger than me lay crying. Her back was to me, but next to her another girl sat drinking orange juice and cookies. Jumping up, I quickly remembered where I was. Placing my hand on my stomach I felt nothing, I had done it, I had gotten rid of my problem. You would've thought that after I had the abortion, I would have felt a sense of relief, but honestly I didn't. That baby probably would've been the only sane thing in my life, at least he or she would've loved me unconditionally.

On my way out, the nurses and staff tried to get me to call a cab but I told them and myself that I was fine. With my head down, I gazed and stared at what was once there.

"Chyna!" a familiar voice yelled.

Looking up, I saw Diane running towards me.

"Momma, what are you doing here?" I asked, shocked.

"I would've gotten her sooner but there was an accident on the highway," she said, while grabbing and hugging me.

"How did you know that I was even here?" I said, still confused.

"Asia called me this morning and she sounded upset. I knew that something was wrong but she wouldn't tell me, I practically had to threaten her in order for her to tell me. Chyna, why didn't you call me?"

"I haven't talked to you in month's momma. What was I supposed to do, call and say, hey momma guess what, I'm pregnant and I'm having an abortion?" I asked her.

"Don't be a smart ass Chyna. Regardless of how you said it, I would've been there for you. No matter what happens, you are still my child and I love you."

"I know," I cried.

"Now, where is Tyreik? Why isn't he here with you?"

"He didn't want to come; he said that he couldn't handle being there when it happened," I lied.

"Don't lie to me Chyna; Tyreik is over Asia and T's house right now. That's why she called me because you told her that Tyreik would be going with you. She said that Tyreik showed up on her doorstep this morning and said that he was not going with you. That's why she called me, because she didn't want you to be alone."

If my face had been glass, it would have sure shattered right then and there. My momma knew more about my own man than I did. Now ain't that some shit? I felt about two feet tall standing there with Diane, because everything that she said about Tyreik was coming true.

"Chyna, I don't know what is going on with you but know that I'm here for you. You are my baby girl and I love you more than I love myself. I never wanted this for you, I only wanted the best, that's why I pushed you so hard. Oh Chyna, how did we get here?" she cried.

Holding my face in her hands, she kissed me on my forehead and held me tight. Sniffling, I held my head down and cried. I think that Diane and me stood in the parking lot for at least ten minutes crying. Diane repeatedly asked me to come home for at least a couple of days, but I kept on telling her that I was fine. I needed to get home to Tyreik so that we could get a few things straight but Diane wasn't having it. She insisted that she would at least follow me home to make sure that I got there alright. Once we got to the house, she then insisted that she come in too.

Looking around, I saw no sign that Tyreik had returned home. While I was checking the call notes, Diane drew me a hot bath that seemed to soothe me some. After seeing that I was safe and okay, she kissed me on the forehead and left. But before leaving, she made me promise to call her before I went to bed that night.

Once I heard the front door close behind her, I tried closing my eyes and letting the silence that surrounded me take me away. Between the bleeding, cramping, tears and rain, I still could only concentrate on Tyreik. I wondered where he could possibly be. I tried calling his cell again but to no prevail. This nigga was literally MIA.

Even after all of this, I wasn't really mad. I felt as though he could have just told me that he didn't want to come and I would have understood that. I just didn't want to hear anybody's mouth (meaning Asia and Brooke) about him not coming. I still hadn't told them that he had cheated on me and gave me Chlamydia. If I had, I would have heard a million "I told you sos".

With my eyes closed, I let the silence take me away to my thoughts. I wanted to feel some kind of remorse for what I had done, but I just couldn't summon up the feelings. My heart had been on E, the only thing I felt was emptiness. It seemed like the only time I felt happy was when Tyreik was around, and he was rarely around, so I was never happy. Asia and Brooke had to have known but they never asked and I never told.

I couldn't get over the fact that Asia had the audacity to tell my mother about the abortion. What kind of friend would do such a thing? My business was my business and she didn't have any right telling her without my permission. But I guess I wasn't doing such a good job of hiding the truth about my relationship with Tyreik. I wanted to be upset with her, but I really couldn't be. She was only trying to look out for me and I loved her for that. I just didn't feel like explaining the reason for Tyreik not being there. I wondered how long I would be able to keep up with this charade.

On the outside, our relationship seemed perfect. I mean everybody knows that Tyreik's a hothead and that I'm irrational, but other than that, we seemed fine. They wouldn't understand that, despite Tyreik's antics, he really did love me. Yes, some of the things that he's done are wrong but I loved him. They would only judge us and I didn't want that. They don't know how the touch of his hand heals any doubts in my mind, and they don't see how he looks at me with so much intensity and desire.

Everyday there was something new. I hurt because of Tyreik but I just couldn't pull myself away. To some he probably treated me bad, but in my eyes, I only saw his love for me. If people knew the cat and mouse game Tyreik played, they would have called me stupid. I used to say that I would never let a man treat me bad, but now I justified every wrong thing Tyreik did with the famous talk show line *"But I love him"*.

Around here, females were itching to get with Tyreik and I was the lucky one who caught and snatched him, and I was not about to let him go for anything. Don't get it twisted, I don't let people run my life just because of what they may or may not say, I just wanted to keep our relationship between the two of us.

Sometimes I questioned our relationship and why I had gotten with him in the first place. I knew there had to be a reason for all of this because I know I had not gone through all this shit for nothing. Tyreik and I were meant to be, but I secretly knew that our ride together was ending. I just wasn't willing to admit it, I still wanted to believe that Tyreik and I would get married and live happily ever after. Yeah, we had gone through some hard times, but doesn't every couple. I loved Tyreik with my soul and without him I didn't think I could live.

Startled by the sound of the phone, I got up hoping that it was Tyreik. Answering on the first ring, I was only let down to hear that it was Asia and Brooke calling me on a three-way.

"How did everything go, are you okay?" Asia asked.

"Yeah, I'm a'ight," I said, getting back into the tub.

"What's wrong, you sound sad?" Brooke questioned.

"Why wouldn't she sound sad Brooke, she just had an abortion, duh," Asia said.

"Shut up, Asia," said Brooke.

"Well it's the truth. Chyna, don't be sitting over there all miserable, we're here for you, you know that don't you?" Asia said.

"Yeah I know you got my back. You got me alright Asia," I spoke, with a sarcastic tone.

"What's that supposed to mean?" she asked.

"Why did you tell Diane that I was pregnant and having an abortion?"

"I thought that she should know."

"Don't you think that you should have been left up to me Asia?"

"You aren't in the right frame of mind right now and at a time like this you need your mother."

"It wasn't your place to tell her though."

"Wait a minute, your momma knows that you had an abortion?" Brooke asked, stunned.

"Yeah, she knows because apparently Asia called her this morning and told her everything."

"Is that true Asia?" Brooke asked.

"Yes and I don't see why you're so upset Chyna, your mother has been worried sick about you. She calls me at least five times a week to check up on you. She loves you Chyna."

"If she loved me so much, she would have never kicked me out in the first place and regardless, you had no business telling her. And why didn't you call and tell me that Tyreik was over there?"

"I didn't know what was going on Chyna. I just did what I thought was best for you once I saw that Tyreik wasn't going with you."

"Hold up, Tyreik didn't go with you?" Brooke asked, stunned.

"No, Brooke, he didn't. He decided at the last minute that he couldn't handle being there," I lied.

"If that's the case, then why are you so mad. Shit, I helped you out," Asia said.

"You helped me out? You helped me out alright by telling all my goddamn business," I said, pissed.

"Hold up Chyna, you need to calm your ass down," Asia warned.

"I don't need to do shit, you need to mind your business sometimes!" I yelled, heated.

"You know what, I will and when your dumb ass gets in over your head again, don't come crying to me!" she yelled back.

"Trust me, I won't."

"Ya'll both just need to chill the fuck out before you both end up saying something ya'll will regret," Brooke said.

"Nah fuck that, I'm sick of people always getting in my business. Asia, case in point, she needs to get a life of her own."

"You know what Chyna, fuck you!" Asia spat, as she hung up.

"Asia!" Brooke yelled.

"She hung up."

"I'm going to call her back because ya'll are tripping."

"She's the one tripping not me, fuck her."

"Chyna, you're talking out the side of your neck right now, you don't mean that, those are just your hormones talking."

"Hormones my ass, I know exactly how I'm feeling right now. So you don't think she was wrong?"

"I mean Chyna, she was only trying to help."

"I don't care," I said, cutting her off.

"Let me finish. Yes, she should have asked or told you but she didn't. Look, this whole thing shouldn't have ever gotten to this point. Frankly, I think both of you are wrong."

"Why am I even talking about this dumb shit? I'ma holla at you later," I said, hanging up without waiting for a response.

I know that I had overreacted, but at the time I really didn't care. I needed to vent and I chose Asia as my target because the person whom I should have gone off on was nowhere to be found.

My bath water was beginning to get cold so I filled it again with hot water. Leaning my head back, I tried to escape when I heard the front door open. My heart began to race as I listened to each of Tyreik's footsteps. First he dropped his keys on the coffee table, then he picked up the phone. I assumed that he was checking the messages. After that, he opened the refrigerator and then closed it. Walking again, he made his way to the back of the apartment. Stopping, he stood in the bathroom doorway and stared at me. We both just stared at each other for what seemed like hours. I guess he didn't know what to say either.

Not being able to hold my feelings in any longer, I asked, "What the fuck happened to you?"

"I had to take care of some business," he spoke, nonchalantly.

"Whatever you had to do it couldn't wait?"

"Nope."

"If you didn't want to come, you could have just said so instead of lying."

"I told you I didn't want to come but you wouldn't let up until I said yes, so I told you what you wanted to hear."

"So that's how it is now, you just tell me anything so you won't have to hear my mouth?" I asked, with an attitude.

Switching the subject, he asked, "Did you go through with it?"

"Yeah I did."

"Okay then, that's all that matters right," he spoke, in a sarcastic tone.

"Yeah, that's all that matters," I snapped back.

Sucking his teeth, he left the bathroom. After quickly bathing, I grabbed a towel and wrapped it around me. Stepping into the bedroom, I noticed that Tyreik was changing clothes.

"Where are you going now?"

"I only came home to check on you and you're okay, so I'm up."

"You're not going anywhere Tyreik!" I yelled, fed up.

"You're getting water all over my floor," he said, ignoring me.

"Fuck this floor, you heard me, you're not leaving!"

"Chyna, I ain't got time for your dramatics today."

"My dramatics, what kind of shit is that? Where is this shit coming from, you don't even talk like that!"

"Don't hate because I'm trying to educate myself and all you want to do is shop."

"Excuse me?"

"You heard me, you need to do something with yourself besides spending my money! Shit, get a fuckin' job, go back to school, do something with yourself! Don't no nigga want a woman who doesn't wanna do shit with herself!"

"Are you serious? I just had a fucking abortion today and you're acting as if I've been at home eating Bon Bon's all day."

"Whatever," he said.

"It ain't no whatever! Did I tell you to go up in me without a rubber every time we fucked!" I yelled, getting in his face.

"You better get the fuck out my face, girl!"

"What you gonna do Tyreik?" I asked, pushing him in his head.

"You're a silly ass lil girl." He said, walking away.

"Nah, come back here!" I yelled, following him.

"Why don't you leave me the fuck alone, damn!"

"Nah, we gonna finish this shit!" I screamed, pushing him.

"Touch me again and I swear to God I'ma fuck you up," he replied, seriously.

"Nigga please, you ain't gonna do shit! You act like you don't even care that I had an abortion today. You're like, oh whatever she'll be a'ight."

"Did I tell you to have the fucking abortion, huh?" He shouted, as he grabbed a picture of us and threw it against the wall. "You the one who didn't want to have the baby. Don't be actin' all guilt stricken now, 'cause I don't feel sorry for ya ass! A real woman would've had the baby whether she wanted it or not, but oh I forgot, you're only seventeen!"

"Nigga back the fuck up! I wasn't only seventeen when you were fucking me. What the hell I look like having a baby by you anyway! The only thing you have done since we've been together is hurt me! You sell dope for a living Tyreik! How the fuck we gonna raise a child under those circumstances! You just mad cause I want more out of life then to be with your sorry ass!" I said, out of hurt and anger.

"Was I sorry when I bought ya ass that truck or all of them fucking clothes and shit you got? I took ya trick ass out the gutter and showed you the game! You ain't know shit until you got wit me! Where ya momma and daddy at? I'm the nigga that raised you, they ain't doing shit for you! When you didn't have a place to stay I took you in! Don't ever forget that shit, wit ya old ungrateful ass! Remember, without me you ain't shit!" He yelled, arrogantly.

"Nigga, have you lost ya rabbit ass mind? You the one who ain't shit, you wanna be John Gotti muthafucker, you ain't no real thug! You got your girl transporting weight for you, nigga that shit ain't gangsta! The shit you pushing ain't nothing but a misdemeanor nigga! How the fuck ya local ass make me? Take ya old Nino Brown, Frank White wanna be, nickel and dime bag ass back to Brooklyn wit that shit you talking! Go try pushing some weight back up there muthafucker, 'cause you ain't running shit here! I have fucked with plenty of niggas and ya ass is small time compared to them! You need to be happy a bitch like me even wit ya ass!" I yelled back, going off.

"I've been waiting for you to fuck up just so I could I give it to ya ass! Let me let you in on something lil girl. You the stupid bitch cause I had ya ass transporting weight for me when I didn't have to. Now what, and I hope you don't think fucking you was all that, cause half the time your lil ass pussy couldn't even keep my dick hard! You wasn't shit but a fuck to me, you fucking tease! I took you in cause I felt sorry for you, and if you hate me that fucking much take ya raggedy ass back home to ya momma, you're a lil girl to me! Take ya trick ass and get the fuck out my crib! Grab ya sunflower seeds, cabbage patch dolls, crayons, backpack, ya Route 66 jeans and get the fuck out, you no class having bitch!" He yelled, while throwing all my stuff out of the closet. "Nah fuck that, you ain't got to leave, you ain't gotta go nowhere cause I'm about to get the fuck up outta of here anyway!"

"You getting ready to run to Rema now? You know what, I don't even care no more! Fuck you, go be with the bitch!" I yelled, slamming the door.

"Don't be slamming my goddamn door!"

"Fuck you and these goddamn doors!" I yelled, slamming another door on purpose.

Walking out of the bedroom, Tyreik marched towards me.

He grabbed me by the neck and said, "Don't make me beat ya ass up in this muthafucker Chyna! What you want, me to beat the shit outta you! Now I told you leave me the fuck alone."

"Let me go!" I screamed, while hitting him in his face.

"I told you to quit fucking with me!" he yelled.

"I said let me go," I cried, while hitting him hysterically. Suddenly a sharp pain ripped through my stomach. "Ty, let me go, my stomach is hurting," I yelled, trying to push him off of me.

"Why the fuck you have to kill my baby?" he yelled. "I ain't done nothing but try to love you and that's how the fuck you repay me!" Easing his grip on my neck, he pushed me against the wall.

"You do not run my life Tyreik!" I yelled, doubled over in pain. "I run my life, I run this shit! You left me when I needed you the most! I needed you and you fucking left me! Why the fuck you keep on doing me like this? I can't take it no more, I fucking needed you," I cried.

"Come on ma, let's just end this shit 'cause this shit ain't working," he spoke.

It took me a minute to realize what he had just said, but when I did I went buck wild on his ass.

"What you think, that's supposed to hurt me! Shit, bye muthafucker! You doing me a favor, get the fuck out, leave! Step nigga, I don't need you! "

Looking at me while shaking his head, Tyreik did exactly like I said and stepped. No matter how much I wanted to run after him, I would not allow myself to do that, I would simply have to move on.

A couple of weeks had passed and Tyreik still hadn't returned home. When the idea of us finally being over was just beginning to sink in, he decided to return home. It was like one in the morning when I was awakened by the touch of his hand on my face. Opening my eyes, I found him on the side of the bed caressing my skin while on his knees. The sight of his face sent tears to my eyes but I tried to hold them in.

"I thought you weren't coming back?" I said, almost in whisper.

"You're driving me crazy girl. I need you in my life, I can't even breath when I think about living without you," he said, kissing me on the forehead. "It's just hard for a nigga to get over the fact that you killed his baby," he said, with tears in his eyes.

"I just wasn't ready Tyreik," I spoke softly.

Climbing on top of me, he kissed me on the lips while still holding my face in his hands.

"I know ma."

"Tyreik, we gotta stop hurting each other like this," I cried, letting the pain seep through.

"I'm going crazy fucking wit you Chyna, for real. I love you," he said, slipping off my nightie.

"I love you too," I cried, even harder.

"We gotta work this shit out ma cause I ain't gonna be able to think straight until we do," he said, kissing my neck.

"Tyreik," I moaned.

"I wanna love you but you have to let me. If it takes the rest of my life to show you how much I love you I'll do it, but I ain't gonna be fucking wit you if you gonna be acting all crazy. If we gonna do this we gonna do it right," he spoke into my ear, while licking and nibbling on it.

"I wanna make things right too baby. I promise that I will not hurt you again," I cried out in ecstasy.

CHAPTER 15

THE END

As I laid there nearing an orgasm, listening to him beg and plead for me to stay, I saw myself. It was like I was having an outer body experience. My spirit stood at the foot of the bed staring back at me with pleading eyes. I saw her crying out for me, I saw her and wanted to return her to my soul but couldn't. I wasn't myself anymore, I was an intruder. The old me would have been gone and moved on, but this new girl was desperate and clingy.

I tried to pretend like the old me didn't exist anymore and that everything he spoke was okay. I ignored all of my doubts, insecurities and tear filled eyes. I was just as tired as he was but I continued to believe that we could work things out. I was not about to lose Tyreik, we were going to make this work no matter what. Who cared that neither one of us were happy, the love that I held in my heart was enough for the both of us, and it was not about to be replaced.

Tyreik began to spend a little bit more time at home but he was still in and out most of the time. I was bored out of my mind, so a week or two later I found myself a job. Since I didn't know how to do much, I got a job washing hair at Premiere Palace. The last girl Coco had washing heads for her quit two weeks prior so I was in luck. It was a cool job for it to have been my first. The only thing I did all day was wash hair and gossip. You could learn the goods on anybody in St. Louis at a salon if you asked the right questions. It was a unisex shop with barbers on the first floor and beauticians in the basement. Every baller in St. Louis came to Premiere Palace to get their hair cut, beard trimmed or lined up. Whenever I had to go upstairs to do or get something, I got much love from the fellas.

It didn't take anytime for me to get my figure back after the abortion. Tyreik hadn't hit it in months and I desperately needed some of that death stroke. Things between Asia and me were still strained, she wasn't even speaking to me and I wasn't thinking about her either. I started to run with a new crew. Adrian, Michelle and I had been hanging tough for a couple of weeks. They liked to get choked and party so they were cool with me.

One Friday night I was home alone bored out of mind so I invited them over. We had a ball watching BET's Uncut, getting blazed and drinking. The weed that night was some heat and I started running my mouth and telling all of my business.

"Ya'll know that ya'll my girls, right," I proclaimed, in a drunken slur.

"Yeah, girl, you cooler than a muthafucker too," Adrian laughed.

"I'm for real yo. Ya'll cool peoples, so cool that I'm gonna let ya'll in on a secret."

"Shit, I love secrets. What is it?" Adrian bounced.

"Okay, but ya'll got to promise not to tell anybody."

"We promise," They both stated, in unison.

"Ya'll my girls and I trust ya'll," I said, staring them in the eyes.

I felt that I could trust them so I finally spilled the beans.

"I fucked Dame."

For a minute neither one of them made a sound, the only thing I saw were their mouths wide open and a shocked look on both of their faces.

"You mean to tell me you fucked your girl Brooke's man?" Michelle asked, in a daze.

"It wasn't something that I planned or anything, it just happened."

"Does Brooke know?" Adrian asked.

"No and she can never find out, it would kill her if she ever knew."

"That's some deep shit," Michelle said.

"Ain't it though, I've been holding this in for months and it's been eating me up."

"I want to know how it happened," Adrian asked, eagerly.

"Like I said, it just happened. Nobody knows about this either, Tyreik cheated on me a while back and I found about it."

"Word?" gasped Michelle.

"Yeah, but it's cool now, we're tighter than ever," I lied. "But when I found out I was devastated. Dame just so happened to call after I found out. To make a long story short, he swooped me up and he was my shoulder to lean on that night. The conversation was flowing and I was hurt so when he kissed me I ain't stop him."

"Word?" said Adrian.

"Word," I answered.

"That's some crazy shit yo," Michelle stated.

"I know, right," I said.

"So Brooke has no clue that her man is a ho?" asked Adrian.

"Not that I know of," I answered.

"So the only people that know about this are the people in this room and Dame?" Adrian questioned.

"Yep," I said, taking another toke of the blunt.

It's funny how when you look back on your life, you realize just how stupid you were at times. Back then I couldn't see how ridiculous my way of thinking was. I justified everything that had happened in my life instead of realizing my mistakes and fixing them.

I wouldn't allow myself to see that things between Tyreik and me weren't going to get any better. I had gotten a job, changed the way I look, behaved and still I wasn't good enough for him. I was determined to make him love me because I could finally taste the love that I had yearned for my entire life. I didn't have a male figure around to really show me how a man was supposed to treat a women, so I basically went off of what I saw everybody else doing. The things that I picked up in the streets were, the more bullshit you put up with meant that you and your boyfriend or girlfriend was meant to be together.

My mom felt as though my pops had the right to know about my abortion, so she told him. Can you believe this nigga called my cell yelling and cursing like he's been around? Now that shit fucked me up, all of a sudden this nigga wanted to play daddy. Where was his ass when I got kicked out seven months prior? I can tell you exactly where he was, sitting somewhere talking shit with a drink in his hand. My momma should have kept her damn mouth shut, so once again she and I were not talking. Dealing with Diane was just added stress that I didn't need.

Asia and I still weren't talking and I had alienated Brooke due to the fact that I was guilt ridden over the Dame fiasco. The only person I had was Tyreik and he barely wanted to be around me. I was sad, guilt stricken, insecure and jealous. Every chick that came through the shop I assumed was fucking Tyreik. I wasn't getting any of his good loving so I wondered who was. Whenever he did break me off, it was always quick and to the point. There was no more foreplay filled with emotions. The connection that we once had had disappeared.

I knew that I had to do something before I lost Tyreik for good so I planned a romantic vacation for two. Trust me when I say it took a lot of pleading and persuading on my part to get Tyreik to agree to go. We were to leave that Wednesday night on a flight to Miami.

Now you know that I had to be fresh to death so I spent the whole day Tuesday at the mall. Time does fly when you're having fun, and I had a ball spending Tyreik's hard earned drug money. I had totally forgotten that Adrian had asked me to take her to her WIC appointment.

After hours of shopping, I sat in my truck and went through my missed calls. I had one call from Michelle and seven from Adrian. Remembering her appointment, I called her back to apologize.

"Hello?" Adrian said, answering her phone.

"What's up girl?" I said.

"What happened to you Chyna, my appointment was at 11:30 this morning?"

"Girl, I'm going on a trip to Miami with Tyreik and I had to go shopping."

"I called and called you Chyna, why didn't you pick up?"

"What don't you understand Adrian, I was out shopping."

"Chyna, my son doesn't have any milk and I missed my WIC appointment so that means I had to reschedule."

"When is your next appointment, I'll be sure to take you to that one."

"You don't get it do you, it's not about when my next appointment is, you should have taken me to this one like you said you would," she snapped.

"Hold up Adrian, don't get it twisted, you cool but you ain't that cool. Now I said that I was sorry, either except my apology or step."

"And you wonder why nobody likes you," she stated, with sarcasm.

"Do you think I give a fuck about somebody liking me?" I yelled.

"Sometimes I wonder how Brooke would feel if she knew about you and Dame?"

"Adrian, I swear to God, if I find out that you told Brooke anything, when I see you I'ma kick ya ass."

"Yeah, we'll see," she laughed.

"Don't let me catch you out in the streets bitch," I warned her, hanging up.

How dare that bitch try and threaten me, I thought rolling my eyes. I wasn't bullshitting either, the next time I saw Adrian her ass was mine. Dismissing Adrian's threats, I went on about my day forgetting about the whole ordeal. Tyreik and I boarded the plane to Miami the next morning. I knew that being in a different environment would help our situation.

As soon as we touched down we began to reconnect. For once we were both smiling at the same time, we were genuinely enjoying each other's company. Our first day there we went sightseeing and shopping. The sound of the ocean waves beating against the current soothed my soul. Being near the beach was so peaceful and serene. Tyreik was finally at peace too and lying there together for the first time, we truly discussed our problems.

Tyreik told me all about Rema and him. He said that they were together for about three years before he moved to St. Louis. She was his first love, which came as a surprise to me. There I was thinking the whole time that I was his first love like he was mine. I couldn't believe that this whole time I had been living a lie, but I laid there and continued to listen.

He said that when she came into town old feelings began to rise. I asked him did he still love her and to answer honestly. With little or no hesitation, he said yes. That yes caused my heart to crawl slowly up into my throat. He told me that things between him and her were over because she had lied to him and he couldn't trust her anymore. I asked him what the lie was and he said that it didn't matter. When I asked again, he finally gave in and said that she lied about being pregnant by him. She did this in hopes of him leaving me for her. I asked him when did all of this happen, he said around the time that I was pregnant. He said that once he found out that I was pregnant, he broke things off with her and she became upset and lied about being pregnant. He said that he wanted to give us another chance because he still loved me. Despite what I had just heard, I put aside better judgment and agreed.

The rest of our time in Miami we made love, only leaving our hotel to eat or shop. My body had been yearning for the touch of his skin pressed against mine. That first encounter had me begging for mercy. Tyreik must have missed me just as much as I missed him because he did my body right that night. We made love slow and hard, retracing and exploring each other's body. It felt good to have him kiss me passionately and with feeling. The only thing that mattered was being in the moment. Every touch that he gave came with a reaction, and I made sure to let him know exactly how he made me feel.

Our four-day stay in Miami came and went by quickly. Before I knew it, we were back on the plane returning home. Unlike our last trip, I returned with my man and a new sense of purpose, we finally were on the same page. The whole trip we spent holding hands and cuddling, Tyreik didn't want me out of his sight. Things felt like they did when we first had gotten together. Walking into our apartment, Tyreik could barely keep his hands off me, I had to practically push him off me.

We hadn't been back into town no longer than an hour before he had to leave out on business, but this time I didn't worry because I knew that he would be right back. Kissing like it was our last, we held each other in a tight embrace. With a peck on the forehead, he told me that he loved me. Searching his eyes, I told him that I loved him also. As I watched him get into his brand new Range Rover, I told him I loved him again, and with a wink of the eye he drove off. Closing the door behind me, I headed to the bathroom, only to be stopped from the sound of the phone ringing.

"Hello?" I said, answering the phone.

"Yo Chyna, did you get my message?"

"Michelle, is that you?" I asked.

"Yeah girl it's me, did you check your messages?" Michelle asked.

"Nah, not yet I just got in, what's up?"

"Look girl, after you and Adrian got into it that day she went and told Brooke everything."

I couldn't believe what I had just heard. It was as if time stood still for a minute, and I swear to God my heart skipped a beat. This shit could not be happening right now.

"Chyna, you still there?"

"Yeah, yeah I'm still here."

"Brooke knows everything, she called me that night to see if I knew. I acted like I didn't know what she was talking about but I think she knew that I was lying."

"Damn, I can't believe this shit!" I yelled.

"So, what are you going to do?"

"I don't know," I said, just as my other line beeped. "Hold on Michelle, it's my other line. Hello?" I said.

"So you fucked Dame?" Brooke asked.

Closing my eyes, I tried to pretend that this shit was not happening. My worst fear was coming true and I wasn't mentally prepared or ready to deal with it yet.

"I want to hear it from you Chyna, did you fuck Dame?"

"I don't know what you're talking about Brooke; I just walked into the house," I lied, trying to play it off.

"Chyna, Adrian called and told me that you and Dame have been fucking around since he moved up here."

Hold up, no this bitch didn't lie on me, I thought.

"You got it all wrong Brooke, me and Dame have not been fucking around since he came to St. Louis."

"But you have fucked with him right?"

I wanted to continue to lie but I was worn out. My heart wouldn't allow me to continue living a lie, so I did what I had been dying to do for months, I told the truth.

"Yes, I slept with Dame but it was only one time Brooke."

"Why, Chyna?" she asked.

"Why what?" I questioned, not understanding the question.

"Why did you do it?"

"It just happened."

"It just happened, what kind of shit is that, it just happened?"

"It wasn't something that I had planned on doing. I was hurting because I had just found out that Tyreik was cheating on me and Dame called the house when all of it was going down and he heard me crying so he came over."

"Wait a minute, Adrian told me that ya'll had sex at his house. And to make matters worse, you had sex with him in the same bed that he and I have sex in."

"We did have sex at his house. He came over and when he got here, he saw that I had fucked up the house so he told me to follow him to his place."

"It didn't run through your mind that what you were doing would hurt me?"

"Yeah, it ran through my mind."

"So why did you do it?"

"I don't know Brooke, I honestly don't know. But what I do know is that I'm sorry."

"You're sorry. Is that supposed to make me feel better?" she asked.

"No, I mean yes," I answered.

"Does Tyreik know?"

"No," I said, gloomy.

"Well, you better tell him before I do."

"Come on Brooke, we've been friends for too long, don't make me do that. We just got things back on track, I can't tell him that. Please, let's just keep this between you and me," I begged.

"Fuck you and Tyreik. You act like that nigga is God. He doesn't give a fuck about you Chyna. You care more about his feelings than you do mine, don't you?"

"It ain't even like that and you know it Brooke. I just can't lose him."

"You are one stupid bitch. You have until tomorrow to tell him or I will," she warned, hanging up.

Throwing the phone at the wall, I screamed, "Fuck!"

Pacing back and forth, I tried to figure out a way to get out of telling Tyreik. He would be returning home at any moment and I knew that Brooke wasn't bullshitting so I had to tell him. Never before in my life had I been more nervous. Pat always said that whatever you do in the dark will come out in the light. I never knew this to be true until now.

"Baby, I'm back!" Tyreik yelled, scaring the shit out of me.

It was now or never, so I met him in the dining room.

"I feel like celebrating, let's go out tonight," he said, excitedly.

"Tyreik, we need to talk."

"We can talk later, go and get changed."

"It can't wait, we have to talk now."

"What's up Dimples, what do we need to talk about?" he said, hugging me.

"I don't know how I'm gonna tell you this," I spoke, starting to cry.

"What's with the tears? I told you we're straight now."

"I know that," I said.

"Well then, what's the problem?"

"Promise me that after I tell you what I'm about to tell you we're still going to be okay."

"I told you I love you, I'm not going anywhere."

"You promise?"

"I promise. Now, I'm about to take a shower, are you coming?" he smiled.

Breathing heavily, I willed my legs not to give out on me. Trembling with fear, I was about to utter the words that no man or woman ever wants to hear.

"Come on let's hop in the shower, who knows what might pop off," he teased.

"Tyreik, I slept with Dame."

For a minute it seemed like time stood still.

"What did you say?"

"I said that I slept with Dame."

Letting me go, Tyreik looked at me with disbelief.

"I'm so sorry Tyreik," I cried.

Standing still, he continued to stare at me. Then out of nowhere he grabbed me by the neck and proceeded to choke me. I tried to push him off me but he was simply too big. The air in my lungs wouldn't allow me to scream. I kind of wanted to die then maybe all the pain would go away. Just when I was about to give up and let nature take its course, he turned me loose. Gasping for air, I tried looking into his eyes so that I could see what he was thinking but that didn't work. Tyreik just had a blank look on his face, not one emotion showed through.

"I never intended on hurting you, you have to understand that."

"When did this happen?" he finally asked.

Still rubbing my neck, I answered, "the night that I found out about you and Rema."

Chyna Black

Nodding his head, I saw that he was putting the pieces to the puzzle together.

"I swear to you that it only happened once."

"You know niggas were telling me that you and him were fucking around but I was like, nah not Chyna. You know I'm like, that's wifey she wouldn't do me dirty like that," he spoke, like he was talking to himself.

"I didn't mean to do it, it just happened. After it happened I felt horrible. There is nothing going on between Dame and me, I promise. I swear to you that the shit meant nothing to me."

"That's what they all say," he laughed.

"I swear, I don't have any feelings for Dame."

"Let me get this straight, you fucked him the night you found out about me and Rema?"

"Yes," I answered.

"So that means the baby that you were carrying could have been that man's child?"

"No, that was our baby."

"Did you use a rubber with that nigga?"

"Of course I did."

"So that was my baby?"

"Yes," I lied.

"My best friend and my girl betrayed me," he said, to himself.

Hugging him, I asked him to forgive me. With his hands by his side, he stood silent.

"You have to forgive me," I said.

Tyriek was silent.

"Please?" I cried. "I'm sorry, you have to believe me when I say this."

"Please forgive me," I cried as Tyriek stood in silence, finally speaking.

"I don't know if I can."

You have to forgive me," I cried. "What more can I say then I'm sorry and that it will never happen again. You are the one that I love, not him. I want to be with you and only you, I love you Tyreik."

"I love you too," he said.

"I'm sorry Tyreik, please don't leave me. Tell me that we can work this out."

"I can't make you any promises Chyna."

"You just said that you still loved me, so I know that we still have a chance. We will work this out, we have too," I cried.

CHAPTER 16

FOR THE GOOD TIMES

I was living in this make believe world where Tyreik loved me and everything was okay. If Tyreik ever really did love me, that love had come and gone a long time ago, but for some reason I still loved him. Everything in my life was falling apart. I had left home, betrayed my friends and lost myself in the process. I had gone from the girl who had everything to the girl who had nothing in less than a year.

I don't know what Tyreik and I called ourselves doing, we barely talked and he never came home, so you know that I was left alone. I was so paranoid that at any moment he would leave me that I stopped eating. My J-Lo physique had quickly transformed into the cracked out Whitney Houston shape on the Michael Jackson special. I knew that I looked bad but I just couldn't help myself. I was even so stressed out that my hair began to fall out. I couldn't concentrate on anything unless it involved Tyreik. Usually I would have had Asia and Brooke to confide in, but I fucked them over so badly that even an apology wasn't good enough.

A week hadn't even gone by and Tyreik and I were at it again.

"Tyreik shut up, you've said the same bullshit before and you know you don't mean it."

"I mean it this time Chyna, we can't be together no more!" he yelled.

"Why not?" I asked, with an attitude.

"Because I need to explore my options."

"Explore your options, what kind of shit is that, explore your options my ass. I have sacrificed too much to be with you Tyreik, you are not just going to up and leave me, I did not go through all this bullshit for nothing."

"It wasn't for nothing, we tried and it didn't work."

"We, we didn't try to do a damn thing. I tried to make it work, not you. Every time you lied, I saw it as the truth. Every time you stayed out late or didn't bother to come home, I justified or looked past it."

"I know you ain't trying to stand here and act like you're a fucking saint, remember you fucked my boy."

"You know what, I was waiting for you to throw that shit up in my face. It happened and I apologize Tyreik. It isn't like it was an ongoing affair like you had with Rema. I forgave you when I found out about that bitch, never once did I throw that shit up in your face. Hell, I forgave you and I tried to forget about the whole thing."

"Well see that's where we're different, I can't forgive that easily."

My heart fell to the floor because it hurt so badly. After all the shit that I had endured during our relationship, I fucked up once and now our relationship was over. This all had to be a joke. We were supposed to be together forever, he couldn't just leave me. What happened to "we'll always be together" and the "I love you's" he'd said to me?

"This is not happening to me, this is just a bad dream," I spoke out loud, to myself.

"Are you going to be okay because I'm about to go?" he asked, unconcerned.

"You're not leaving Tyreik!" I screamed.

"Look, I don't want to leave you like this but I got to go," he said, walking to the door.

"I'm not playing Tyreik, don't walk out that door," I warned.

Without even a hint of hesitation, he opened the door and left me standing there alone with a fog of tears streaming down my face. I tried to stand up but my legs wouldn't support me. For almost an hour, I laid there on the floor drowning in my tears. After the sadness faded, anger started to rise.

"Why!" I screamed. "Why is this happening to me God, why? Why are you doing this to me? What did I ever do to you? Why did you bring him into my life if you knew all along that you were going to take him away?" I cried.

A few days had passed and I still sat in the living room crying. I hadn't talked to anyone in days, and I didn't care whether I lived or died at that point in my life. My momma had tried contacting me, but every time I saw her number on the caller ID, I would ignore it. My daddy even picked up the phone and called me, can you believe that shit? I most definitely was not about to talk to him. I couldn't give a fuck about what he had to say. He hadn't been there for me in all these years, so why should he start now.

The only thing that I was excited about was T's birthday party. Even though I looked like a crack head, I still wanted to attend. I had been preparing for it that whole week. This would be the first time since my argument with Asia and my betrayal of Brooke that I would see them both. I was hoping that I could reconcile with the two of them that night. I know that I shouldn't be going to T's party in my condition but I had to see Tyreik. I was content in believing that we would be back together.

I couldn't go to the shop since I had just up and quit on Coco without calling or saying anything. With the best of my abilities, I tried to pull myself together enough to look halfway decent. I weighed about a buck 05 and my hair was steadily shedding but I didn't care.

T's party was being held at The Living Room downtown. As I pulled up to the club, I saw people waiting in line to get in. I heard that T had rented out the entire club so I knew that I wouldn't have to stand in line long. T had required that everyone wear white and gold, so I rocked an off the shoulder white fitted top, and matched it up with a pair of white tuxedo pants and some gold Jimmy Choo strapped heels. Since my hair was falling out, I put it up once again in a ponytail, which I rocked to the side. On my ears, neck and wrist, I sported Baby Phat Jewelry. Grabbing my gold Louis Vuttion purse, I stepped out of my truck and strutted into the club.

The Living Room was packed with every hustler and hoe in St. Louis. 100.3 The Beat was in the house as well as some of the Rams players. Nelly and The Lunatics were in attendance too. Nervous was not even the word to describe how I felt, everybody that hated me was in the club. Despite what had happened between Brooke and me, T still had love for me and I would love him forever for that.

Taking a deep breath, I made my way upstairs to the VIP section. I swear to God it seemed like as soon as I hit the last step all eyes were on me. Now mind you, nobody had really seen me since before the abortion and I don't think anyone expected me to show up, but once again I Ain't Neva Scurred!

Brooke, Asia, Adrian and Michelle eyed me up and down. Searching through the crowd of people I found T, and making my way over to him, I tapped him on the shoulder.

"Happy Birthday, nigga," I joked.

"What's up baby girl," he smiled.

"You, that's what's up."

"Oh, for real."

"Yeah nigga," I laughed.

"Nah for real, I'm glad you could make it. You're a little on the thin side though ma, you okay?"

"Yeah I'm cool, here's your gift," I lied, switching the subject.

"Can I open it now?"

"Yeah," I smiled.

"Damn, a $500 gift certificate to Hat Zone," he gushed.

"I hope you like it, I mean I didn't know what to get for a man who has everything."

"I do have everything, don't I?"

"I'm happy for you T, at least somebody's happy."

"I heard about you and Tyreik."

"Damn, news sure does travel fast. We just broke up, what a week ago."

"I'm sorry though."

I saw the worry in T's eyes, but once again I tried to ignore the warning signs.

"Well look, I got plenty of food and drinks so have fun, a'ight. I got to go mingle, Asia's giving me the evil eye."

"She always was a perfectionist."

"Yeah she is, but I love her."

"Oh T, that's so wonderful."

"Don't get all sentimental on me now."

"Okay, I won't," I grinned.

"Let me go before she kills me."

"A'ight have fun and happy birthday!" I shouted over the noise.

Standing by myself, I surveyed my surroundings. I quickly noticed Brooke and Adrian across the room giving me the evil eye and, if it wasn't for T, Adrian would have gotten her ass kicked right then and there. I wanted to go over to Brooke and apologize but my pride wouldn't allow it.

Instead, I went over to the bar and ordered a Cosmopolitan. I had been sitting there for about ten minutes before I noticed Tyreik holding hands with Rema. I don't know why, but I was shocked. There was still a part of me that believed it wasn't over. I mean, I thought that I really meant something to this nigga. But honestly, he looked happier than ever. He held Rema's hand and gazed into her eyes like he used to do me. Couldn't he even wait a couple of weeks to flaunt her ass around town? I guess my feelings weren't important. I wondered if he even knew that I was there.

Pulling my mirror out, I checked my face. Even with the lights dimmed I still saw the bags and dark circles around my eyes. I really was beginning to look like Skelator but once again, me being me, convinced myself that I looked okay.

Focusing my attention back to Tyreik, I noticed that he had left. The Cosmo was taking its effect and I began to see things in a different light. Tyreik wasn't really over me, he was only trying to make me jealous, yeah that had to be it. I kind of felt sorry for Rema because he was only using her and she was too dumb to realize it. By the end of the night I would have my man back and things would be back to normal.

"Excuse me, can I get another…" But before I could finish, I was rudely interrupted.

"Let me get a Heineken and get this beautiful young lady whatever she wants." He smiled.

"Jaylen!" I screamed, with delight.

"What's up baby girl?"

"You, nigga! Look at you all iced out and shit."

"I'm trying to hang with the big dogs. What's up with you though, you're not looking good ma."

Jaylen was the only person with guts enough to state the obvious.

"I'm a'ight, I just haven't been feeling well that's all."

"Don't tell me you tripping off that lame ass nigga Tyreik."

"Look at you trying to be all tough," I laughed.

"I'm serious C, fuck that nigga, I got you."

"Oh word, you got me?"

"I've been trying to tell you for months that I got drafted to the NBA."

"Word?"

"Yeah, I was the #3 draft pick. I got drafted to the Detroit Pistons."

"Oh, my God, Jaylen, I'm so proud of you."

"But, enough about me. How have you been and tell the truth?"

Just as I was about to tell Jaylen about all the drama that was in my life, I spotted Tyreik again and this time he was standing alone. This was the perfect opportunity for us to talk.

"Hold that thought Jaylen, I'll be right back," hoping down off the bar stool, I left Jaylen once again in mid-sentence.

The VIP area was so packed that I thought I wouldn't make it over to Tyreik in time. With his back turned to me, I gave myself the once over then tapped him on the shoulder.

"What's good?" I asked, as he looked at me.

I could tell that he wasn't pleased with my presence but I ignored it and kept on talking.

"I wasn't expecting to see you here, especially with Rema," I said.

"Chyna, what did you expect, we're not together anymore," Tyreik said.

"I know that, it's just hard to see you with somebody else, especially her so soon. I mean damn, we just broke up last week and didn't that bitch lie to you about her being pregnant."

"Yeah she did but I forgave her."

"Oh, so you can forgive her but you couldn't forgive me?"

"I don't know what to tell you."

"Tyreik, just answer me this one thing and I promise I'll leave you alone."

"What?"

"Do you still have feelings for me?"

"I will always have feelings for you."

"Okay, do you still love me?" I stressed.

"I don't know," he answered.

For a moment, I tried to pretend as if he had said yes. Then I tried to pretend like I hadn't asked and he hadn't answered. We stood looking into each other's eyes, mine filled with tears and pain, and his filled with hatred and frustration, but I was still determined to get him back.

"Ty, I said that I was sorry, why can't that be enough for you. It was enough for me when you cheated on me."

"I'm not you, I can't be back with you after you fucked my boy!" he yelled, causing a scene.

"Yes you can. I still love you and you still love me," I cried.

"Didn't he tell you that he doesn't want to be with you anymore," Rema stated, coming up behind Tyreik and standing by his side.

"You need to mind your own business," I said to Rema, wiping my eyes.

"He is my business, Tyreik is my man now. He doesn't want you, so go get a life."

"If you really believe that, then you're dummier than I thought. Can't you see he's only using you to make me jealous? Trust and believe, that in a few days he'll be right back at home with me," I spat, checking her.

"Why would he come home to you? Look at you, you look like you've been freebasing his product," she laughed.

"Are you gonna stand there and let this bitch talk to me like that? You better check her Tyreik," I demanded.

"Chyna go home, it's over. Look at you, I mean really look at you!" he yelled. "You're a sleezeball and I'm not trying to be with you after you fucked my boy."

"Tyreik dog that's enough, let's just have a good time," T spoke, trying to pull Tyreik away.

"Nah fuck that T, let him finish. I'm a sleezeball is that right? Yeah I fucked Dame and it was better than fucking your lame ass!" I yelled.

His nostrils were flaring so I knew that I had him right where I wanted him. The nigga was heated.

"Yes boo boo, the dick was all of that. That's why I fucked him, now what?"

"Yeah, a'ight, whatever."

"I know it's whatever!"

"Bitch, fuck you!" Tyreik spoke, walking away.

"What did you say?"

Charging towards me, he said, "I said fuck you bitch!"

"Oh so, now I'm a bitch?"

"I ain't got time for this shit," he said, trying to walk away again.

"Naw fuck that, so I'm a bitch now?" I asked again, grabbing his arm.

"Get the fuck off me!" he yelled, snatching his arm away from me.

When he snatched his arm away, he caused me to lose my balance, causing me to fall.

"I told your dumb ass not to touch me. Now look at you!" he yelled, into my face.

"Come on Chyna sweetie, get up," I heard a sweet voice say.

As I looked up, Asia grabbed my hand to help me up.

"You better get your girl Asia before I hurt her for real," Tyreik warned.

"Tyreik, get the fuck outta here, just go home!" Asia snarled.

"Now it's my fault? She's the one that came in here tripping. What the fuck am I doing explaining myself? I'm up, come on Rema!" he shouted.

"Are you okay?"

"Yeah, I'm a'ight," I said, dusting myself off.

"Okay everybody, the main event is over, drinks are on the house!" Asia yelled, over the crowd.

As soon as they heard free drinks, the crowd dispersed and started back partying.

"Chyna, what is wrong with you coming up in here tripping like that?" Asia asked.

"I don't know what's gotten into me Asia. I need help, it's like I'm going crazy fucking with this nigga. What does she have over me, I'm just as pretty as she is? Why is he treating me like I ain't shit?" I cried.

"Girl, I don't have the answers to that. It's going to be okay though," she assured, hugging me.

"Where is Jaylen? I need to talk to him," I whined.

"Jaylen left right before you and Tyreik got into it. What you need to do is go home and get some sleep, you look like you haven't slept in days."

"Okay," I whispered.

"I tell you about dumb hoes," Adrian said to Michelle, loudly enough so that I could hear.

"What the fuck did you say?" I asked, targeting my anger towards her.

"I said, I tell you about silly ass hoes," Adrian stressed.

I hadn't forgotten by a long shot that I owed Adrian an ass whooping, so the bitch and her mouth caught me at the right time because what I couldn't do to Tyreik was about to be taken out on her. Snatching Asia's drink from out of her hand, I walked over to Adrian and threw it in her face.

"Bitch!" she yelled, shocked and soaked.

"Call me another bitch," I said, punching her in the mouth. "You're gonna learn to shut the fuck up sometimes!" I yelled, still hitting her.

With her hands covering her face, Adrian repeatedly asked me stop hitting her but I couldn't stop. I might have looked like Ally McBeal, but I was whooping on old girl like I was Laila Ali.

"Chyna, get off of her!" T yelled, pulling me away.

"Nah, fuck that T, the bitch had that shit coming!"

"Cool, you whooped her ass, now take you crazy ass home girl."

That night I knew that I had lost my grip on life, and if I didn't hurry up and get help, I was going to lose my sanity for real.

CHAPTER 17

STRAIGHT PLAYED

The next day, I was awakened out of my sleep by a loud thud on the front door, instantly I was pissed. Grabbing my robe, I stomped to the door and without even looking to see who it was, I opened the door.

"What the fuck do you want?"

"I came to tell you that you are officially being evicted."

"Excuse me?"

"Oh honey you're excused. Let me explain so that you can understand. Tyreik knows that you were the one that messed up his car last night. Your little cry for attention didn't work he wants your ass out, you've over stayed your welcome and it's time for you to bounce," Rema grinned with pleasure.

"You can kiss my ass because I ain't going nowhere until I hear it come out of Tyreik's mouth."

"Well, if that's the only thing keeping you here then here's my cell. Call him up and ask him yourself. Go ahead, call," she urged.

Snatching her cell, I walked into the dining room. The bitch had lost her mind coming to my house with this bullshit. Tyreik may not want to be with me but he would never just put me out on the streets like that.

"What's good mommy?" he spoke, thinking I was Rema.

"What's good poppy? I see you had to send your bitch over here to do your dirty work for you."

"Why the fuck you fuck up my truck?"

"I didn't touch your funky ass truck."

"I don't even give a fuck, it ain't like I can't get another one."

"Okay then what's the big deal?"

"Haven't you had enough Chyna? I'm sick of arguing with you, just get your shit and leave."

"You mean you're actually kicking me out?" I asked him amazed.

"Chyna, I'm sick of talking to you. Leave the keys to the truck. Just get your shit and get the fuck out of my life!" he yelled, hanging up on me.

I couldn't believe this nigga was dead serious, he really wanted my black ass out. Going back to the front door, Rema stood in the doorway with a huge smile spread across her face. Throwing her phone back at her, I hit her in the head with it. Laughing, I told the bitch to suck a fat dick and then I slammed the door in her face. With some gratification, I leaned against the door and smiled. It seemed like it had been ages since I truly smiled.

Now what was I going to do? I didn't have any other place to go but home, and I really wasn't sure if Diane would even allow me to return home. Tired of thinking, I went to the closet and grabbed my Louis Vitton luggage. I filled each suitcase to the brim with each designer piece that I had acquired. When those got full, I got seven trash bags and filled them with the rest of my clothes and purses. I had to get four plastic bins from out the storage closet for my shoes alone. Packed and ready to go, I took one last look around the bedroom. I still couldn't fathom the fact that I was really leaving. I had spent so much time alone in this house that I wasn't used to the outside world anymore. After two hours of packing, I took a shower and threw on an all black Juicy sweat suit. With my hair pulled up in a ponytail and my Mac lip gloss on, I looked halfway decent for a change.

Placing an order for a cab, I remembered Tyreik's secret safe. I had only gone in it once before and that one time, I ran across 40 g's. I hoped that my luck would be just as good today. Putting in the code 6,9,6,9, the safe opened. Tyreik's ass would have a freaky code like 69 69, I laughed. You don't understand how tight my fingers were crossed. I hadn't saved a penny while I was with Tyreik, I needed there to be some real money in the safe. With one eye open and the other one closed, I cracked the safe's door open and saw only one stack of dough in it. Taking it out, I skimmed through it and estimated that it was only 5 g's.

"Damn," I cursed. A bitch like me could run through 5 g's on one outfit. But shit I couldn't complain, it was more than I had a minute ago. Securely placing the money in my Hermes Birken bag, I headed to the door.

As soon I hit the door, the red & white County Cab came speeding up the street. The driver's eyes grew big once he saw how much shit I had but he perked up when I placed a Benjamin in his hand. While the driver put my things in the car, I decided to have a little fun. Taking my keys, I made a trail from one side of the truck to the other. That nigga wasn't just going to take my jeep away without any repercussions, and for once I finally felt a sense of relief.

"Ma'am, are you ready?" asked the driver.

Placing my oversized Fendi glasses on, I answered, "Yes."

It had been almost a year since I left home. Pulling into the driveway, I saw that things had changed drastically. Diane had had a walkway built into our yard. She had added a deck onto the back of the house and flowers were everywhere, the house looked beautiful. Stepping out the cab, I told the driver to wait.

Opening the screen door, I rang the doorbell and prayed for the best. It was a Sunday morning so I was pretty sure that she would be home.

"Who is it?"

"It's me momma."

As she opened the door, I saw a little hesitation in her face.

"Hi, momma." I spoke, softly.

"What's going on, what are you doing here?"

"I came to see you. I wanted to know if I can have my old room back?"

"Well, Chyna, you know that if you come back and live here that you will have to follow my rules. There will be no staying out into the wee hours of the morning. You will have to get a job because I will not take care of you. You are eighteen now and it's time for you to grow up. You have to get your GED and I don't want Tyreik anywhere near my house. Do you understand?"

"I understand."

"Now that that's settled, go and get your stuff," She smiled.

Once I settled back into my old routine, things were pretty much like they used to be but better. Diane did her thing and I did my thing. We didn't try to crowd each other, which was good. Not once since I had been back did she ask what happened between Tyreik and me and I appreciated that. We talked a little more now, which was also good.

More than anything, it seemed like Diane was always cooking or fixing me something to eat. She told me that I had gotten skinny so she fed me everything under the sun until I was back into a size six. I had to admit, I did look a hell of a lot better. The dark circles and bags were now gone from my eyes and my hair had finally stopped falling out, I was even talking to my dad. Since I had moved back home, we had long talks and aired out our problems. I mean, don't get me wrong, some things will never be forgotten but they can be forgiven.

I really didn't have that many skills besides book smarts and shopping, so I got a job at Express in the Northwest Plaza. Things were going good but Tyreik still weighed heavily on my mind, I had to make a change for myself. I couldn't go back to that way of living again. A few days after I had moved back in with Diane he called my cell.

"Hello?"

"Where is my money?" he yelled, into my ear.

"What money?" I snapped back, wanting to laugh.

"I know you took my money out my safe Chyna."

"I don't know what you're talking about," I laughed.

"You think that shit is funny? I want my money back or else."

"Or else what?"

"I'ma kill ya ass, that's what!" he yelled.

"Yeah whatever, kill this muthafucker," I said, hanging up.

It was kind of sad because I still wanted him back.

Asia and I were back hanging tight despite the fact that Brooke still hated me. I hated the fact that we all couldn't kick it together anymore. Asia would always have to choose whom she would ask to go places with her. I wanted desperately to have Brooke's friendship back but there was only so much begging that I was willing to do.

It was a typical Friday at the mall, niggas were looking fine and females were shopping trying to find their club outfit for the night. I, on the other hand, was taking a late dinner break. It was about 6:30 p.m. and I hadn't eaten a thing since nine that morning, so a sista was starving. Working at Express kept me up on the latest fashion, I stayed fresh looking. I mean it wasn't what I was used to but it would do for now.

It was October and I rocked a crisp white fitted button up shirt, a pair of pinstripe wide legged slacks with some suspenders and my all black Gucci stiletto boots. My hair was healthier than ever since I hooked up with my new beautician, Miesha. She hooked me up with a fresh wrap so you know my shit was bouncy. My silver hoops and bangle bracelets completed the look, I looked like a fly ass Al Capone.

By me working in the mall, niggas tried their hand with me daily but none could compare to Tyreik. I had been accustomed to a certain way of living and none of these niggas could compete with Tyreik's bank. I also knew the game and how it was played. Half these niggas just wanted to get with me because I was Tyreik's ex girl. They wanted the opportunity of saying that they had me, but I wasn't having it. That was until I ran into an old flame whom I hadn't seen in years and who I didn't recognize on sight. I was making my way back from the food court when I stopped at The Lark to do some window shopping.

As I checked out their latest display, this voice from behind me said, "You like what you see?"

"As I matter of fact I do," I answered, playing along.

There was something about the person standing behind me that felt familiar. His breathe smelled like honey and his cologne was commanding my attention. I was already attracted to him without even seeing face.

"I bet you don't even know who you're talking to?" the person said.

"If I didn't know who I was talking to, I wouldn't be talking to you now would I?"

"You still got that smart ass mouth I see."

"And you know it."

"It's funny running into you like this because I was just thinking about you."

"Oh word? Well it was nice talking to you but I gotta go," I replied, walking away.

"Hold up Chyna," he said, grabbing my arm and turning me around.

A smile appeared on my face once I realized who I was talking to.

"LP!" I yelled.

"What's good ma?"

"Shit, you nigga, that's what's up," I said, hugging him.

Turning him loose, I got a good look at him. The boy most definitely was doing the damn thing. LP had gotten his weight up over the past couple of years. He wasn't the same old school driving, skipping school to shoot craps boy I knew from high school. His arms were covered with tattoos and his grill was filled with platinum and diamond teeth. I would later find out that they were the detachable kind. LP was Eko'd out from head to toe and his Cartier watch and earrings were blinding me. He was a lot more muscular now and he sported locks now instead of braids.

"So, how have you been girl? I heard about what happened at your boy T's party ma. I can't believe that nigga played you out like that."

"It's nothing, I'm good," I said, trying to avoid the conversation.

"Fuck that nigga, I see you still looking good. Shit, you look better than I remember. I can't believe you're all grown up," He smiled, giving me the once over.

"Yeah, I'm all grown up now. I'm not the same naive Chyna from back in the day," I stated, letting him know what's up.

"I feel you, I feel you," He grinned, licking his lips. "So you work here?"

"Yeah, I work at Express and I have to get back to work, I'm already late as it is."

"Chyna Black got a job, the world must be coming to an end," LP joked.

"Whatever," I laughed.

"But nah for real, why don't you let me call you some time?"

"I don't know LP, you know that I just got out of something."

"Yeah I know that, but a nigga like me bugging out over you for a minute now. I'm not about to let you go after all this time," he replied, seriously.

I didn't know what to do. My heart still belonged to Tyreik and I still had hopes that we would get back together. On the other hand, LP was looking good and he was saying all the right things. The more I contemplated it, talking to LP wasn't such a bad thing because, after all, Tyreik would be out of his mind with jealousy. While we were together, whenever I mentioned LP's name Tyreik would always become aggravated and annoyed. He knew that LP was the only guy, besides him, that I had feelings for. Fucking with LP would be the perfect get back in my eyes so, me still being me, gave in and gave LP my cell number.

With our scheduling conflicts, it took LP and me a minute to get together. For our first couple of dates, we did the usual dinner and movie deal. I learned that LP had a son and another one on the way by the same girl. I was a little shocked by this but I didn't care, he was with me now so whatever happened before me was none of my business. The whole going out to eat thing was cool, but you know a chick like me gets bored with that real quick. LP caught on and stepped his game up.

It was our fifth date and I expected the same old boring date but I was surprisingly pleased. LP blindfolded me and ordered me to chill and go along with the ride. When we finally reached our destination, he helped me out of his F-150 and walked me into what I figured was an empty building. I didn't know what LP was up to, but whatever it was, I was enjoying the suspense. Suddenly, after a minute or two of walking, we stopped and LP opened a door. Leading me into the place, he held my hands.

"LP, where are we?" I asked, for the umpteenth time.

"You ready for your surprise?" he asked.

"Yes," I giggled.

Gently he lifted the blindfold from over my eyes and revealed my surprise. After the blurriness left my eyes, I focused on all the jewelry cases surrounding me, and in front of me stood a white gentleman who looked to be in his fifty's and above his head was a sign that read Cartier.

"LP, what's going on?" I asked, confused.

"I want you to take off every piece of jewelry that you have on," He demanded.

"Are you serious?" I asked, dumbfounded.

"I'm dead serious, I don't want you wearing anything that nigga bought you when you are around me."

"Do you know how much these pieces cost?" I laughed.

"Yeah, I estimate that you have about 45 g's worth of ice on, and once you get rid of that shit, I plan on doubling it."

Now this was a date. Even though the jewelry held sentimental value, I was no fool. If LP wanted to spend his hard
earned drug money on me, I was all for it. That night, LP purchased almost 20 g's worth of bling for me. He said that as long
as I was good to him, that he would be good to me. He said that
over time, he would buy me even more jewelry but I had to
prove my loyalty to him first. From that point on, I was in love.
LP spoiled me with any and everything that I wanted. The lack
of time that I spent with Tyreik, LP more than willingly picked
up. But even though I was feeling LP, my mind was still focused
on Tyreik.

Every time we went somewhere, I hoped that we would run
into Tyreik. I wanted him to see how well I was doing without
him and for him to realize what a big mistake he had made by
leaving me. LP and I had been dating for about a month when
my wish was fulfilled.

One Saturday night after we had finished watching movies at
his crib, he decided that he needed to check on one of his clubs.
I was unaware that the club that he owned was a strip club in
Brooklyn, Illinois. Now mind you, I had only been on the
Eastside a couple of times so I wasn't in my element, and I
thought the nigga was trying to kill me or something cause it
seemed like we were in the goddamn woods. Once we got off
the country deserted like streets, we came to a brightly lit building with a ton of cars in the parking lot.

Once we pulled in, I saw that the parking lot was filled with
cars. LP said what's up to the bouncers and introduced me as his
girl. I began to blush because never before had he introduced
me as his girl. Holding my hand, he escorted me into his estab-
lishment. As soon we stepped into the club, my mouth dropped.
There were females walking around naked and hoes were giving
lap dances. Whenever one of the strippers walked past a guy, he
would just slap her ass as if it was nothing. I was surprised to find
so many females in the club kicking it. While I continued to
stare, LP led me over to the bar.

"Close your mouth Chyna," he laughed.

"I can't believe these girls are degrading themselves like this," I said.

"Hey, we all got to make a buck someway," LP shrugged. "But listen, I got to go take care of some business. Stay right here, I'll be back in a minute."

"I know you're not about to leave me here by myself," I whined.

"I'll only be gone a minute Chyna, be cool, a'ight."

"Whatever," I said, rolling my eyes.

"You know I love it when you pout," LP smirked.

Holding my Marc Jacobs bag tight, I summoned the bartender over.

"Welcome to Soft Lips, what can I get for you?"

"Let me get a Long Island Ice Tea."

"One Long Ice Tea coming up," he replied.

Ten minutes had passed and I still didn't have a drink. You know me, I became impatient after one minute.

Just when I was about to flag him down again, a thick New York accent from behind said, "Ay dog, don't you know that this is the owner's girl you got waiting."

My heart literally sank when I realized that it was Tyreik.

"I didn't know you got down like this ma, you like hanging out in strip clubs now?" he teased.

Facing him, I smelled liquor all over him. I had never seen him so pissy drunk before.

"What do you want Ty?" I asked, with an attitude.

"Damn, it's like that now?"

"What other way could it be? We don't have anything to talk about so leave me alone."

"Now we both know that you don't mean that," he smiled, deviously.

"Who are you here with, because I know that you are not here by yourself?"

"I came up here with my niggas T, Keith and Dame."

"Oh, so you can kick it with that nigga but you couldn't try to work things out between you and me?"

"I'll never let a bitch come before my niggas," he laughed.

"You know what, fuck you Tyreik, you need to step before LP comes back," I warned.

LP hated Tyreik with a passion, he hated everything that he stood for. He had already said that if he ever caught me with Tyreik he would split my wig.

"Fuck that nigga, I'm Tyreik James, every nigga in here know about me," he boosted, like he couldn't be touched.

"Whatever, Tyreik."

Touching my hair, he whispered into my ear, "Rema can't satisfy me like you Dimples."

"Get the fuck off me Tyreik!" I yelled, angrily.

As I pushed him off me, I saw LP standing across the room watching my every move.

"Oh, so you just gonna play me like that just cause you with that nigga?"

"Yup, just like you did me with Rema," I spat, walking off.

"What the fuck was that nigga doing all up in ya grill?" LP barked.

"Chill with that shit LP, we were just talking," I said.

"How you gonna let that nigga disrespect me in my own club?"

"I told him to step, so why you tripping?"

"Fuck that," LP declared, walking towards Tyreik.

"What's ya problem dog? Why you all up in my girl's face like the shit is all gravy?"

"Calm down new money, I was just seeing how my ex-wifey was doing. Ain't no harm in that, is it?" Tyreik smirked.

"It's disrespectful homey, Chyna's mine so remember that shit nigga."

"That's enough LP, let's just go," I pleaded.

"Naw Dimples, let your man do his thing. He think he's a big boy now so let that nigga play with the big boys. Your girl knows how I get down so you need to listen to her. You think cause you copped a couple of bricks that you the man? I see the look in your eyes you want to be me, but you can't be. Yeah, you got my old flame but nigga I can always get her back," Tyreik said, in his drunken state.

"Come on LP, let's just go home, fuck him," I begged, as I watched LP's chest heave up and down.

"Listen to ya girl dog, you need to check yourself new money. You're feeling yourself way too much. Don't step out of line cause your peoples are around. Never mind what you might have heard, I'm Tyreik James, BITCH."

Tyreik, Dame, T and Keith all cracked up laughing.

"Yo dog, I'm Rick James, BITCH," Keith laughed, damn near falling over.

"Ya'll niggas watch too much Dave Chappelle," T laughed, shaking his head.

"Oh, so ya'll niggas think this shit is a game," LP grimaced, pulling out his gun.

The music halted, the strippers stopped dancing and everyone in the club sat frozen, too afraid to move.

"LP stop, you've proved your point, let's go," I said, petrified.

"Naw fuck that, this nigga got the game all fucked up. You ain't moving weight no more nigga. Not only do I have your girl but nigga, I got the whole Southside on lock so you can quit stunten partna. Now stand the fuck up and kick rocks nigga," LP said, cocking the gun.

Taking one more swig of beer, Tyreik stood and smiled at LP. Why don't this nigga hurry the fuck up, I thought.

"Yo dog, you ain't gonna handle this shit?" T asked, ready to bust a cap.

"It's cool man, let's burn out," said Tyreik.

After winking his eye at me, Tyreik and his crew left.

"Turn the muthafuckin' music up and get back to work!" LP shouted, as he placed his nine back in his pants.

"Take me home, I'm ready to go," I said, heated.

"What's ya problem?" LP said, confused.

"All that shit wasn't even called for LP. You could have easily just gone on about your business, but no you just had to say something to him, didn't you? Whatever animosity you have towards Tyreik is something that you have to deal with, not me. And I don't appreciate you throwing me up in his face like that. I will not be a part of your little game," I said, walking away.

Walking as fast as I could, I made my way to the restroom. Standing in the mirror, I tried my hardest not to cry.

"It ain't even like that Chyna, why you tripping, I love you!" LP yelled, walking into the restroom behind me.

"Will you get out, you're in the ladies restroom."

"I don't give a fuck, I own this muthafucker. I see pussy everyday so a bitch's pussy don't faze me."

"Whatever, I'm ready to go. I've had enough drama for tonight."

"I know you heard me when I said I love you."

"Yeah, I heard you and I ain't trying to hear that shit," I said, rolling my eyes.

"Why not?" standing in my face, LP smiled.

Damn he is fine, I thought.

"You don't believe that I love you?"

"Nope."

"If I didn't love you would I have laced your pretty little ears with four karats worth of diamonds?" He replied, kissing me.

Damn, his kisses are so sweet, I sighed.

"Come on," LP said, grabbing my hand.

Dragging me across the hall to his office, LP locked the door behind us. Standing in the middle of his office, I wondered if I should give him some. We had been talking for a while and I still hadn't given up the pussy. Pulling his Padre jersey over his head, LP showed every muscle and tattoo that he possessed. You know that song *"Take My Breath Away"*, well that shit was playing in my head on full blast.

LP did say that he loved me and he laced me with some jewelry, with the promise of more if I acted right, I contemplated. Fuck that, my pussy was throbbing and his dick was calling me so I gave up the drawers.

Grabbing my waist, he pulled my pale pink poncho over my

head revealing my pink satin bra. Kissing my neck and chest, he made his way to my breast. Picking me up, LP roughly placed me on his desk. Ripping my jeans off, he realized that I didn't have any panties on. Hungrily he pushed my legs opened and feasted on my kitty. Biting down on my bottom lip, I tried not to scream. Licking me softly, LP massaged my thighs.

"Um, that feels good," I moaned.

"I've wanted to taste you since I saw you at the mall."

"I wish you would've told me," I said, about to cum.

It had been months since I had some fire head, so I enjoyed every minute of it. After I came all over LP's face, he lifted my right leg up and placed it on his shoulder. Stroking me with his fingers he, without asking, entered me. Now normally I would've checked his ass but I trusted LP enough to let him slide up in it raw. That night I came twice and I forgot all about Tyreik and LP's beef.

A couple of weeks later, LP and I were barely speaking. He started playing the same old bullshit games that Tyreik used to play. All of a sudden the love that he said he had for me didn't exist. He didn't know how to pick up a phone, and the nigga all of a sudden lost his directions to my house. I knew the signs, so I dropped his ass not knowing that I was a couple weeks pregnant.

LP and I had been broken up for about two weeks when I learned that I was pregnant. I figured that telling him would be easy and that he would be happy about the news. I wasn't looking for us to be back together, I just wanted him to take responsibility for his child. LP was a pretty understanding man, I thought he wouldn't trip when I told him, but guess what, once again I had played the fool.

After taking the pregnancy test and crying for damn near an hour, I decided it would be best to call and tell him.

"Hello?" he answered, annoyed.

"You busy?"

"Nah, what's good?"

"Look, we need to talk."

"Talk about what Chyna?"

"I know that we don't fuck around no more and that's cool. You got the chance to throw me up in Tyreik's face, so mission accomplished."

"I told you that ain't have shit to do wit me not wanting to talk to you no more, I just wasn't feeling the situation no more," He lied.

"Whatever, I couldn't give a fuck about that right now."

"Well, what the fuck you call me for?" he snapped.

"I called to tell ya ignorant ass that I'm pregnant," I snapped back.

"What the fuck you mean you're pregnant?" LP yelled.

"Hold the fuck up! Who are you yelling at? You heard me, I'm preg...nant," I stressed into the phone.

"What you telling me for, the shit ain't mine."

"What?"

"Don't try and act like you're a fucking angel. You fucked Tyreik's best friend. How I know you wasn't fucking around while you was wit me?"

"Nigga please, be for real. Don't act like me being pregnant is a shock to you. You the one that wanted to slide up in it all the time without using a rubber. I wasn't with nobody but you!" I yelled, shocked at his comment.

"How am I supposed to know that?"

"I'm not even gonna argue wit you LP. You know damn well that this baby is yours, so if you don't want to help me then fuck you," I said, hanging up.

Can you believe that nigga? Just when I thought I had my shit together, here I go and fuck it up again, but this time I knew I would be keeping the baby. Everything happens for a reason right? Even though I had just had an abortion seven months prior, I knew that this time the baby was a blessing and not a burden. I needed to have this child because I needed something to give me the strength to finally make a change in my life. I needed to sit my black ass down and reflect on the past year. All of the pain, heartache, desperation and frustration were leading up to something big, I just didn't know what that big thing was.

Diane was gonna kick my ass, I thought. There really wasn't any good way to tell her so I decided to tell her one morning while she got ready for work.

"Momma you got a minute, I need to talk to you about something."

"I'm really in a rush Chyna, can it wait until later?"

"Nah, I need to talk to you now."

"Well, what is it?" she asked, while putting on her shoes.

"I'm pregnant."

"What did you say?"

"I said I'm pregnant momma," I cried.

"Chyna, you mean to tell me you done gone and got pregnant by that old trifling ass nigga again?"

"No, it's by somebody else."

"What nigga you fucking now?"

"The guy LP that I've been going out with lately," I answered.

Sitting on the edge of her bed Diane could do nothing but shake her head, I had disappointed her once again.

"You ain't learned shit from the first time, did you?"

"Momma, I know that I messed up but it's happened and I have to deal with it," I cried.

"I hope you don't think that you're gonna get another abortion?"

"Nah, I want to keep my baby."

"I know you're gonna keep that baby. You need to realize that the world does not revolve around you, and you having a baby is what's gonna teach you that. Yes, I have not been the world's best mother but I have always tried my best. Despite what you may think, I do love you Chyna. You are my baby girl and the only thing that I have ever wanted for you is the best. That's why I've been so hard on you, that's how Pat raised me. She raised me with tough love and it may have not been the best way to love, but that's all I know. It hurt me when things between your father and me didn't work out. I can admit now that my ill feelings towards your father may have been misplaced, instead of me dealing with him, I took my feelings out on you," She said, crying too.

"Momma, it's okay."

"No it's not and I don't ever want you to think that it is because it's not. You have a life growing inside of you that is going to love and adore you."

"I know," I sniffled.

"Now is LP going to help you with this baby?"

"No," I cried, even harder.

"And why the hell not?" Diane yelled.

"He's saying that the baby ain't his."

"Well, is it his?"

"Yeah it's his, I ain't been wit nobody else."

"Okay, fuck him. You're gonna raise this baby on your own. If he wants to act like a damn fool then let him. But you cannot, and listen to me when I say this Chyna, you cannot take your feelings towards LP out on that baby. Now I'm willing to help you but you have to remember I'm only the grandmother, and Lord knows I'm far too young to be somebody's grandmother," Diane said, laughing to herself.

"Momma, I know that my situation is messed up but I'm gonna have my baby, get my GED and get a job. None of this stuff is gonna slow me down, I'm still going to make something of myself, I promise."

CHAPTER 18

STARTING OVER

Five and a half months into my pregnancy tragedy struck. The beef between LP and Tyreik escalated, leaving casualties. Tyreik couldn't go out like a punk that night, so he, Lonnie and Boog shot up LP's momma house thinking he was there, and word spread across town quickly that it was Tyreik. Of course, LP had to retaliate, so he had a couple of his boys roll up on T and Tyreik while they sat in front of T's apartment in T's truck.

It was about two o'clock in the morning when I was awakened out of my sleep by a hysterical Asia.

"T is dead!" She screamed, before I could even say hello.

"Calm down Asia. What happened?"

"They were sitting in front of T's apartment, Brooke was in the house sleep. I guess they were out there talking and getting high because they never even saw LP's boys coming. They shot T's truck up and Tyreik got hit twice, once in the shoulder and once on the side. T got hit five times in his back and died instantly. When Brooke heard the shots and ran outside to see what happened, Tyreik was coughing up blood and T was slumped over the steering wheel. One of their neighbors called the police because Brooke passed out. The three of them are at the hospital now. Brooke's mom told me that Tyreik is in emergency surgery and Brooke had to be sedated," Asia wailed.

Asia had to be lying, there was no way that T could be dead, he was like a brother to me. Hell, I was closer to him than I was to Cantrell. I wanted to go up to the hospital but Diane wouldn't let me. She said that it would only be more added stress on the baby and me. I cried the whole night for T.

He was only twenty-three years old. How were Mr. and Mrs. Mayes supposed to cope with the fact that their oldest child was dead? How would Brooke survive without her mentor and brother? Had Asia and T just found each other to only be torn apart? And how would Tyreik react when he came out of surgery and found out his best friend was dead? Most importantly, how was I going to live knowing that my child's father was behind the hit on T and Tyreik? The more I thought about it, the more I hated LP. I wanted to call him and yell until I could yell no more, but what would that solve? T would still be dead and LP would still be living.

The funeral for T was a couple days later. Diane didn't think it was such a good idea for me to go, but I had to go to show my love and respect for T. Unity Chapel Baptist Church was filled from wall to wall with T's family, friends, ex-girlfriends and acquaintances. T was well known and respected in the hood, even other dealers came to show their respect. Asia and I attended the funeral together. It took us forever to find my fat ass something to wear. I ended up buying a black DKNY dress with a pair of black three-inch DKNY heels. I had Miesha flat iron my hair to the back and I wore my all black Jackie O glasses.

As soon as we walked through the church doors, Asia and I broke down. I knew that I had to be strong for Asia and my baby, so I pulled myself together. We found Brooke sitting in the front pew by herself crying. Seeing Asia and me watching her, she jumped up and hugged Asia. I really wasn't quite sure how she would react to me being there so I laid back in the cut.

"He's gone Asia, why did he have to die like that? I can't live without my brother Asia, I won't do it, it ain't right," Brooke cried.

"I know Brooke, I know," Asia said, while stroking her back.

Pushing Asia away, she looked me up and down and said, "What are you doing here?"

"I came to say goodbye to T and to be here for you Brooke," I said.

"Well, I don't want you here. Get out, it's your fault my brother's dead anyway."

"No, it's not Brooke, why would you say something so mean?" Asia asked.

"It's okay Asia, she's right, it is my fault. Everything is my fault, if it hadn't been for me, T would still be alive," I cried.

"You're not to blame Chyna, none of this is your fault. You didn't make T go with Tyreik and shoot up LP's momma house, and you didn't tell LP to put a hit out on Tyreik. They did what they did and now we're all suffering the consequences. Brooke, I know that you're hurting but you need Chyna right now. We all need each other right now so ya'll have got to put all that mess that happened behind ya'll. Chyna is having a baby and Brooke you lost your brother. One life had been taken away but another one is on the way. Ya'll both need each other more than ever, so put your differences aside and make up," Asia demanded.

I wanted to run over and hug Brooke but I didn't know if she would hug or hit me.

"I said make up, I'm not playing," Asia snapped.

We had never seen Asia more serious in our life, so we both walked towards each other and embraced. At first it seemed fake and unnatural, but after a minute we both were holding onto each other for dear life. The funeral ended up lasting about an hour and a half. Mrs. Mayes fainted when they opened T's casket, she couldn't stand seeing him lying there so lifeless. Asia, Brooke and me walked up to the casket together to pay our last respects to T. I kissed T and told him that I loved him. Brooke and Asia did the same. When the funeral ended, we all went back to Brooke's parents house to eat. My fat ass couldn't wait to get my grub on.

Just as I finished fixing my plate, I spotted Tyreik. I thought that he was still in the hospital so I didn't expect to see him. Standing in the middle of the dining room, I stared in his direction. He looked good despite being shot twice. He looked like he had lost a little weight but, all in all, he looked the same. Out of nowhere, my baby started moving all over the place.

"Chyna, are you okay?" Brooke asked.

"Yeah I'm a'ight, the baby just moved," I smiled, while rubbing my belly.

"For real, let me feel," Brooke said, placing her hand on my stomach.

As soon as she placed her hand on my stomach the baby moved again.

"How does it feel, does it feel funny?" she asked.

"Yeah kind of," I laughed.

"Can I feel too?" Tyreik asked.

"What's up Tyreik, I thought the doctors said you wouldn't get out until tomorrow?" Brooke asked.

"I had to get up out of there. You know they can't hold me," he smiled.

"How you holding up?" she asked.

"I'm a'ight, I don't want to talk about it though," he said, "You a'ight?"

"I feel a little bit better. My mom ain't doing to well though," Brooke said.

"Word, where she at?"

"She's in her room laying down."

"I'ma go and check on her but let me holla at ya girl first," he said, looking at me.

"A'ight then, I'll check you later," Brooke said, leaving.

"I heard that you were pregnant but I ain't believe it," he said.

"Well, as you can see I am."

"You know what you're having?"

"Yeah, I'm having a girl."

"You still wit that nigga?" he asked, sternly.

"No, we broke up before I knew I was pregnant," I replied. "Where is Rema, why ain't she here wit you?"

"I wanted to come by myself, is that a'ight," he said, with an attitude.

"I just asked you a question Tyreik, you don't have to get smart."

"Everything is an argument with you, ain't it?"

"Whatever, I ain't got time for this," I said, pulling myself away from the situation.

You don't understand how good it felt to leave Tyreik standing there alone for once. I didn't want to but I had to do it, I had a baby on the way and I could not continue to play the same old stupid games with Tyreik.

Throughout the rest of my pregnancy, Brooke, Asia, Diane,

my dad and even Cantrell stood by my side. Once Cantrell found out that LP had played me, he stepped up and became my baby girl's surrogate father. LP went around telling everybody that the baby wasn't his. He told people that I was a liar and a whore. It kind of hurt but I knew that he was lying, so I knocked the dirt off my shoulders and kept it moving.

On September 18, 2002, I introduced India Renee Black to the world. Weighing in at nine pounds zero ounces, my baby girl was beautiful. India looked just like me when I was a baby, she had a head full of curly hair, slanted eyes and dimples. Whenever I looked into her eyes, I knew that she was a blessing from God.

We connected immediately, she was a mini me. Diane and Cantrell fell in love with her immediately. Cantrell would come over to the house just to dress her up. My dad spoiled her rotten with clothes and toys, and Asia and Brooke came to get her almost every other day.

With me not being able to work because I didn't have anyone to watch her, it put a strain on my pockets so I did what I had to for my child. Two weeks after India was born, I went down to the Department of Social Services and filed for temporary assistance. Sitting at a table with India by my side in her car seat, I almost cried. How did I get here, I asked myself? I was class president in high school and in the running to be class valedictorian. I went from being the most likely to succeed to a welfare recipient. I still hadn't gotten my GED and I wasn't qualified for any type of position besides cashier.

Most of the girls there were around my age or younger, there were Blacks, Whites, Latinos and Asian girls all there needing some of type of help or assistance, and it seemed like a thousand children were running around or crying. I wanted so bad to get up and leave but I couldn't because I had my baby girl to take care of, so I set my pride aside and did what was best for her at the time.

"Chyna Black," a social worker called out.

Looking around the room, I hoped that no one there knew who I was.

"Hi, it's nice to meet you. My name is Marie Gibson and I'm going to be your caseworker," she smiled.

"Hi, nice to meet you too," I smiled back.

Walking to the back, she found her cubicle and asked me to have a seat.

"That's your little girl?" she asked.

"Yes."

"What is her name?"

"Her name is India," I said, proudly.

"Well, Chyna, she is beautiful."

"Thank you."

"So you're here for temporary assistance and food stamps?"

"Yes and I'm here to file for child support also."

Marie and I talked like we were old friends. She was really nice and seemed to want the best for India and me. She didn't make me feel like a statistic, she made me realize that I had a second chance to turn my life around. I qualified for temporary assistance and food stamps. Since LP's name wasn't on India's birth certificate, we had to take a paternity test to prove that he was her father. Anita told me that the courts would be summoning LP to take the test. A week later, the courts summoned LP to take the paternity test but he failed to show. They summoned him again, this time with a warning that if he didn't show he would face jail time.

India was about three months when LP decided to pop up over my house. I had just gotten done giving her a bath when I heard the doorbell ring. I was at home by myself so I had to carry

India to the door with me. I damn near dropped India when I saw LP on my doorstep.

"What do you want?" I asked LP.

"I came to see my baby," LP said.

"Oh, now it's your baby since you had to take a paternity test? You wasn't claiming her while I was pregnant. What do you want to see her for now, you ain't been trying to see her," I snapped.

"Well I am now."

Even though LP was an asshole, I had already said that I would never deprive him of seeing his daughter. India didn't have anything to do with him and his bullshit, and she needed to be around her father.

"Come in LP."

Stepping into the house, he stood by the door.

"You look good," he said, smiling.

"Thank you," I said, rolling my eyes.

"So we have a little girl?"

"Yeah, her name is India Renee Black."

"Why you ain't give her my last name?"

"Why would I give her your last name, you ain't did shit for her?"

"I know I haven't but I am now since I know that she's mine. Let me see her."

"You knew she was yours in the first place," I said, handing her to him.

"I know, but to be honest wit you, I got you pregnant on purpose," he laughed.

"Are you fucking kidding me?"

"Naw, I wanted you to be my baby's mom so I got you pregnant on purpose. Damn, I make some pretty kids," he said, looking at India.

"So you mean to tell me that you put me and your daughter through all of this bullshit for nothing?"

"Naw, it wasn't for nothing, we got a baby out the situation. Now I got two boys and a baby girl," he said, rubbing India's face.

"Nigga, I went through my whole pregnancy wit people coming up to me saying that you was telling people that I was a liar and that my baby wasn't yours. You sitting up here pushing a brand new Mercedes Benz while me and your daughter are on welfare!" I screamed.

"Calm down, I said that I was gonna help you."

"Fuck that, give me my daughter and get the fuck out!" I demanded.

"You're not gonna let me spend some more time with her?"

"Hell naw, get the fuck out, step."

"A'ight, but I'll be back later on with her some diapers, clothes and shit."

"Don't waste your time." I said, slamming the door behind him.

That day ended up coming and going and I never heard from LP. I really didn't care though because I didn't want him to be around India anyway. What type of positive influence could LP possibly bring to India's life? He sold drugs for a living and he owned a titty bar for God's sake. What the fuck was I thinking when I laid down wit his ass?

CHAPTER 19

ME, MYSELF AND I

A couple of months later, I finally found someone trustworthy of watching India for me while I worked. Her name was Janea Stewart, she was a friend of my mother's from way back. Since I finally had a babysitter, I found a job working at the local Shop 'N Stop. The pay wasn't much but my hours were flexible and the people were cool, especially this girl named Tiara. She was in the same situation that I was in except she had two girls. We bonded over our love of books, but I told her that I hadn't read any interesting books in years.

"Girl, you been sleeping, it's this book out called *'Flip Side of the Game'* that's killing the game right now," Tiara said to me one day.

"Who is it by?" I asked, while checking a customer out.

"The author's name is Tu-Shonda Whitaker. There's also a book out called *'Every Thug Needs a Lady'* by Wahida Clark and one called *'Little Ghetto Girl'* by Danielle Santiago. Girl, you better go pick these books up, you will not be able to put them down, trust me."

So when I had some money to spare, I went to Barnes and Noble and picked up those books. Tiara was right, I couldn't put them down. My passion for reading was revived and after that, I began putting money aside to buy at least two books a month. I didn't realize how many urban hood novels were out, and reading all of those tales of ghetto, sex and drugs prompted me to start writing my own book.

I didn't let anyone know that I was writing a novel because around here haters are always ready to knock your dreams. Diane kept on bugging me about getting my GED but I had others plans, I was going to be a writer.

It was a Saturday afternoon and I was out with Brooke while she did some shopping.

"Chyna, wait on me!" Brooke yelled, from inside of BeBe's.

"I'm going outside Brooke, I need to feed India," I lied.

I didn't have any damn money and I didn't want to be anywhere near clothes that I couldn't afford. Leaning down into India's stroller, I tickled her stomach. She was such a happy baby that she made me happy despite our situation. India had any and everything that she wanted and that was all that mattered. No, I couldn't afford the same luxuries that I had become accustomed to, but that was okay, I still looked fly. I had gotten my shape back in no time, and to me, my body looked even better after I had India.

It was March 2003, so I had on a pink fitted shirt, an old pair of Seven jeans and a pair of pink and white Puma's. I had started to rock my hair back curly so I had it up in a ponytail with some big pink plastic earrings in my ears. Picking India up, I sat her down on my lap and sat on a bench while I waited for Brooke to finish shopping.

"Hey my sweet baby," I said, while bouncing India around.

"So is this Miss India?" a thick New York accent spoke.

Looking up, Tyreik stood before me causing my heart to stop beating. He had gained his weight back since the shooting and he looked sexier than ever. I had thought about him every now and then. I still loved and wanted him back in some weird kind of way. Sometimes I felt like I would never get over him.

"How do you know her name?"

"Brooke and her parents talk about her all the time. I go over there and check on them from time to time," he stated.

"Well yes, this is Miss India Black," I smiled.

"Can I sit down with you?" he asked.

"Yeah sure," I replied, patting the seat for him to sit down next to me.

For a while we just sat there staring at India. I think we both looked at her and wondered what could have been.

"She looks just like you," he finally spoke.

"Is that good or bad?" I joked.

"You know that's a good thing. She's going to have long hair just like you," he spoke, while stroking her curls, "you look good."

"Thanks."

"You here by yourself?" he asked.

"Nah, Brooke's in BeBe's trying on clothes."

"I'm surprised you're not in there trying on clothes and buying up the whole store wit her," he laughed.

"My funds ain't like they used to be, my baby comes first now," I shrugged.

"I feel you. What, that nigga ain't helping you take care of your daughter?"

"Nah, I'm doing it all by myself."

"Damn, that's fucked up," he replied, shaking his head.

It had been a long time since Tyreik and I had had a civilized conversation. Us having a calm conversation seemed foreign to me. Tyreik seemed different now, he seemed at eased and settled.

"You've grown up a lot Chyna, I'm proud of you," he said, while gazing into my eyes.

"I had to, I have somebody else to think about now besides myself."

"Tyreik, where are you at?" Rema said, walkie talking him on her Motorola cell phone.

"I'm at the mall?" he said, talking back.

"Hurry up, I miss you," she said.

"Look, I gotta go, I'ma holla at you," he said, kissing me on the cheek.

Watching him leave was hard but for the best. He still was with Rema and that's where he needed to be. The sound of that bitch's voice still irked the shit out of me. I thanked God right then and there for allowing her to call, because for a minute there I thought that we might have had a chance to reconcile. Tyreik hadn't changed, he was still playing games and the sooner I learned that, the better off I would be.

India was almost a year old when I ran into Jaylen again. I had just gotten off work and was sitting at the bus stop waiting for the bus. I had my notebook out and was trying to think of my next scene. I didn't care where I was, whenever I could find time to write I would. That day the bus was running late and my feet were hurting like hell. I was trying to come up with the ending to my book, so I was deep into thought and not paying attention. I was so deep in thought that I didn't even notice Jaylen driving by.

"Is that really Chyna Danea Black I see sitting at the bus stop?" he teased.

"Jaylen," I smiled, delighted to see him.

Making a u-turn in the middle of the street, he pulled over and swooped me up.

"Damn Jaylen, you pushing a Navigator? You doing the damn thing boy."

"I told you I had my shit together but you wasn't trying to hear me."

Giving Jaylen the once over, I realized that Jaylen was no longer the scrawny basketball player from high school, he was a grown ass man now. The boy had muscles and tattoos on his arms. He sported a low cut with waves and he even had a mustache. Shit, Jaylen had my nipples hard just on sight. I hadn't had sex in over a year and the way Jaylen was looking he could most definitely get it. Hold up, what the fuck was I thinking, Jaylen is like a brother to me besides, he's in the NBA, what the hell would he want with me, I thought.

"But nah, I wasn't trying to hear you back then and I'm sorry for all those times I blew you off. I was all fucked up in the head and I took my problems out on anybody that was around. But I have grown up a lot since the last time you saw me."

"Hold up, did I pick up the wrong person? Where is the real Chyna Black at 'cause I know you ain't Chyna," he joked, grabbing my face and twisting it from side to side.

"It's me Jaylen," I giggled.

"So what brings about the sudden change of attitude?" he asked.

"I just realized that the life I was leading wasn't cool for me. I had had way too many bad times and the good times were few and far in between, you know. I wasn't happy and I had to deal with a lot of shit that had been brothering me, and plus I had somebody really wonderful come into my life," I grinned.

"Oh really, you got another nigga now?" he asked, annoyed.

"Since you're dropping me off, you might be able to meet my special person," I smiled, trying hard not to laugh.

"Ah Chyna, I'm not really up to meeting anyone right now. I'm just gonna holla at you later, a'ight," Jaylen said, pulling into my driveway sounding sad.

"Come on in Jaylen, it'll only take a minute, I promise."

"A'ight," he sighed.

"Chyna, is that you?" Diane yelled.

"Yeah it's me and I got somebody wit me."

"Who?" she asked.

"Just come and see woman," I called out to her.

"Jaylen!" Diane screamed when she saw him.

"Hi Miss Peoples, how you doing?" he said, hugging her.

"I'm doing well. Look at you all grown up and just as handsome as can be," Diane flirted.

"Okay momma, that's enough," I joked, pulling her away from him. "I told Jaylen that I had somebody very special to introduce him to," I hinted.

"Oh, okay, it's in your room," she smiled.

Leading Jaylen to my bedroom, I opened the door and showed him my surprise.

"Jaylen, I would like for you to meet my daughter India," I said, picking her up.

"Damn Chyna, she's beautiful, she looks just like you," he smiled, admiring India.

"Thank you."

"So, is this you and Tyreik's child?"

"No, you remember LP don't you?"

"Yeah, I remember that nigga."

"Well after me and Tyreik broke up I got with him, and to make a long story short, I got pregnant again but this time I kept the baby."

"So you mean to tell me you had abortion and then turned around and got pregnant again by LP?" he asked, shocked.

"Yeah," I replied, uncomfortable.

"That's some deep shit Chyna but you've changed so that's all that matters," he said, rubbing my back.

"Thanks Jaylen," I smiled, while looking into his eyes.

Checking myself, I quickly looked away because despite what Jaylen said, he could never truly want to be with a chick like me.

"Let me see her," he said, taking India from me.

"Say 'hi' India," I said.

"Hi," she said, while slapping Jaylen in the face.

"Like momma like daughter," he laughed.

"That's right," I laughed too.

From that day on, whenever Jaylen was in town we were together. He seemed to love spending time with India, and I always anticipated his calls. He would always come over to the house and play with India or he would shower her with gifts.

239

Even when he was on the road, he would call at least once a day to check on her. A lot of time had passed and things in my life were getting better and better by the moment.

It was September 18, 2003 and India's first birthday party was under way. Diane's back yard was filled with people. Asia, Brooke, Brooke's parents, my peoples from both sides of my family, Tiara, Janea, Michelle and Jaylen were in attendance. I had gotten India a Winnie the Pooh cake and decorations and Diane had barbecued and cooked. Kids were running around everywhere and the sun was shining bright. Jaylen came with a truck filled with gifts and another birthday cake for India.

"Jaylen, why did you buy her another cake?" I asked.

"India is my baby girl, she deserves to have the best of everything."

"Okay, but two cakes," I laughed.

"Yes, India has two cakes. Now hush and have a good time," he said, kissing me on the lips and slapping me on the butt.

I stood there shocked and turned on all at the same time. Jaylen had actually kissed me. Jaylen had never been so forward with me before. Looking over in his direction, he winked at me.

"Close your mouth Chyna," Asia teased.

"Come here, you too Brooke," I said, pulling them into the house.

"What's wrong with you?" Brooke asked.

"Jaylen just kissed me."

"Okay," Asia said, unfazed.

"What do you mean okay? The boy just kissed me," I stressed.

"Chyna, Jaylen has liked you since we were in elementary

school, you just were too busy being a ho to notice," Brooke stated.

"Fuck you, bitch," I laughed.

"You know you like him. Girl, you better get on him and stop bullshitting around," Asia added.

"See, that's the thing, I love Jaylen but just not in that way. He's like a brother to me."

"Well, if you feel that way then you need to tell him because that boy is feelin' you," Brooke said, seriously.

"Ya'll really think that I should tell him that I don't like him like that? It might break his heart."

"Chyna get over yourself, you're cute and all but you ain't all that mamma," Asia said, scrunching up her face.

"The hell wit you ho," I laughed.

"Now come on so we can go sing happy birthday to my Goddaughter," said Brooke.

"Heifer, she's my Goddaughter too," Asia replied.

"Oh shut up Asia and come on," Brooke said, while pulling Asia back outside.

Following them back outside, I searched the backyard for a little girl with curly hair and a bright yellow dress on. It wasn't very hard to find India, she was sitting in her favorite spot, her sandbox.

"India, look at you, got all this sand in your hair, I should whoop ya butt," I fussed, while dusting the sand out of her hair.

"Momma," India laughed.

"You get on my nerves lil girl, come on," I smiled, while walking with her.

"Happy birthday to you, happy birthday to you, happy birthday dear India, happy birthday to you!" everyone sang.

"Blow out your candles India," I said.

Leaning her over her first cake, India and I blew out her sparkle candles. Everybody clapped and cheered her on. Giving her to Jaylen, they blew out the candles to her second cake.

"Yeah!" I yelled, as she blew out the candles.

Turning around so that I could grab a paper plate, I spotted Tyreik walking up the driveway. For a second, I just stood there and stared at him in amazement.

"Chyna, hand me the plate," Brooke said, awakening me from my daze.

"Is that really Tyreik I see?" she whispered.

"Yes it is," I answered, overwhelmed.

"Ah, somebody's got a problem on their hands," Brooke cracked up laughing.

"Shut up Brooke."

"Don't be getting mad at me cause ya boo here," she teased.

"What are you doing here?" I asked.

"Nice to see you too Chyna," he smiled, "I came because I overheard Brooke telling her mother the other day that she was going to your daughter's birthday party, so I decided that I would go out and get India something, is that alright with you?"

"I don't mind you being here, but my mother is a whole another story."

"I got you're momma, don't worry about that," he said, giving me that devious smile.

"Chyna, your daughter wants you," Diane said, behind me.

"Hello Ms. Peoples, how are you doing?" Tyreik said, all polite.

"I'm doing fine and you?" she said, with an attitude.

"I'm doing well, I don't mean to intrude or anything but I wanted to give India her present in person. I also remember Chyna telling me that your birthday was in October. I know that it's a little early but I went on ahead and got you something now," he said, handing her a long black jewelry box.

"Oh why thank you," Diane replied, perking up, "can I open it now?"

"Please do."

"Oh my Lord, Tyreik, thank you," she smiled.

Taking a three-karat tennis bracelet out, Diane showed it to me.

"I know you ain't come bearing gifts and didn't bring me nothing," I said, jealous.

"Oh Chyna hush, Tyreik baby, thank you, go on over there and fix yourself a plate."

"How do you know that I even want him to be here?" I asked, aggravated.

"Who cares what you want, this is India's day not yours. Now quit playa hating and go feed ya baby," Diane said.

As I stood there and watched Diane treat Tyreik as if he were her long lost son, Jaylen came over to me.

"We need to talk," he said.

"I didn't invite him here if that's what you think."

"I know you didn't, but I still don't like that nigga being here."

"I know you don't and I'm sorry, but Jaylen we have to come to some sort of understanding."

"Yeah we do. I know that you know that I want more than a friendship from you."

"I love you and care about you a lot Jaylen, but I'm not willing to jeopardize our friendship for anything, you mean too much to me for me to do that. I hope that you can understand that and that we can still be friends. "

"I kind of figured that you wasn't feeling me like that, but I don't see why not 'cause a brotha is kind of fine," he joked.

"Whatever nigga, you look a'ight," I laughed, "you know who I think would make a perfect match for you?"

"Who?"

"Brooke, she needs a man like you in her life."

"I'll see what's up, but look I gotta go because I got a flight to catch. I know you love that nigga so go and be with him but just be smarter this time around," he said, hugging me.

"Thank you Jaylen, I love you and be safe."

"I will," he said, over his shoulder.

When everybody was done eating ice cream and cake, I began to open India's gifts for her. For some reason, as soon as India laid eyes on Tyreik she wouldn't let him go, so while I opened her gifts she sat on his lap. I had gotten her a ton of Playskool toys and clothes. Diane gave her a three hundred dollar savings bond. Cantrell got her a little girl's vanity set. Brooke and Asia went in together and bought her a pair of diamond stud earrings. Tyreik went all out and got her a platinum necklace with a heart pendant. Jaylen also got her Rocawear, Baby Phat and Baby Gap clothing. And last but not least, he purchased her a motorized Barbie jeep. My baby was in toy heaven that day.

Back inside the house, I had began washing dishes since the party was winding down. India's first birthday had been more overwhelming then the day that I had her. First Jaylen kisses me and then Tyreik shows up. I didn't know what his ass was up to but whatever he had planned, I wasn't feeling it one bit.

"What you thinking about," Tyreik asked, sneaking up on me.

"You," I answered.

"What about me? I hope it ain't nothing bad," he said, while wrapping his arms around me.

"I'm wondering what is going on, I mean did you really come over here just to give India a birthday gift or did you come over here to see me?"

"Honestly, I came to see the both of you."

"But, why?"

"I wanted to see your daughter again because she reminds me of what we could have had and I missed you."

"How can you say that you miss me, but yet you're still with Rema? You're still playing fucking games Tyreik and I ain't got time for that shit," I said, becoming angry.

"Calm down shorty."

"Look, thanks for coming by and for the gift but I think it's time for you to go."

"That's cool, I'll leave but this conversation is not over by a long shot," he said, kissing me on the forehead.

"Whatever," I said, rolling my eyes.

Right before I sent *'Me & My Boyfriend'* off to Triple Crown Publications, I told Diane and the girls about my dream of becoming a writer. To my surprise, everybody was ecstatic and supportive. Jaylen, of course, was enthusiastic about the news. He had always told me that I would do something great with my life. Our friendship was still intact and we had become even closer.

He and Brooke were now talking and going out on dates whenever he was in town and I couldn't have been happier for them. Jaylen had even offered to help me get my own crib but I would always say no. I had had people taking care of me my whole life and I was finally making it on my own, I was barely making it but I was making it.

On December 14, 2003, my dream came true. It was a Saturday and I was at work. My shift was almost up and I thankful because it looked like a blizzard outside. My neck and feet were killing me and I couldn't wait to get home. All I wanted was a hot bath and to snuggle under the covers.

Just as I was about to check out my last customer, my manager came to tell me that I had a phone call.

"It's your mom, she said that it was emergency," Ray said.

"I hope nothing's wrong with my daughter," I replied, panicking.

"She's on line one, go and talk to her, I'll finish your line up."

"Hello Momma, what's wrong?"

"Chyna, guess what?"

"What?" I asked, confused.

"Triple Crown sent you a letter saying that they want to give you a two book deal!" Diane screamed.

"Are you for real momma, don't play with me," I smiled.

"I'm not playing, I have the letter right here in front of me. It says that they liked the first four chapters of *'Me & My Boyfriend'* and they want you to send in the rest of your manuscript."

"Oh my God," I cried.

After talking to Diane some more, I hung up and told everybody I knew. Asia and her crazy self kept talking about how we were going to be famous and how she was finally going to be in one of 50-Cent's videos. Brooke's old Suge Knight ass kept telling me that she wanted to be my manager.

That night it was raining cats and dogs outside and I was snuggled up underneath the covers knocked out. It was about 3:30 in the morning when I heard a knock on the front door. India and I were at home alone so I was kind of afraid to answer. Diane had taken a second job at the Sheraton Hotel for extra money.

"Who is it?"

"Me!" Tyreik yelled.

"What are you doing here?"

"I needed to see you."

"It's three o'clock in the morning Tyreik. My momma might like you now but she don't like ya ass like that."

"Whatever, I missed you," he said, while hugging me.

Taking me by the hand, he led me to my bedroom. Sitting on the edge of my bed, Tyreik removed his shoes and got into bed with me. Lying face to face, we held each other.

"My old man called me today," Tyreik said.

"For real, how did he get your number?" I said shocked.

"He always had it, we talk about once or twice a year."

"What did he want?"

"He called me to tell me that Lizette died," he spoke softly.

"I'm sorry to hear that Ty," I said, while stroking his face

"It's cool, she's in a better place now."

"How did she die?"

"She died from an overdose of heroin."

"How is Redd doing?"

"He's cool I guess, he said that he's happily married to one of his hoes named Honey."

"Ya daddy still pimping?"

"Pimping is in his blood, what can I say."

"So how do you feel about Lizette being dead?"

"She wasn't no kind of mother to me so it really don't bother me too much."

"Well, you know that I'm here for you if you ever need to talk."

"You know that I still love you, don't you?"

"I don't know how you feel Tyreik."

"I want you back Chyna."

"I don't know Tyreik, I have to think about that," I said, becoming overwhelmed.

"I hear you Chyna, but I can't wait on you forever."

"I don't want you to wait forever, I just want you right here and right now," I said, kissing him.

I needed to feel a man inside of me, it had been far too long so I gave Tyreik a piece of myself hoping that would be enough for now. Lying on top of me, Tyreik

kissed my eyes, nose, ears, lips and cheeks. Slowly caressing my body, he peeled off my silk nightgown. Massaging my breast, he licked and sucked them slowly.

"Mmm," I moaned.

Trailing kisses down my stomach, he stopped to tickle my navel with this tongue. Making his way in between my legs, Tyreik made me scream with pleasure. No matter how much I begged him to stop because I couldn't take anymore, he would persist.

After about an hour of giving me nothing but head, Tyreik eased his way back up my body and turned me over. He traced his fingers down my spine and stopped once he reached my tattoo. Kissing me slowly, he traced his tongue along each letter of his name. Flipping me back over, he kissed me on the lips. Pulling his shirt over his head, I saw that he had gotten my name tattooed on his shoulder.

"I told you that I love you," He said, staring me in the eyes.

Tyreik took his time with me that night, he wouldn't stop until I was thoroughly satisfied. I knew that he was making love to me but I wasn't sure just yet if I felt the same way. Lying in bed next to him, I remembered that when he woke up he would be going home to Rema. I couldn't believe how stupid I was to sleep with him knowing that he was still with her. This thing between Tyreik and I had to end, but I just didn't know if I would ever be able to get over him.

CHAPTER 20

THE BEGINNING 2 THE END

Five months had passed and 'Me and My Boyfriend' was finally about to be released. The whole lead up to the book coming out was pretty easy. I just couldn't wait to see what people thought of it. Jaylen was so supportive that he threw me a huge book release party at The Chase Park Plaza Hotel.

With my advance money, I was able to quit Shop 'N Stop and get off welfare. I was grateful for the job but I couldn't wait to tell them to kiss my black ass. I had made a lot of friends while working there and a lot of them were at the party. Tiara, Stephanie, Chris, Tory, Jackie, the two Nicole's and Ray, my manager, were all there. Local celebs like Nelly and the Lunatics, Chingy, J Kwon and Marshall Faulk were all in attendance. Jaylen and some of his teammates were even there.

As soon as I arrived, people were all on my tip. You know a sista had to come clean so I had purchased an all white suit from Gucci. I didn't have a shirt or bra on underneath it so you know my shit was crucial. Miesha had given me a roller set so my hair was filled with big pretty curls. A gold pair of earrings, necklace and gold Jimmy Choo's completed my look.

Asia and Brooke were also looking fabulous. Asia sported a Diane Von Furstenberg wrap around dress while Brooke rocked a Chanel mini dress. I had gotten Big D from Q.95 to DJ for me.

While I was on dance floor shaking my ass to Fat Joe's *"Lean Back"*, I spotted Tyreik coming through the crowd. My eyes had to be playing tricks on me, I had invited him but I didn't think the nigga would actually show up, but as usual I was wrong. The nigga looked good though. He had on a plaid buttoned up shirt with a white T on underneath, a pair of LRG jeans and all white S. Carters. His baseball cap was tilted to the side and I swear he had on every piece of jewelry he owned.

I was getting my groove on to *"Goodies"* by Ciara when Big D switched to *"Hood Hop"* by J Kwon, and when J Kwon got up on stage and rapped along to his song, the party really started jumping. Asia, Brook and I started doing the Mono like it was going out of style.

Everybody started screaming, "Go Chyna, go Chyna go!"

Looking over at Tyreik, I saw him watching my ass sway to the beat. Giving him a look that said you can look but you can't touch, I kept on doing my thing. When *"Hood Hop"* went off, I vacated the dance floor in search of a drink. I didn't even make it halfway across the room before Tyreik grabbed me.

"Can we talk?" he asked.

"We don't have anything to talk about," I replied, walking away.

Instead of getting something to drink, I decided to leave out and get some fresh air. Sneaking out the back, I stood on the side of the building and inhaled deeply. I called home to check on India. Janea told me that she was doing fine and that she was in her room sound asleep. Closing my flip phone, I got ready to go back inside when I was stopped by the touch of a hand.

"I thought I might find you out here."

"Tyreik, what do you want? Why are you even here?"

"You did invite me didn't you?"

"Yeah I did, I just didn't think that you would actually show up," I stated, bluntly.

"That's fucked up," he grinned.

"Shut up, it ain't even like that," I laughed.

"So you wrote a book, huh?"

"Yeah I did."

"There better not be anything about me in it," he joked.

"Trust me, it's not," I said, rolling my eyes.

"I'm glad to see you did something with yourself despite all of the bullshit you been through."

"We all go through stuff," I said, waving him off.

"Nah, you've been through a lot of stuff ma. You had to deal with your old bird, plus you had to put up with my bullshit."

"I'm passed all of that, I'm over it," I lied.

Taking my hand in his, he said, "Nah, I ain't treat you right when I had you ma. I mean I fucked up and I'm man enough to admit that. I'm also man enough to admit that I need you back in my life."

"What happened to Rema?"

"I told her I ain't want to be with her no more, I don't love her, shit I never did. As a matter of fact, we've been broken up for a while. I know you thought that night when I came over that her and I were still together but we wasn't, I wouldn't have done you like that. When I was wit you, I wasn't ready to deal with being in a serious relationship, but now I'm ready. You just have to give me another chance ma."

"I don't want to talk about this anymore, I got to get back, people are going to be wondering where I'm at," I said, nervous and confused.

"I can't let you go Chyna, I won't," He said, grabbing me and holding me tight.

"Tyreik, you can't do this to me, I won't let you. I just started to get my life back together. I tried to make you love me but you didn't. And to be honest with you, if it wasn't for you I wouldn't be where I'm at now. I thank you for all the tears and stress because look at me now, I have a man who loves me and my daughter and I think I love him too," I lied, with tears forming in my eyes.

"Fuck that nigga! That nigga can't make you feel the way I do. You love me and I love you. Shit, that's all that matters. I know things were fucked up back then but I've changed. We can make it work now ma," he said, stroking my hair.

"I'm not saying that it's all your fault, because I made it okay for you to do me wrong, but I just can't go back Tyreik," I cried.

"Yes you can, you know you want to," he said, holding my face in his hands.

"I've got to go Tyreik. Just let me go, please."

"I love you," he said.

Holding me, he looked me dead in the eyes and kissed me. Hungrily we explored each other like it was the first time. I knew at that moment that me kissing Tyreik would have lasting effects, but I didn't care. It couldn't be more wrong but it felt so right being in his arms again. I needed Tyreik more than I needed air to breathe. The thought of how he used to treat me and cheat on me crossed my mind and then I started to feel stupid all over again. Fed up, I pushed Tyreik up off of me. Staring at him, I hated him for making me feel the way he did.

"How dare you try to come back into my life and fuck things up."

"Ma, be quite, you know I got you."

"I…. don't…. love you… anymore," I stressed. "Tyreik you left me, I tried to love you but you wouldn't let me. I knew that eventually you were going to leave me. I sat in that house every night and cried because I knew you were wit Rema. Shit, crying never kept ya ass home anyway. I had plenty of opportunities to leave you and I didn't and that's my fault. I just can't go back," I said, trying to convince myself.

"Stop crying ma, I know I fucked up but I promise I'ma make it right this time. I know that I didn't show you enough attention back then, but you the one that I want to be with. I can't live without you ma, I tried but I can't," he said, rubbing my back and kissing me on the face.

"Let me go Tyreik, please."

"I love you, can't you see that," he said, trying to kiss me on the lips again.

Aggravated and fed up, I pushed him off of me and yelled, "didn't I tell you to stop! Fuck you and you're so called love, 'cause it or you don't mean a damn thing to me! You said that I drove you away and that everything was my fault! You didn't give a fuck about me and I don't need nor want you in my life Ty! You are nothing but a burden to me now, so let that be the reason ya ass stay the hell out of my life!"

"Ma, kill all that noise, you don't mean that shit. Tell that to your heart," he said back.

"Whatever Tyreik, I gotta go, I can't do this anymore."

Running back inside, I rushed past Asia and ran into the bathroom. Standing in the bathroom mirror I searched deep inside of my soul. You did right, you had to let him go. You have to let go no matter how much it hurts Chyna. You have to let go, I said out loud to myself.

It was the middle of June 2004 and I was preparing to go to my GED graduation. Yes, I had finally gone and taken my test and I passed it on the first try. My book was doing extremely well and I was getting good feedback from fans. It had even made it on the Essence Best Seller List. India was growing and learning more and more each day. Every time I looked at her, she looked more like me. Jaylen's team had won the NBA championship that year and he and Brooke were now a couple. Asia was interning at the Barnes Hospital for nursing. With the money that I had made off my book, I found me a nice two-bedroom apartment right around the corner from Diane's house.

Standing in front of my full-length mirror, I gave myself the once over. I looked pretty damn good in my cap and gown. For the first time in my life I felt complete. I was making it on my own through the grace of God and I was happy. I felt strong, confident and blessed that I had come this far and made such a change in my life. Grabbing my purse, I ran downstairs to meet everyone.

The ceremony didn't last long, it was short and to the point. When my name was called a smile a mile wide crossed my face. Everyone in my family cheered. Diane, Cedric, Cantrell, India, Asia, Brooke and Jaylen were all there to support me.

After the ceremony, we all sat and had juice, cookies and cake with the other graduates and their family.

"I'm so proud of you," Diane said, hugging me tightly.

"I can't breathe ma."

"I'm sorry, I just got a little choked up. I love you, I just wish Pat could have been here to see you."

"She is and I know that she's proud of me too. I love you too ma."

"I love you too," my daddy Cedric added.

"I love you too daddy."

"You really think you're the shit now, don't you?" Asia teased.

"Damn right I do."

"I'm so proud of you girl," she said.

"Yeah, keep doing your thing girl," Brooke replied.

"I'm gonna try ya'll, I just got to take things one day at a time."

"That's all that you can do. You know that we're here for you whenever you need us," Asia said.

"I know and I love ya'll so much," I cried.

"Oh Lord, here she go with the tears," Brooke teased.

"Shut up," I said, wiping my eyes.

"Momma," India cried.

"What is it baby girl?" I asked, picking her up.

"Her funky self boo-booed," Asia said, holding her noise.

"Leave my baby alone," I laughed.

"I'll go and change her," Jaylen offered.

"Boy please, you can barely put your clothes on let alone change a diaper," Brooke teased.

"Well then, why don't you teach me," he said, kissing her.

"I'll teach you something alright," she said, kissing him back.

"Ya'll two are so sickening, go and get a room," I said, acting like I had to throw up.

"Don't hate, congratulate," Brooke laughed.

"Go and change my baby's diaper and get out my face," I laughed too.

"Looks like somebody's got a visitor," Asia said, eying the door.

Turning around, I found Tyreik walking through the door. His showing up out of the blue all the time was starting to get on my nerves.

"I think I'll leave you two alone," Asia said, trying to walk away.

"You better not leave me by myself with him," I hissed.

"Chyna, he loves you and you love him, stop fighting it. What's in the past is in the past. I would give anything in this world to have one more day with T. You are being given another chance at love with Tyreik, don't let your pride get in the way of that. Now handle your business," she said, kissing me on the cheek.

"You look good Dimples," he said.

"Thank you, you do too," I said, nervous.

"Here, I got you something," he said, pulling a bouquet of pink roses from behind his back and handing them to me.

"Thank you," I smiled, while smelling them.

I had never been given flowers before so the gesture was very welcomed.

"I'm glad that you went on ahead and got your GED, I'm proud of you."

"Thanks," I said, not knowing what else to say.

For a minute we just stood there in silence, then out of nowhere I just blurted out that I loved him.

"I know you do," he said, grabbing and hugging me.

"If we are going to do this, we have to take things slow."

"That's cool ma, I'm just glad that you finally stopped fighting me."

"If you start bullshittin' again it's over Tyreik and I mean it."

"I got you ma, this time we gonna make things right, a'ight."

"Okay," I inhaled deeply.

"Mommy!" India yelled, running towards me.

Picking her up, I held her in my arms. Running his hand through her hair, Tyreik kissed her on the forehead.

"Da da," India giggled.

I couldn't believe how my life had changed so drastically. All my drama began when I was fifteen. That's the year that I broke loose, learned how to fuck a man real good, strip him of all of his dough and scream fuck the world while waving his cash in my hand. But now I'm twenty-one and all the drama that once was is all gone. We all have a story and this is mine.

You know it took me a minute to realize that life ain't always what it's cracked up to be. It ain't always rainbows and butterflies like I thought growing up, the shit is complicated. One minute you're happy and the next minute you're sad. I had spent most of my life walking around feeling sorry for myself and blaming everybody else for my problems. You know the heart has a long memory and mine has plenty of scars. I had to come to the conclusion that we all are dealt heartache and pain, but what I've learned is that there is always a lesson to be learned. You just have to learn from your mistakes, dust yourself off and keep moving. If you believe in life, love, hope and God then you will be fine. My heart is full and I'm determined to live my life to the fullest.

This is not the end of my story, this is only the beginning of me, Chyna Black.

"MENAGE A' TROIS Sexy Flicks"
The Ultimate in Visual Entertainment

Experience visual entertainment at its best! Our photos of sexy ladies will take you far and beyond your imagination.

Order a Sampler Set today for only $9.99*   (Assortment of (10) Hot photos)
Send $2.00 for a preview Color Catalog
Send $6.00 for a multi-page Color Catalog

Quantity	Item	Price
	"Sampler Set" (Assortment of (10) Hot photos)	$9.99
	Preview Catalog	$2.00
	Full Catalog	$6.00
	Merchandise Total	
	Shipping & Handling (**FREE** For a limited time)	**FREE**
	Total	

Send All Payments To:
MENAGE A' TROIS
2959 Stelzer Road Suite C
Columbus, OH 43219

*The Sampler Set is pre-selected
This is a limited time offer.